THE FORGOTTEN MAID

MAID

Jane Cable

SAPERE
BOOKS

THE FORGOTTEN MAID

Published by Sapere Books.

20 Windermere Drive, Leeds, England, LS17 7UZ,
United Kingdom

saperebooks.com

ISBN: 978-1-80055-313-2

To the afternoon crew at 'The Tinners'. You know who you are.

ACKNOWLEDGEMENTS

The first and most important acknowledgement has to be to Lawrence, the man who really talks to ghosts, for letting me use his gift in this story. And to him and his mother for taking the time to read the manuscript. My husband Jim's knowledge of and enthusiasm for the Napoleonic wars has been invaluable. There are also many local people who have given me a leg up along the way: the house steward and volunteers at Trelissick, including neighbours who work there; Sue Grace, who introduced me to the wonders of the Courtney Library; Leigh Ibbotson for his insights into planning regulations; Caroline Palmer for her local history books; and my author friend and talks partner Sue Kittow for her extensive knowledge of Winston Graham and his works.

This is the first time I have written anything historical and I found it really difficult at first, even with the wealth of information about the Regency period provided to me by fellow author Cass Grafton. However, after a long lunch of writerly conversation with the marvellous Claire Dyer, her sage advice helped me to see the wood for the trees and everything fell into place.

The support of other writers is always important, and I would also like to thank my word count partner, Kitty Wilson, for daily chivvying and support. On the home front I am forever grateful to my friend Sally Thomas for her constant interest, for reading the manuscript no less than three times, and for our literary adventures together.

This is the first novel I have written with a publishing contract already signed, and I thank Amy Durant at Sapere Books for seeing the potential in the story.

Last, but not least, the locals at 'The Tinners' and the wonderful, warm community at 'Porthnevek' for welcoming Jim and me and helping us to make Cornwall our home.

PROLOGUE

The blackness is intense. Deeper, darker, thicker, magnifying. In the distance the crash of waves beats against the cliffs. I put out my hand. The rock is damp, the roughness of it scraping my fingers as I trace an arc above my head.

Something is scurrying behind me. A breath of fur against my ankles and I stifle a scream. *Courage. Take courage.* I close my eyes and picture the gleaming expanse of ocean lying ahead.

A light flares in front of me, his face in profile as he bends over a stub of candle. The flame settles and I step forwards into the circle of light.

He scoops more scraps of candle from the floor and places them in my hand, closing his fist around mine. "Follow me," is all he says before he turns away.

The flame climbs the walls ahead of him, quartz sparkling in the bouncing light. It circles him like a halo, my protector in this place without stars and sky. A shiver runs through me from head to toe. *The sea. Think about the sea.* I pause for a moment; yes, I can still hear it.

I have no way to measure distance except by the pounding of the waves. The tunnel narrows where a tumble of rocks has spewed from the wall. He tests it with his boot. It is solid and he clambers over it, leaving me in darkness.

"Pass me a fresh candle."

I reach out and he touches the ends of my fingers as he takes it. A rustle of the fabric of his coat. A click. And once again we have light.

He holds the stub high and I scramble over the rocks, their sharpness digging into my palms as I steady myself. What if there is another fall? Panic clasps my chest but I must not allow it to take hold. Therein lies the path to madness.

Time stretches as we edge forwards. His silence becomes increasingly heavy, as though his spirit is crushed by the weight of stone above. Perhaps he is concentrating, navigating us through this unfamiliar land. *Think of the sea. Moonlight on the ocean. Home.*

The roof is lower now and we have to stoop. He is bent over the candle, the flickers behind him dim. I want to ask if he will light a stub for me but I dare not. Something about his manner closes me down. And we may need every last scrap to light us to the end.

My shoulders hunch. My back aches. I consider crawling, but the floor is too rough. Just keep moving, keep moving. And trust him. Because I have no choice.

All of a sudden, he is upright in front of me. He holds the candle above his head, and it fails to reach the furthest corners of the cavern. For the first time, his mouth curves into a smile. I brace myself against the wall and straighten my spine.

"What is this place?" Water is trickling somewhere to my left, its music almost lost in the wash of the waves below. *Not distant. Not above. Below.* My heart sings a silent prayer of thanks.

He walks the perimeter, tracing the walls with the light, a curious zigzag up and down, up and down. I sink onto my haunches as I watch him. The flame gutters.

"Bring me another candle."

I follow the last flickers across the floor, then darkness closes around us. I stop. "Where are you?"

Footsteps. His breath warm in my ear. "No-one would ever find you here," he whispers. His fingers are tight around my wrist. The stubs of candle rattle softly as they fall to the floor.

PART ONE: 2015

CHAPTER ONE

I lean on the gate in the bright Cornish October sunshine. Below me, the valley slopes steeply away, a tumble of gorse and weeds fed by the long, damp summer. Thistles, nettles, couch grass and dock jostle for position between the overgrown bushes and crawl over the mounds of reddish-brown shale.

Our new glamping site will begin some two hundred yards ahead of me, near where something called a Clwyd Cap is marked. I balance on the bottom bar of the gate and crane my neck, but all I can see is the conical tip of a metal frame. Must be it. My pencil swirls as I mark a ring around it.

The sharp *ca-cack* of a jackdaw breaks the silence. I climb the gate but stop as I'm astride it. I can see the sea. A glimmer of turquoise ahead of me, half hidden by the angle of the hill. A childish excitement ripples through me. Of course, I spotted it in the distance as I was driving here, but I didn't realise the valley had a view.

I allow myself to rest on top of the gate to enjoy the sunshine. Our valley, currently un-named on the map but which will soon be known as Wheal Dream, runs parallel to the cliffs. At the bottom of the field I can see a group of chalets, so I guess beyond them a road runs down to Porthnevek, but most of the village is hidden from view. A few houses cling to the hillside opposite before it becomes too steep and rises to a cliff at the far end.

My phone trills in my pocket. A text. My palms begin to sweat. *Good god, Anna, you're forty next year. Words cannot hurt you. Pick the damned thing up.*

Instead, I slide from my perch and make my way through the gorse to the flatter land in the centre of the valley, where couch grass forms a thick mat over the shale. To my right, a pasture curves upwards, a herd of cows lowing as they feed. Above them is Nevek Cot, my lodgings for the next ten or so months. It squats low in front of the farm buildings, its gable window glinting in the sun. I probably should be unpacking, but there'll be time enough for that when the clouds roll over.

When I reach the metal gate marking the boundary between our land and the chalets, it is wedged open. I run my fingers over my mobile as I gaze at the tyre tracks into the field, the grass worn away beneath them. A grubby van and an old Vauxhall are parked there, and I suspect more will follow later in the day. No reason to move them on now. Making enemies from day one is a bad idea. So is making enemies full stop. I whip out my phone, but the text is just a message from my service provider and my shoulders slump with relief.

Beyond the chalets, a single track road dips towards the village, but to my right is a footpath leading to the cliffs. I round a corner and for the first time have a clear view of the beach. The tide is out, revealing a huge expanse of flat, damp sand. The waves are dotted with surfers, seal-like specks in their wetsuits, bobbing beyond the breakers.

Something about the view takes my breath away. The emerald hue of the ocean, the waves crashing against the cliffs in the middle distance, the changing colours of the sky as the clouds roll across. There's a wildness to it, making me tingle, and I hug my clipboard as I take it all in.

"Got you, has it?" The man's voice is soft with a Cornish bur. I look up to see sandy hair and a beard flecked with grey; green eyes as deep as the sea.

"It has rather."

He nods. "Does that to people. Claims them. For better or for worse."

What a strange thing to say. I stand aside to let him pass.

I follow the track until it joins the main coastal path on the cliffs overlooking the beach then skews back inland to the village. The main part of Porthnevek is nestled in a narrow valley behind a tongue of dry sand extending inland towards a stream. I walk past a grey pebble-dashed community hall and a boarded-up pub. A bus is pulling away, its gears grinding on the beginnings of the hill. I cross the road behind it and find myself standing in front of a row of shops.

The first is empty, but the second is the village store. Next door is a hairdresser and beauty salon, and beyond that a conservatory juts onto the pavement, filled with decorative driftwood in every shape and size, from seahorse mobiles to dining tables. It's obvious that outside the summer season Porthnevek is a quiet backwater, so it must be quite a precarious way to make a living.

I am filled with childish delight when a bell rings as I open the door of the village store. A woman in her fifties with close-cropped hair and a stud in her nose is behind the till.

"Good afternoon," she says. "Cracking day out there."

I smile. "It is, isn't it?" Then I start to browse the shelves. I don't need anything, but it's useful to know what they stock, and the answer is a bit of everything. You could get by, shopping here, and the prices aren't too steep either. I feel I should buy something, so I select a card with a view of the beach to send to my boss Cecile.

14

Purchase complete, I study the price list outside the hairdresser. The notice on the door tells me they're closed today, but maybe I'll come down later in the week. I could do with a cut, and a manicure wouldn't go amiss either. A woman of about my own age with blonde hair tied up in a scarf drags a chair and bucket around the corner of the conservatory. Despite her baggy dungarees, she is more Audrey Hepburn than Hilda Ogden, and there's something familiar about her eyes I can't quite place. She smiles at me.

"They don't open on Mondays. None of us do. Not a lot of point, really."

"It does seem rather quiet."

"It's good to have a breather after the season. I'm Wednesdays to Sundays now. Pippa does Tuesdays to Saturdays."

"That's handy. I might pop down tomorrow to book a haircut."

"You living here, then?"

I nod. "I arrived yesterday, so I'm trying to find my feet."

"Oh, bless you, that shouldn't take long. There's lots going on at the community hall: yoga, art class, book club — depends what you're into. Now the pub's closed, the social life revolves around Stars café on the beach, and the village has a couple of Facebook pages."

"That's very kind, thank you. I have to say it feels really friendly — everyone speaks to everyone."

"Proper community, Porthnevek, and proud of it. I'm Serena, by the way."

I hold out my hand to shake hers. "Anna."

"Why don't you drop back some time when I'm open and have a coffee? I'll fill you in on who's who and what's what. Like every village up and down the country, there are always a few awkward ones you can't trust further than you can throw them," she says with a wink.

"That's fantastic — so kind of you. I certainly will."

"No worries, hon. Any time."

Steaming coffee in my hand, I power up my laptop — one of the few things that made it out of the boxes yesterday evening. The drive down and the sea air must have exhausted me, because even after an early night I slept well, tucked under the eaves with the window open to let in the breeze. And I could hear the sea. Incredible. The smooth wash of the waves in the distance lulled me to sleep in no time at all.

I turn the radio down a notch as I open my emails. I'll deal with the urgent ones first, then go through the site plans again. They'll make far more sense now I've seen the lie of the land, and I'm meeting the planning consultant this afternoon, so I need to be ready.

Two coffees and a bowl of cereal later, I am lost in the background reports. This was mining country; in fact, the valley itself was the result of early opencast works. It was only later the rich seams of copper were chased underground when Wheal Nevek was built.

I set up the printer on the dining table that will serve as my office until the portacabin arrives on site. That will happen after we have planning permission but before work starts. I pull a planner from a crate and stick it to the wall with Blu Tack. With a thick red pen, I mark the target dates for appointing contractors and finalising budgets. When we get the green light, I'll add everything else and we can get on with the build. My pen hovers around the end of June. I should have settled the permanent manager and sorted out any teething problems by then, so I'll be up and away.

There's no time to pick up any baggage, and that suits me since my divorce — everything I own fits into my trusty Peugeot, and I'm proud of it. Plus, I get to live in some of the most beautiful places in Britain. Apart from the fact I could do my job in my sleep, what's not to love?

My phone trills. Convincing myself it's probably nothing, I pick it up.

'You can't run away forever.'

I quickly hang up and close my eyes, my nails digging into my palms. I'm not running — I'm working.

CHAPTER TWO

It's more pleasure than business that takes me to the village the next morning. Rather than use the road, I approach on the cliff path, the rise and fall of the coast towards St Ives mesmerising in the autumn sunlight. I stop for a moment to breathe in the salt air and watch the fulmars circle below me, then turn the corner and head down into Porthnevek's valley.

Serena is sitting at one of the tables in her conservatory shop, threading wooden starfish onto a string. She looks up when she hears the click of the door and smiles.

"Anna! Your timing is perfect. I was just going to put the kettle on. How do you like your coffee?"

"With milk if you have it, otherwise black's fine." I study her handiwork. "That looks fiddly. Do you make everything yourself?"

"No, my brother does some of it. The tables, the benches — the larger mirrors."

"It must be nice to share a talent."

"Oh, we're very close in all sorts of ways. He's only eleven months younger than me, so we grew up in each other's pockets. The only time we've ever really been apart was when I went away to art college."

"So you live together?"

"Oh no. I have a partner, teenage kids. And much as I love him, he's too chaotic for me. He lives up in Nankathes and his place is an absolute tip."

"Nankathes?"

"You probably haven't found it yet. It's at the bottom end of Wheal Nevek valley."

"Oh, the place with the chalets."

"It looks like we'll have a battle on our hands with some cowboys who want to build a glamping site up there." The kettle boils and she pours water into the mugs. "They've frigging started already — putting nasty notices on cars. People have been parking in that field for years. It's a bloody cheek."

"That was a mistake."

Serena looks over her shoulder. "A mistake?"

"Overzealous planning consultant. I told him to remove them as soon as I found out. Look, I have to come clean, Serena, that's why I'm here. To supervise the build."

She turns, hands on hips. "There won't be a build. You'll never get planning. We'll fight it all the way."

"I was rather hoping to be able to work with the village to create something that will benefit us all. Once Wheal Dream's up and running, it'll create jobs and money."

"Wheal Dream — more like frigging Wheal Nightmare. You have no idea how crammed this place gets in the summer — the last thing we need is more tourists."

"We're confident we can extend the season, bring money into the village for longer. The yurts have log burners and…"

She steps forwards and I take a step back. "You don't get it, do you? There won't be any yurts. We're not going to stand by and let you ruin our valley. It would be better for everyone if you just packed your bags and went back where you came from."

I shake my head. "That isn't my job."

"Then if all you're concerned about is your job, you'd better go off and do it. But don't expect any help from me."

Her venom takes my breath away, but I have to remain calm. "That's a shame. It's derelict land, after all. Isn't there any way we could find some common ground?"

She folds her arms. "Not a chance." Her body is rigid, her eyes like fiery emeralds.

"Then I'm sorry." I close the door quietly behind me.

It's only later I begin to consider Serena's reaction a little extreme. Surely someone running a business like hers would benefit from extra tourists? I may even have considered buying some of her furniture for the yurts. I ponder it on and off over the next week but find it impossible to fathom. Apparently she isn't the only one who feels this way. First I am blocked from the community Facebook group. Then the woman in the village store is monosyllabic when I go in for some milk. The final nail in the coffin is when I fail to book an appointment for a haircut any time before Christmas. I should be angry, but for some reason my overriding emotion is closer to sadness.

CHAPTER THREE

On Saturday morning I wake to the beat of rain against my bedroom window. A grey cloak has settled across the valley. Once I've made myself a coffee, I take my iPad back to bed. According to the forecast, the weather will improve later, and I need to do something, go somewhere and not mope around here. I open the National Trust app to consider the possibilities.

There are three local properties I could visit. East Pool Mine catches my eye, but a large part of it is closed for renovation. Otherwise, there are two stately homes: Trelissick and Trerice. The former promises gardens and riverside walks, and the photographs of brilliant autumn colours seduce me. Even better, I can drop into Truro on the way back to find a hairdresser.

By the time I park at Trelissick, the sun is already creeping out from behind the clouds. I stroll towards some outbuildings, signposted as the café and second-hand bookshop, and am just considering a coffee when I see a poster advertising a volunteer information talk at eleven o'clock. It's almost that now, so I ask at the ticket desk if there's still time to attend and they point me towards a room above the bookshop. I slide into the back row with not a moment to spare.

As I catch my breath, I realise what a crazy thing volunteering would be. Okay, it could work from now until about January, but after that who knows how I'd find the time. And I'm only here on a temporary basis anyway — surely I'm not worth training? But on the other hand, perhaps the basic skills are transferable to other properties. I look around me. The room isn't exactly packed.

The iron-haired, rosy-cheeked lady giving the welcome speech sits down and is replaced by a broad-shouldered man in his thirties. His fair hair is tousled and he wears a navy fisherman's jumper. He's not good-looking, exactly, but he has a strong jawline and a beguiling smile that are eye candy enough to sweeten his talk. He introduces himself as the volunteer co-ordinator for Cornwall, so he's probably the main event.

I watch as he perches on the edge of a table and outlines the opportunities available. I don't much fancy working outside in the winter but they also need room guides, which sounds a great deal warmer. It would be interesting to learn about the history of the house too. Plus, volunteering would be a way to make friends, although looking around I'm about twenty years younger than most of the others.

They're a sociable bunch, though, and I find several people to chat to as we're given coffee and melt-in-the-mouth chocolate shortbread. In a corner are two small tables where the speakers will talk to each of us individually, and although I'm not sure I have too much to offer, it would be rude to leave now.

The room is almost empty by the time I am called forwards by the volunteer co-ordinator. He introduces himself as Luke Hastings, his handshake firm and his smile wide.

As soon as we sit down, I come straight to the point. "I'm only in Cornwall for a temporary contract, so in truth I don't know how useful I can be."

He leans back in his chair. "How temporary is temporary?"

"Until next June, July."

"And how much time could you give?"

"Quite a bit up until January. Weekends, at least. Afterwards, maybe less, but I would try to do something most weeks if you needed me."

"To be honest, beggars can't be choosers." He grins. "What do you fancy doing?"

"I'd prefer an inside job in the winter. I'm interested in history, so room guiding appeals. You said you look after the whole county... I don't suppose there's any scope to work at East Pool? I'm getting quite interested in mining heritage."

He smiles at me. "Trelissick has mining connections too."

"Really?"

"Have you heard of Guinea-a-Minute Daniell?" I shake my head. "His son made the house what it is today, but it was a bit of a story of clogs to clogs in three generations. Ralph Allen Daniell, the middle one of the dynasty, was said to make a guinea a minute from Wheal Nevek mine alone in its heyday."

"Wheal Nevek?"

He leans forwards. "You sound as though you've heard of it."

"Porthnevek is where I'm living and working."

"Then I have just the job for you, Anna, especially in the run-up to Christmas. Tell me, do you like dressing up?" There's laughter in his eyes and a flash of something else.

I can't resist teasing him, so I lower my voice to a husky whisper. "That all depends on the costume."

Before I commit, I want to see the place for myself. Luke leaves me at the entrance, pressing his card into my hand and telling me to call when I've thought it through. Out of the corner of my eye I watch his broad back disappear into the shop, then I follow the line of a red brick stable block towards the house.

It is a grim, grey place, the walls still damp from the morning rain. The front porch is graced with an afterthought of cream Palladian pillars, which seem at odds with its austerity. I push on the dark blue front door, and to my surprise I see another set of pillars inside the far end of the entrance hall. What a terrible aberration.

A lady in her early sixties wearing a floral jumper steps forwards to greet me, asking if I've visited the house before. When I shake my head she gives me a potted history, including the money spent by one Thomas Daniell on upgrading Trelissick in the 1820s, which left him bankrupt and fleeing for France. I look at the pillars again. *Serves him right.*

It's as I move into the drawing room at the front of the house I begin to change my mind. Huge sash windows look out over open parkland and the sweep of the River Fal beyond. So broad is the water that the view extends almost to the sea, the port of Falmouth hidden between two distant promontories. Absolutely jaw-dropping.

Most of the rooms open to the public face this way. The drawing room leads to a narrow space lined with china cabinets then on to a lavish dining room set in Georgian fashion. Beyond that is a library with comfortable leather chairs placed at the windows and low tables with binoculars and nature guides. Two small children bounce around on one of the seats, their grandmother desperately trying to control them before the room guide intervenes by showing them photographs of deer in the park. Could I do that?

I ponder my decision in the tearoom in the old kitchen. I pick up a packet of sandwiches and a bottle of sparkling elderflower and carry my tray up a half flight of steps to a small table next to the window. No stunning view here, just a neat enclosed garden with a stone-built cottage on the other side of the lawn. But I suppose views weren't for servants. All the same, there is something about this room that draws me in.

Something about the house, to be fair. Is it the connection with Porthnevek? It was a brief but important one. It's not too fanciful to think the ore taken from my very own little valley, and the sweat of the villagers, were frittered away on this place. A bloodline, almost, tugging me into its spell. I close my eyes, and the clatter of cups and knives fades to the solid ticking of a clock and footsteps on a wooden floor. I shake my head. For goodness' sake, Anna, what's got into you?

I finish my sandwich and stroll outside and across the terrace in front of the house. More wedding cake pillars. But turn your back on them and the view must be one of the best in Cornwall. The gentle rolling slope with so many shades of green is a total contrast to the wild ruggedness of the north coast, which made all this possible. I wonder, did the Daniell family even think of it?

More to the point, what do I think of volunteering here?

CHAPTER FOUR

I wake on Sunday with a head full of cobwebs. I have no idea why. I consider going back to sleep, but my skull is beginning to pound, so I swallow some paracetamol in the kitchen while I wait for the kettle to boil. It is only once I'm back in bed that I look at my phone. I wish I hadn't.

Don't think you can hide, Anna. Facebook is such a great help when it comes to finding people.

Holy shit.

I stumble down the stairs and sit shivering at the dining table while my laptop warms up. I type in my password then log out of my Facebook account before opening an incognito tab. I search my name but my public profile is clean, locked down. As I knew it would be. Even my new profile picture, taken on holiday in Rome, gives nothing away.

But something has — or someone. Or else it's a bluff.

The shivering's taken hold, so I climb the stairs and snuggle back under the duvet with my rapidly cooling coffee. Bringing up Facebook on my phone, I can see anyone with access to my profile could take a reasonable guess where I am from the pictures I've posted. And who has access? Friends. Mutual friends. It would only take a casual word from one of them and the trail would be wide open.

There are people I don't want to lose from my life, but I can't risk it. Once I've finished my coffee, I jump into the shower to try to give myself some much-needed zing. It sort of works and I spend the rest of the morning setting up a new Facebook profile then individually messaging people to tell them my old account's been compromised and any new friend request from me is genuine. Although whether I'll dare post anything even there seems unlikely.

Caught up in domestic tasks, it is mid-afternoon before I'm lured outside by the warmth of the sun. I stand on the terrace and gaze down at the valley, where a man and a liver-coloured spaniel are picking their way through the gorse. Technically they're trespassing, but at this stage it doesn't matter. With Serena hellbent on whipping up a storm, the fewer feathers I ruffle the better.

A walk seems like a good idea, so I pack a bottle of water and an OS map into my rucksack and head out through the farmyard towards the cliffs. Some of the cows are in the barn, their lowing and the sweet smell of silage filling the warm air. A dry stone wall, partly overgrown with vetch, marks the field boundary and I follow it towards the scrubland and sea beyond.

There is no gate or stile, so I clamber over the stones and drop onto the footpath below. Two hundred yards of gorse, grass and tangled heather roots separate me from the cliff edge and the sparkling turquoise lure of the ocean beyond. It shimmers and dances, fading into the distant blue of the sky. Half a mile or so in the opposite direction to Porthnevek is the towering wall of a ruined building. I head towards it.

For a while I walk on grass, but as I breast the gentle slope, the terrain changes. Here it is more like the floor of Wheal Nevek valley: slivers of shale in russets and greys, which crunch beneath my walking boots. Even so, the ubiquitous heather and gorse have colonised the area, and swathes of brilliant yellow glow in the sun.

I am beginning to recognise this as mining country. The map marks the ruin as Wheal Catharine, with its sister Wheal Clare on the opposite side of the valley ahead. From where I'm standing, I can't see what's in the dip between them, but the remains of Wheal Clare are more complete, perched dramatically on the cliffs with the sea washing the rocks below.

Once again, the view robs me of my breath. Despite the sunshine it is elemental and wild, ugly and beautiful at the same time. I close my eyes and instead of the empty scrub and the wash of the waves, I imagine miners filling the plateau, smoke belching from the chimneys, the clatter and clang of ore being broken and moved.

I shake myself then skirt Wheal Catharine, heading down into the valley and towards the shore. The tide is out and damp sand stretches below the cliffs until a promontory seals off the wide beach just beyond Wheal Clare. I pick a middle path across the beach and turning away from the glistening sea, I look upwards as I walk.

The old mine's chimney is perched close to the edge of a seemingly precarious slope. Its grey-brown silhouette rises from the scrubby grass, the clear blue sky behind it. The cliffs are fractured and fissured, and I wonder how much is natural and how much is due to the labyrinth of tunnels which must lie behind them. A father and two small children are making their way into one of the wider cracks. Rather them than me.

Once I leave the beach, I explore the remains of Wheal Clare's buildings, admire the view, then return to the bottom of the valley to follow the footpath inland. A stream gushes beside me, screened by shrubs and small trees festooned with unpicked blackberries starting to shrivel. Even here autumn is beginning to grip.

At the end of the path, I climb a steep road and find myself opposite a pub called The Tinners. Do I or don't I? I'm not that far from Porthnevek, so will I be shunned here as well? I stand on the grass verge opposite, weighing up the possibilities. One way or another, it would be better to know.

The pub resembles a child's drawing of a house, with a door in the middle and four sash windows looking towards the road. It has a low wall in front of it, built around what appears to be a six-foot granite cross that must have fallen over some time in the dim and distant past. Balanced on top of it is a chalkboard advertising Sunday roasts, but I have a joint of pork at home. Just a drink, then. And probably a quick one.

The bar is directly opposite the door from the lobby and stretches partway along the wall. There are half a dozen stools in front of it, the three closest to me occupied by men. Nobody turns, nobody stares. That's a promising start. Even better when the barman smiles and says hello.

Through an arch come the clatter of cutlery on plates and the bubble of conversation, the scent of roasting potatoes filling the whole pub. Towards the back wall are four small tables, and at the one in the far corner sits the man who made those strange comments about being claimed by the view when I saw him on the cliff.

I study the labels on the pumps as the barman asks what I'd like.

"I'm not sure. I generally have a golden ale or something similar."

He picks up a small glass and pumps an inch of beer into it. "Try this."

I take a sip and it's fresh and hoppy. I nod at him. "Half, please."

While he pours my drink, he asks if I'm on holiday. The moment of truth.

I shake my head. "I've just moved to the area."

He smiles. "Then you need to remember to ask for Lushingtons."

As I put my glass to my lips, a bearded bloke at the far end of the bar raises his pint in my direction. "Welcome," he says, then returns to the newspaper he's studying with the thin, fair-haired pensioner next to him.

I thank him but decide not to strike up a conversation. A family with a booking for an early supper arrive, and the barman shows them to their table and prepares their drinks. I take a sip of beer, attach my phone to the Wi-Fi and scroll through the BBC website. The man next to me slides off his barstool and disappears through a door to the garden.

The pensioner looks up at me. "Don't mind Ray. He's never very sociable until he's finished his second pint." His accent isn't local and verges on the plummy.

"Thanks for the heads-up." I smile at him then go back to my drink, half listening as the men discuss their crossword.

"British filmmaker responsible for romcoms like *Notting Hill*, seven and six. Second letter I, last letter S. How the blazes would I know?"

The bearded man replies. "It's general knowledge, Tim, you either know it or you don't."

"It's Richard Curtis," I tell them.

Tim nods. "Looks like you could be useful."

"Throw the odd clue in my direction and I'll see what I can do."

After a while, Ray returns and continues his silent sipping of his pint. The barman comes and goes as people arrive and depart, a friendly word for everyone. In a quiet patch, he asks me what brings me to Porthnevek.

It's important I give my answer loud and clear. "I work for the company planning the glamping site in Wheal Nevek valley."

"It's about time someone did something with that overgrown rubbish pile," says Ray. Tim nods.

"I don't think everyone's so pleased about it," I venture.

"Well, they won't be. That's folks, isn't it?" Ray picks up his pint again and I sense the conversation is at an end.

After a while, the bearded man calls across the bar, "Hey, Gun, this one's for you. Peer of the realm, the young Queen Victoria's trusted adviser. Begins with M."

A voice I recognise comes from behind me. "Sorry, Keith. I'm listening to George."

I frown. Another strange choice of words. I glance over my shoulder. The man from the cliffs is sitting alone.

When I turn back, Ray is laughing. "George is the pub ghost," he tells me. "An old mine captain who was a regular about a hundred years ago. Gun likes to have a chat with him."

"Really?" My eyes must be out on stalks.

Tim chuckles. "Take no notice. Gun's shot away."

As I finish my drink, I contribute a few more answers to the crossword and begin to relax. For the moment at least, I have a small foothold here, but I don't want to outstay my welcome. As I am gathering my bag from the floor, Gun approaches the bar.

"Sorry, Keith. If you don't have that answer yet, it could be Melbourne." He turns to me, his green eyes stopping me in my tracks. "Been out on the cliffs again?"

"Yes. It's so beautiful. When the sun's out, it's hard to stay away."

31

"So I was right about them claiming you. What's your name?"

"It's Anna."

"Then I'll see you again, Anna." There's a gentleness about him that's unusual, beguiling, and I can't help but return his smile.

"Yes." I pull my rucksack over my shoulder and take a step towards the door. "Goodbye, all. Enjoy the rest of the crossword."

Ray murmurs, Keith waves and Tim bids me good afternoon. Gun leans against the barstool I've just vacated, his eyes on me as I walk away.

Outside, the air is crisp and cold, ahead of me to the west a faint orange glow of sunset. I cross the road, taking the footpath, but I regret it almost at once as the last of the light fades and I step in a puddle, water splashing over my trainer and up the leg of my jeans. This is a popular spot for dog walkers, so goodness knows what else I'll tread in if I'm not careful. I switch on the torch on my phone.

I soon reach the road to the farm and, sweeping the tarmac ahead of me with the narrow beam, I stride out. The sweet smell of silage permeates the air, and I can hear the cattle rustling in the field between me and Wheal Dream. On the other side of their pasture headlamps track the main road to the village, but then another light catches my eye, deep in the valley. I stop to try and pinpoint it, but it's disappeared. Maybe it was just a reflection.

The cottage is warm and welcoming. A long soak in the bath is tempting, but I really need to sort out my emails and diary ready for the new week, so I head to my makeshift office in the dining room.

In the moment before I turn on the light, I am sure I see something flickering in the valley, but by the time I slide open the patio doors and step outside it is in darkness again. I stand for a few minutes, watching with my arms wrapped around my chest, but there is nothing more, and very soon the cold defeats me.

At the top of my inbox is an email from Luke Hastings, asking if I've given any more thought to doing some hours at Trelissick. He suggests we meet for a coffee to discuss it. They must be absolutely desperate to go that far, but he says they have special plans for the run-up to Christmas he thinks I'll enjoy. I mull it over and come to the conclusion there's no real reason to refuse.

CHAPTER FIVE

To my surprise, Luke arranges to meet at a cider farm a few miles away rather than at one of the National Trust properties, but after a solid morning preparing my responses to planning objections, I am more than ready for a little Tuesday truancy. They are all fairly predictable — but some of them are pretty vitriolic, and it makes me wonder what might happen during the build if we do win.

Luke is waiting in the courtyard outside the farm's restaurant. He's leaning against the wall wearing a thick jumper with a bright red scarf wound around his neck. As he holds out his hand to shake mine, I remember what a nice smile he has. It creases the corners of his blue eyes and gives him a couple of dimples, which seem completely at odds with his strong bone structure. Combined with the scarf, his expression gives him an almost boyish charm.

He finds a seat close to the wood burner in the centre of the room and, as it's lunchtime, he suggests we have one of their famous baguettes. I tell him I'll eat anything except egg, and he strides towards the counter. I sit back on the low sofa and close my eyes, enjoying the warmth. I probably should light the burner in the cottage more often instead of relying on the central heating.

Luke returns with a tray laden with a cafetiere of coffee, cups and saucers, and two enormous baguettes cut into two.

"One's sausage and mustard and the other cheese and chutney. I thought we could share, if that's all right with you?"

"Perfect." I smile at him.

He rubs his hands together. "Right, sausage first because it's hot."

It's also delicious, and I try not to fall on it like a ravening wolf. Instead, I ask him how he came to be in Cornwall.

"I was born here. My dad was in the navy and he was stationed at Culdrose at the time, and of course we moved around, but I always wanted to come back. I couldn't believe it when I saw this job advertised. I've worked in the charity sector since I graduated, so it was perfect — like coming home."

"Have you been back here long?" I take another bite of baguette, careful not to let ketchup ooze down my chin.

"Almost five years. Time just flies. I should probably be looking for my next promotion, but I keep forgetting to." He laughs.

"I've been doing the same job for the last eight," I tell him, "but I move around so much I don't get bored."

"So what exactly is it you do? You just put project management on your application form."

"I work for a glamping business, looking after the development of new sites from planning through to a few months after opening. Then I hand over to the permanent manager and move on."

"Sounds interesting."

"And it can be challenging, because very often the locals don't like it."

Luke laughs. "Well, you can open as many as you like in Cornwall. We need all the tourists we can get."

"Plus, it would be worth training me as a volunteer if I was to stick around a bit longer. Although I guess the skills are transferable."

He puts down his baguette and looks directly at me. "So are you seriously considering it?"

"Yes, I am."

"Well, that's great news, because we really need you, Anna. You may have noticed you're rather younger than most of our volunteers, and I can't see any of them dressing up as French maids." He winks, but somehow it isn't creepy.

"What, suspenders and a tiny black skirt?"

He fans himself with a menu and we both laugh. "Now that's an image to conjure," he says.

I feel myself starting to blush, so I ask him what he really means.

"Oh, I do mean French maid, but in the Regency sense. They were very fashionable, and I'm sure the Daniell family would have had one. This Christmas we're decorating Trelissick as it would have been in 1815, and I'm asking each volunteer to dress up as a member of the household. So of course it would be great to have someone from a slightly … er … younger generation."

"Are you sure about French maids in 1815? We'd been at war with France for so long it surprises me."

"A lot of the French aristocracy fled to London during the revolution, so perhaps they started the trend. I'm no historian, but the house steward seems to think it's right. And I can promise you the costume would be a rather demure plain grey dress."

"Thankfully." I grin at him. "I'm not getting my legs out in December — for anyone."

"Then you're looking at one disappointed man. But seriously, Anna, will you? Just weekends and one or two evenings when we open late? You wouldn't have to do all of them, although a few shifts in November too to get you up to speed would help."

Luke's smiling at me and honestly, what would be the harm? "All right." I open the calendar on my phone. "When did you say the induction was?"

"A week today. It starts at six thirty."

"Oh. That's the day of the planning meeting, and I've been warned it could go on a bit."

He puts his hand gently on my arm. "Get there when you can, Anna. I assure you it would be no hardship at all helping you to catch up on the bits you miss."

I manage to stay away from The Tinners until Thursday, but after another vicious text from up country I need a drink. As I wrap my anorak around me against the cold, I try to convince myself their bullying is entirely normal and actual face to face confrontation is extremely unlikely. Logic doesn't stop me having nightmares about shadows lurking around my front door, though, and I find myself glancing up and down the lane before setting out.

The pub is practically deserted, with only Gun perched on a barstool chatting to Rich, the barman.

"Where is everybody?" I ask.

"Gone to a wake," Gun tells me. "Eric — used to be a local here before you arrived."

"And you weren't invited?" I tease.

He shrugs. "I don't see the point."

Rich laughs as he pours my beer. "It's pretty meaningless for you, Gun, isn't it? You can still chat to Eric whenever you like."

Gun shakes his head. "It's not like that."

I can't say I'm comfortable with this conversation, but I'm curious all the same. "Then what is it like?"

He turns to me, green eyes piercing mine. "It isn't up to me. Rich makes it sound as though I conjure up spirits at will, when the reality is they decide if they want to talk to me."

"I'm sorry, but I don't really understand."

"Well, it's like … say … remember the day we first met on the cliffs? Well, it was up to you whether you stopped to talk or not, and you did."

"But you started the conversation."

"You're not a ghost."

"So if you did see a ghost out on the cliffs…"

He puts down his glass. "Which I do, all the time…"

"I'm sorry, Gun. This is so weird."

He smiles. "Well, at least you've got the guts to say so to my face. Shall we change the subject? I'm glad everyone's piping down about having to pay 5p for a plastic bag. We need to do something about the environment, don't we?"

Although we chat happily enough for a while, I decline Rich's offer of a second drink.

"I'm off too," Gun tells me. "I can just as easily walk your way as any other."

"Do you live in Porthnevek?" I ask.

"More or less. Nankathes."

"So you don't walk down through the valley?"

He holds the door open for me, shaking his head. "Not now it's private land."

"Some people do. I saw lights there the other night."

He tucks his chin into his collar and we cross the road. He pulls a torch from his pocket and we walk in silence for a while, following its beam. Halfway down the track, he stops. "There used to be a huge mine here — bigger than Wheal Clare, even. Strange how not a trace remains."

"What, Wheal Nevek? I wonder what happened to it?"

"Ran out, closed. George can remember the foundations of buildings. The last of the stones were taken for the smelting works by the stream."

"So fairly recently, then?"

Gun laughs. "No. Remember George died in 1913."

A shiver runs through me from head to toe. "Stop it, Gun. You're freaking me out."

"Best walk you home, then, Anna. But there's really nothing to be scared of. I promise."

CHAPTER SIX

The sulphurous lights in Cornwall Council's car park do little to improve the planning consultant Roland Tresawl's cadaverous looks, but he is smiling. He's an exceedingly stuffy man and can have an annoyingly overbearing manner, but at this precise moment he has every reason to look pleased with himself.

"May I buy you a drink to celebrate?" he asks.

"No, thank you. And I'm not being difficult, Roland, you did a fantastic job in the planning meeting. It's just I need to be somewhere else."

He nods. "You were rather impressive yourself. Stood up well to the abuse."

We start to walk briskly towards our cars. "It was pretty nasty, wasn't it?"

"Especially when they realised they weren't going to win. As I said at the beginning, there's always opposition, but I've rarely seen anything like this. Not unless there's wildlife involved." He rolls his eyes.

"Do you think they'll appeal?"

He looks at me over his glasses. "They'd have to go to the powers that be in Bristol if they did, and the development's too small for that."

"Then we're watertight. Though I do worry they might try something when we start the build."

"It would be most unusual, but the bad feeling does seem to be genuine. I wonder why?"

"If we could have got to the bottom of 'why', I could have nipped it in the bud. But the village closed ranks. And the formal objections were rather predictable. As you told me they would be." I look at my watch. "I'm sorry — I really must be going. Thank you again for all your help."

As I climb into my car, the adrenalin is still coursing through my veins. The last thing I want to do is listen to a lecture on health and safety and customer experience at Trelissick. At least the lecturer passes as eye candy. I find myself wondering if Luke's single. I slap the thought back down. He's probably just flirtatious, and at the moment that's good enough for me.

It's a few jobs since I've had a man in my life, and even then it was pretty casual, but since my marriage ended so badly I haven't wanted to risk anything more. My last boyfriend suited me perfectly — he was a pilot flying in and out of Gatwick when I was, according to some protesters, ripping up trees in rural Sussex. He was renting the flat above mine and we met on the stairs. It was a very ordinary relationship between ships passing in the night. Companionship, sex and no thought of permanence. We still text sometimes; he winds me up with photos of his food in exotic hotels. I generally reply with a jacket potato.

One of the last conversations I had with my mother was about whether I'd ever settle down again. She'd given up hoping I'd have a family, but she still reckoned I needed some roots. Maybe she was right, or maybe it was the pain of having her precious roots ripped away from her that made her say it. But I can't go there now — and anyway, I'll never know one way or another. I glance at my phone. She'd hate what else is going on too, but that isn't my fault.

I was hoping to disguise my late arrival at the induction by sneaking into the back, but given there are only six of us there's no obscurity in numbers. As I slide through the door, Luke glances in my direction and smiles.

"Anna — you made it. Help yourself to a cuppa and take a seat." Then he carries on explaining the National Trust's customer charter.

I recognise one of the women from the recruitment talk and sit down next to her. Once Luke has finished, we troop after him towards the house for a detailed tour from Julie, the steward. My new friend introduces herself as Liz and we shake hands. She's bouncy and blonde and a newly retired nurse, and suddenly I feel tired next to her. All I want to do is sleep for a week but I keep nodding and smiling, wondering what the hell I've taken on.

Although I try very hard to listen to the tour, little of the information sinks in and I'm relieved when we're each given a lever arch file of papers to take away to study. As room guides we could be placed anywhere, and the whole of the downstairs is open to the public. Much of upstairs was updated by the last owners, so it's being used for offices and storage.

At the end of the tour, Luke pulls me to one side in the kitchen corridor as the others file towards the front door. "Would you like me to fill you in on the parts of my talk you missed?" he asks. "Maybe over some supper?"

The post-adrenalin heaviness is like a lead cape around my shoulders. "I'm sorry, I wouldn't take it in. I've had a bit of a long day."

"You do look a little tired, but still beautiful all the same." He touches my cheek. "Perhaps another time?"

The warmth from his fingertips flows through me. "Yes, another time."

"Friday? I'll book somewhere and pick you up at seven. Your address will be on your file."

"You're sure it isn't too much trouble?"

He grins. "It will be my absolute pleasure."

CHAPTER SEVEN

My breath forms clouds as I step onto the patio, the first rays of sunshine filtering into the valley below. There's the faintest sparkle of frost on the top of the hawthorn, and the berries packed on its naked branches seem to glow in the early light. What a glorious day to start work on Wheal Dream.

The locals won't expect us to move so quickly. Just a few days after planning, and on a Friday at that. But I had the clearance contractor booked anyway, and it should only take a day or so for a man with a digger to grub up the brambles and gorse, so when the paperwork comes through from the council we can start to level the centre of the site. I finish my coffee and stride along the lane to unlock the gate from the main road at the top of the valley.

I spend the first half of the morning marking out the area to be cleared with the digger driver while his workmate attacks the overgrown edges of the site with his strimmer. I'm half looking over my shoulder in the direction of the village but we suffer no interference, although I fear it might be the calm before the storm. I very much doubt the protestors will simply fade away.

It is almost dusk when the digger falls silent, and the driver phones me in my makeshift office at Nevek Cot to say they'll be back for a while tomorrow morning to finish off and get rid of the rubbish. Day one complete. I power down my computer and head upstairs. I have what may very well pass for a date tonight, and a long soak in the bath will get me in just the right frame of mind.

To be honest, I'm feeling pretty good about life anyway. I love the start of a new build, the thrill of possibilities. Out with the old — the couch grass and gorse — and in with the new. A different chapter in the valley's life. I think of Luke and wonder if the coincidence means he'll be a new chapter in mine, but is there a page I need to turn over first? For the moment, the unwanted texts and calls have stopped, so that's a question for another day.

By the time I drain the bath and wrap myself in a towel, night has properly descended. I pad across my bedroom to close the curtains, but as I glance down into the valley I notice something. There is a tiny flicker and the beginnings of an orange glow.

My trousers and jumper are on the floor. I haul them on and, grabbing the fire blanket from the kitchen, race across the cattle field to the valley, stumbling over tussocks of grass before heading towards a gap in the hedge and vaulting the barbed wire.

Halfway down, the smoke begins to reach my nostrils. Somewhere to my right is a massive bang, which almost floors me, but as an eerie glow lights the sky I realise it's a firework. I scramble the last part of the bank, thankfully strimmed this morning. Now I can see the orange glow properly — it's a very small fire in a corner of the pile of grubbed up gorse, right next to the digger. I whip the fire blanket out of its wrapper and throw it over the flames, pressing it down with my bare hands to take out as much air as I can.

The choking smoke fills my nose, my mouth, my throat, making it almost impossible to breathe. But I can't give up, although I'm coughing and wheezing and my hands are beginning to burn. I have to put this out. The night is split by another firework and in the corner of my eye I see a shadow.

It pounces and I'm pulled away.

"What are you doing, you stupid woman?"

There's a moment of terror before I recognise the voice, but what with the smoke and having the air knocked out of me as I escape from his arms and hit the ground, I can't reply.

I roll onto my side to see Gun wrench a fire extinguisher from under the digger's seat and spray it on the flames licking around the edge of the blanket. I never thought of it, but I'm too busy coughing to berate myself any further.

Slowly I sit up, but breathing is tough. Gun's elongated silhouette is black against the dying embers and the drifting smoke gives him a wraith-like appearance. I can't help but shudder, and the shudder turns into uncontrollable shivering. There's a final blast from the extinguisher and the orange glow dies away.

Gun turns and holds out a hand to help me to my feet. It's only when he grasps my palm that I realise it hurts and I snatch it back. He crouches next to me in the darkness.

"What is it, Anna?"

"My hand. I might have burnt it."

"The whole lot of you might have gone up in flames."

"No, I…" I start to cough again.

He pulls his torch from the pocket of his walking trousers. "Hold them out."

I do as I'm told and we inspect my palms together. They're red in places, but not blistered.

Gun shakes his head. "You are one stupid, stupid, woman. Why the hell didn't you use the fire extinguisher?"

"I didn't think."

"Come on, let's get you home and soak those hands in cool water."

This time he takes me by the elbow to help me into an upright position. I ache all over and I'm still shaking. He takes off his coat and wraps it around my shoulders. When I protest he'll get cold, he simply shrugs.

Rather than take the shorter route through Nankathes, he guides me up the dirt track to the main road, his torch scanning the path ahead.

"They made a good start down here today," he says.

"Yes. We need to crack on before the weather turns." He grunts. "Gun, you've never said. Are you for or against the development?"

"It's not my concern. And my name's Sebastian, by the way."

"Sorry, Sebastian. You don't like being called Gun?"

"It's not the name, it's the reason for it I don't like. But it's not too bad with the guys in the pub. *They* don't mean any harm."

"They told me it's because you're shot away, but right now you seem the least shot away person on the planet."

He stops and looks down at me, but in the darkness I can't see his face. "Exactly," is all he says.

When we reach Nevek Cot, there is a car outside and a figure at the front door. Luke.

He steps into the road. "I thought you'd stood me up," he says. He glances at Gun. "You haven't, have you?"

"There was an emergency on site," I tell him. "A fire. G— Sebastian helped me to put it out." I delve into my trouser pocket for my key, wincing.

"Anna's burnt her hands," Gun says. "Make sure she puts them in cool water for a while. Then maybe some honey on them later to stop them blistering."

"It's all right," says Luke, "I'm a qualified first aider."

The door swings open and I turn on the light. Luke is in chinos and a jacket. Gun is looking as dishevelled as I feel. I shrug his coat from my shoulders and hand it to him. "Thank you for everything."

"It's fine." Gun nods and strides down the lane as Luke ushers me inside.

I lead Luke through to the kitchen, where he inspects my palms then cleans the washing up bowl with anti-bacterial wipes before filling it with cool water and setting it on the table in front of me. I plunge in my hands and although they tingle at first, the pain begins to recede.

"Thank you."

He leans on the back of a chair. "Whatever happened?"

"There was a fire. I was trying to put it out."

"With your bare hands?"

"No, with a fire blanket."

He shakes his head. "I see you're going to need extra fire safety training too." Then he smiles. "But not tonight. How about I cancel the restaurant and get us a takeaway? There's a really good Chinese in Redruth."

"That sounds perfect."

"I guess I'll be about forty minutes — longer if there's a queue. Is that okay?"

I nod. I'm beyond tired. He drops a kiss onto the top of my head and then leaves.

I gaze around the room while my hands soak, my brain beginning to mull over the possible causes of the fire. Sabotage or a stray firework?

The cuffs of my sweatshirt are black, and I become aware I stink of smoke. I drag myself to my feet and up the stairs. The warm water in the shower and the shampoo sting my fingers, but I need to get clean. The towel is rough against my damaged skin, so I pat myself dry then dress in a long denim skirt and my favourite green jumper. I'm just spraying myself with perfume when I hear a knock on the door.

Luke's on the step, clutching the Chinese. He grins when he sees me. "That's a proper transformation."

I laugh. "I didn't realise how smoky I was. I still feel a bit like a kipper."

"You don't smell like one — that's lovely perfume. How are your hands feeling now?"

"Sore, but they're okay."

In the kitchen he sets out our meal and shows me his other purchases. There's antiseptic cream for my burns; I smooth it over them while he opens a bottle of wine. Finally, he pulls out a pack of plastic gloves, explaining I need to keep my hands clean until I'm sure they won't blister.

I smile up at him. "You are just the kindest man."

"And a sucker for a damsel in distress. Come on, let's eat."

At first we talk about food; his preference for Chinese, mine for Italian. Then we move on to my holidays there and the evening passes quickly. The wine dulls the pain for me, but one glass is his lot when he's driving. I apologise there's no spare bed.

"It's okay," he tells me. "I need to get back to Kelly."

"Kelly?"

"Didn't I mention I have a dog? She'll be crossing her legs by now, I shouldn't wonder."

"Maybe you could bring her over here for a walk sometime?"

"She'd like that. As would I. It's been a lovely evening, Anna, despite the fact it wasn't as I'd planned. Now, will you promise me you'll soak and dress your hands again before you go to bed?"

I stand to see him out. At the front door, he turns and drops a single kiss onto my lips. "I'll call you tomorrow to see how you are."

I watch as he climbs into his car, then I go back inside to run water into the bowl.

I wanted more than just one kiss. Hopefully that's for another time.

CHAPTER EIGHT

I'm down in the valley looking for clues before the clearance guys arrive, my second cup of coffee in a thermal mug balanced on one of the large stones near the Clwyd Cap. I don't know what I expect to find, but as I rake through the charred gorse there's nothing, not even a matchstick. A jackdaw calls, startling me, and the sea beats the cliffs in the distance, but otherwise all is still.

I pick up my coffee and walk towards the Nankathes end of the site, wondering how Gun is this morning. It will take me a while to get used to thinking of him as Sebastian; Gun somehow suits his lone wolf ranginess, the enigmatic edges of his character. Sebastian is softer, somehow, calm in a crisis.

I turn back towards the valley and take a sip of my coffee. Now the gorse has been cleared from the central area, I can see it's as flat as the surveys suggested and will make quite a decent platform for the yurts as it is. The groundworks guys will have their work cut out tucking the services building into the side of the valley below the cattle field, and putting in a proper road from above will entail a fair amount of earth-moving too.

In my mind's eye I'm seeing the finished development, but the reality in front of me is an ugly swathe of naked earth. A thick band of vegetation has been left at one side as a nature corridor, and it clings to the bottom of the steep shale slope below the main road like a drunken caterpillar. My hands are beginning to sting. It's probably time to go home and soak them again.

I become aware of footsteps behind me and I turn around.

"How dare you rip our valley apart!"

Serena. It would be. Flanked by half a dozen other people, some of whom I recognise from the planning meeting.

"I dare because I have permission to build. Planning permission. As you know."

"But you can't start yet."

Do they know it will be a week or so before I have that precious planning certificate? But even so, I've done nothing wrong. "We haven't started, just cleared the ground. Which we don't actually need planning permission for. So perhaps you can tell me just exactly what you're doing here?"

"None of your frigging business," a man calls. He's short and thickset with a grey tinge to his beard.

I take a step towards them. The gate has been locked now we've begun work, and I'm glad of its steel bars. "But it is my business, isn't it? And despite the bad feeling at the planning meeting, I'm still open to working with the community to reach some sort of compromise."

"We don't want a compromise. We want you to stop." Serena's hands are thrust deep into her pockets. Mine start to throb against the warm metal of my thermos as I grip it.

"You need to accept that isn't going to happen."

"We don't need to accept anything."

I take a step forwards. Those startling green eyes are so full of anger. "I'm sorry, Serena. I'm happy to sit down and talk about this rationally, but not to have a slanging match. It doesn't achieve anything."

"You'll be sorry!" she yells.

The digger driver appears behind me. "Trouble, love?"

I don't take my eyes from Serena's. "Are you threatening me? It sounded a bit like a threat."

"You've raped our valley. What do you expect?" Her voice is cracking and she turns away, leading her band of followers back through Nankathes towards the village.

It's not until much later in the morning I begin to wonder about those eyes. There's a simple way to see if my hunch is right, and I head onto the cliffs for my normal circular walk to The Tinners. But a sea fret is swirling up the coast and even the stark outline of Wheal Catharine is obscured, so instead I hug the grass-topped wall which bounds the farmland, the damp silence enveloping me. I don't meet even one single dog walker.

The pub is more than welcoming, though. Ray is smoking in the shelter outside the back door, and Keith is sitting at one end of the bar, crossword in front of him.

"Hi, Anna. It's this bloody general knowledge one on a Saturday. Any idea what the capital of Sicily is?"

"Palermo?" I unwind my scarf and hang it on a hook behind the door before shrugging out of my anorak.

"Fits."

Rich has a half-pint glass poised. "Lushingtons?"

"Please." I take the empty stool next to Keith and scan the paper in front of him. "What else is left to do?"

I try to keep my hands in my lap or wrapped around my drink. Just one blister has appeared, a small one in the soft flesh at the base of my index finger, and overall the redness is beginning to fade. After a while, I ask, "No Gun today?"

"Said he's run out of money. Doesn't want to add to his tab when he can't pay it off," Ray tells me.

"How much is on it, Rich? Are you allowed to say?"

"It's not too bad. Not by Ray's standards, anyway. Not a big drinker, is our Gun."

I take my debit card out of my purse. "Then I'll pay it off."

Ray whistles. "Fancy paying mine too?"

I laugh. "Not on my salary. Gun did me a favour last night and I owe him."

"Fair enough," says Rich.

Nobody asks. I like that about this pub. But I tell them anyway. "There was a fire on site. Gun spotted it and helped me to put it out."

"Arson?" asks Keith.

"I can't be sure. It just seems a bit of a coincidence it was the day we started work down there. Luckily the contractor left the digger overnight, and Gun knew where to find the fire extinguisher. Is that what he does?"

"What, put out fires?" Ray rolls his eyes.

"No, does he drive a digger?"

"I've not known it, but he has laboured on building sites. Anything really, when he has to. Always hand to mouth, is Gun."

"He's a joiner by trade," Keith chips in. "A bloody good one at that. But there isn't always call, and he doesn't exactly push himself. Can't push himself, some of the time. Makes stuff for his sister's shop, though — keeps his hand in."

Bingo. I was right. Owners of startling green eyes like that just have to be related, and I remember Serena telling me about her brother. How close they are. An uncomfortable thought slides into my mind — how did Gun know about the fire? He was pretty noncommittal about where he stood on the development.

CHAPTER NINE

Hungover is not the best way to start my career as a volunteer at Trelissick. Yesterday went from bad to worse; as I was walking home, the texts began again.

You'd better get yourself up here. Oh, but you never were here, were you? Not when it mattered.

So instead of a quiet evening slumped happily in front of *Strictly*, I ended up sobbing into a bottle of Chianti instead.

I'm not on duty in the house until twelve, so I force down a bacon roll and two cups of black coffee in the café in Trelissick's yard before taking a brisk walk around the boundary of the parkland. At the top of the staff car park is a Victorian-style round tower, straight from the pages of a fairy story, and through a nearby arch in the brick wall is the road. It sinks between high banks as I follow it down to the river, the shudder and clank of the chain ferry at the bottom reverberating through my skull. A wooden sign points the way and I climb a few steps onto a muddy path, skeletal trees and frost-damaged vegetation on either side.

To my left is the River Fal, deep and dark green. There is a mooring platform and further along cages for growing mussels. To my right the bank rises steeply towards Trelissick's gardens, glossy camellia leaves above me as damp vegetal smells mix with the salt tang of the air. The breeze is in my face, blowing up from Falmouth harbour and weaving through the trees, its freshness doing more to cure my churning stomach and aching head than the coffee did. The cool air is taking the last of the sting out of my hands too, as they hang loose and gloveless by my sides.

The path curves slowly around a headland between the main channel and one of the deep inlets that characterise the Fal. Ahead I catch glimpses of a pebbly beach, but it isn't until I'm almost upon it the house comes into view, majestic at the top of its rise, its white portico gleaming despite the grey morning. From here it almost looks like three houses jammed together, and I rack my brains for what we were told about its evolution. I'm sure something was here before 'Pillars' Daniell got hold of it — a farmhouse, I think my information file said. But his contribution of the mini-Parthenon is certainly the standout feature, although to its right is a rather pleasant, restrained Georgian style house, and beyond that the orangery, which has had a white-pillared porch stuck on it for good measure too.

I prepare for a long, slow trudge across the parkland and up the hill, but my body copes rather better than I dared hope. My phone bleeps and I stiffen, but I make myself look at it and I'm glad I did — it's Luke, wishing me luck. All the same, I'll be happy to lock my mobile away in the staffroom for a few hours.

I'm filling in today, while we take it in turns to have our costumes fitted for the Christmas extravaganza. Liz is on duty in the hall and gives me a message from Julie that I'm to go first, so I follow her instructions and duck under the rope at the bottom of the stairs.

Whoever decided not to open the first floor wasn't wrong. It's fine as far as the prying eye gazing upwards can see, but turning back along the landing there's almost a tidemark where the perfectly decorated period walls end and the 1950s wallpaper begins. Along the landing and up a few more stairs a door is open, and Julie peeps around it, beckoning me to come in.

The room over the entrance hall is light and airy, despite the paper peeling from the corners and the threadbare chintzy carpet. Half of one side is taken up with a rail of clothing: richly coloured frocks, dazzling red footmen's uniforms and next to them drab navies and greys. Consulting her clipboard, she leads me to this section.

"Luke's got you down as the French maid. Is that okay?"

I laugh. "It'll have to be. No, seriously, Julie — whatever fits in with everyone else."

She pulls a grey dress from the rack. "You don't mind the plain costume?"

"Oh, no. I like to blend into the background."

Although it boasts little in the way of decoration, the dress has a tight-fitting bodice and a skirt that will fall from just below my boobs. The material is softer than I expected and has an almost satin-like quality, so I ask Julie about this.

"Very often lady's maids would have been given their mistresses' cast-offs, which they would alter to suit their status. Most were fine seamstresses — it was an important part of their job."

"Oh, lord — I hope you don't expect me to sit in a corner sewing."

"Nothing like that. In fact, we need to exercise a certain amount of licence in your role because you'd have been mainly working upstairs. But there's going to be a set piece every weekend afternoon where the coach and horses arrive from the stables and you and Mrs Daniell climb in and drive away to deliver Christmas goodies to the poor. All very theatrical."

I pull my jumper over my head and start to unbutton my trousers. "And is that likely to have happened?"

"Oh yes; we don't have that many records about the Daniell family, but a diary kept by the vicar at Porthnevek records Elizabeth visiting to dispense food and medicines to the elderly and unemployed miners, and her maid would have surely gone with her." She holds the dress open for me and I step into it, turning away from her so she can do up the zip. "There would have been tiny buttons if the dress was real. Thank goodness for modern technology."

The dress is a reasonable fit, but it gapes a little around its square cleavage so I stand still while Julie pins it how it should be. "I wondered," I ask her, "so soon after the Napoleonic wars, whether Elizabeth Daniell really would have had a French maid."

"Oh yes, we even know her name. Although to be honest, it could have been an English girl pretending. If the high class couldn't actually get one from France, they would give their lady's maid a French name anyway."

"So who am I to be?"

"Thérèse. Or possibly Thérèsa."

"If there isn't much information about the Daniells, how do we know?"

"There's a letter mentioning Thérèse in an archive relating to the artist, Thomas Chalmers. He was some sort of relative." She secures the last pin. "Now, see how it feels to move in. Walk to the other end of the landing and back."

The sleeves are quite tight, but the fabric isn't too heavy and the dress falls to just above my ankles. I try to imagine what it would have been like being a maid here, scurrying around, fetching and carrying, forever at your mistress's beck and call. But as it is I glide serenely along the landing, past the faded wallpaper into the Georgian area with its still life of flowers at the head of the stairs. As I turn to retrace my steps, I notice a door is ajar. I catch a glimpse of a small fireplace and a low antique chair with a heart-shaped back next it upholstered in the most beautiful green brocade.

"How is it?" Julie calls.

"It's fine. Perfectly workable. Now, what should I have on my feet?"

"Do you have any black pumps?"

"No, but I can always pick up a pair. They'd come in handy for work, I'm sure."

Julie unzips the dress and I change back into my own clothes. As I head for the stairs to relieve the guide in the dining room, I notice the bedroom door is closed. The chair looked beautifully preserved, and I make a mental note to ask Julie about it when she has more time.

PART TWO: 1815

CHAPTER TEN

Red was a useful colour for soldiers' uniforms, Thomas thought. Not so the white of their breeches. Of course, as an artist his eye sought the contrast, but the red was in danger of taking over. Red and muddy brown. And the blackening buzz of flies as the sun lifted higher over the horizon and began to find some warmth.

For the finished work, his watercolours would be of no use. Not sufficiently visceral. That was the word in sentiment, if not in literal meaning. But how to portray the stink of putrefaction, the damned waste of lives? To show it as it was would offend the sensibilities, make the viewer recoil. No, he was paid to celebrate the glory. He'd heard in the town last night Napoleon was on the run with the ragtag remains of his army. Perhaps now the killing was over.

He shifted on the log and turned the pages of his leather-bound sketchbook. Herein the reality lay. A lifeless hand stretched as though in supplication, a face barely recognisable as such with fair hair matted and soaked in blood, the guts spilling from a horse. On another page, a woman in a shabby dress pulled teeth from a corpse. Everywhere corruption of flesh and soul.

But for now they were objects, shapes. And he must complete his work before the day became too warm, the stench overpowering. On a fresh double page he sketched the lines of the hills, the ruined hovel at the edge of the woods, the patterns and shapes of the red and blue uniforms that would form the outline of the finished canvas.

The trees behind him offered some protection from the sun, but his throat was becoming dry. He tucked his book under his arm and dropped his graphite into his pocket before standing and stretching to return to his horse. It was enough. The real work could be done in the comfort of his London studio.

When he first saw the young woman, he thought he was imagining her. She clung to a shattered tree, dark hair straying from her mob cap, her face hidden by her raised arms. Her grey cloak flowed around her shoulders with such fluidity she gave the appearance of a wraith, shimmering between this world and the next. Even from twenty yards her posture screamed anguish, and before he knew it Thomas was feeling for his pencil.

No. She needed help. He allowed himself a moment to commit the scene to memory and then approached her.

Even when he was within touching distance, she did not turn. He could see her shoulders were heaving, although her sobs bore the bitter silence of despair. He cleared his throat. Still she clung to the tree.

In the distance he heard hoofbeats. Four, five horses. English voices, coarse words. Flashes of red through the trees.

He reached out, the grey fabric of her sleeve smooth against his fingers. She jumped and let out a gasp, arching her back against the trunk as she faced him.

"I mean you no harm."

Her eyes were grey, empty. Devoid of life and comprehension. Red spots of colour lit the pallor of her cheeks and she swayed a little.

The soldiers' voices were closer, and Thomas judged they were riding along the edge of the wood. He tried again. "Mademoiselle?"

Her eyes closed. Her mouth moved in a vain attempt to form some words before her knees gave way. Thomas caught her in his arms, her body so light it felt as if her dress and cloak were empty.

At the moment of waking, Thérèse believed she was in her father's house in Roscoff. Something in the lumpiness of the mattress, the horses passing beneath the window, gave her a fleeting impression of security that vanished when she opened her eyes.

Seeing a man standing at an easel just feet away, she bit back a cry and closed them again. Who...? But the question was only part formed when a torrent of anguish burst inside her. Paul. He was gone — gone. How could she ever live without him?

Her instinctive response was to curl into a ball and weep, but in a strange room with a strange man that was impossible. Instead she clenched her teeth together, willing the tears away, and forced herself to think before she was entirely overtaken by the waves of grief running through her.

As best she could she tried to piece together the nightmare fragments of the morning. Through the hours of darkness, the small band of cantinières and other camp followers had stumbled against the tide of the retreating army, searching for their menfolk. Seeing faces she'd recognised, she'd asked about Paul, but no-one had seen him since the action at Quatre Bras. She moved from group to group, man to man, until eventually the look in one soldier's eyes had told her all she needed to know. She'd pressed him and he'd simply shaken his head before urging her to turn back and take whatever protection the army could still give.

But the cantinières had continued towards the battlefield, finding their first corpse in the grey of early dawn. A perfect man, save for his bloodied blue artillery trousers. She'd kept her distance while the others searched his pockets for anything of value and Marie-Louise cut the buttons from his tunic. If Paul was dead, would someone do that to him?

The group had moved on and she'd followed a little way behind. *If Paul was dead. Paul was dead.* She'd rolled the words around her head, trying to make them fit. She had no reason to disbelieve the soldier. There had been truth in his eyes. And yet — she'd felt no pain. And dawn was still breaking around her, another day beginning.

The second corpse had ripped her dormant feelings from their shell. A crater for a stomach, his face blown half away. Dark hair like Paul's. But not Paul's. What if Paul… A scream had risen through her, and she'd turned and run until she'd cannoned into a tree and clung to it.

Through half-closed lids, she now observed the artist. She could not remember who he was or how they had come to be in this room. There was something, and she grappled for it. The warm, dusty smell of a horse. The jerking motion of a trot.

And what now? Had he taken her to use her, or was he kind? She studied his profile. His long nose had a bump in it and his lips were thin, but he had an expression of serenity as he sketched, one moment leaning to look out of the window and the next his pencil flying across the sheet of board.

He glanced towards her and smiled. A stream of words tumbled from his mouth, but she understood none of them. Was she losing her mind?

He cleared his throat and spoke more slowly, in French this time with a heavy accent. "Excuse me, Mademoiselle. I forgot myself. I suppose you understand no English?"

English. The enemy. She pulled herself up the bed and clung to the mahogany post, staring at him.

He put down his pencil. "I mean you no harm. Truly. There is no reason to be scared. Napoleon is captured — the war is over."

Then it was all for nothing. Nothing. "Paul!" The word escaped in a breath ahead of her sobs.

She heard the artist's footsteps cross the wooden floorboards, then the scrape of a chair. He positioned it some feet away from the bed and leant on its back. "Can I fetch you anything? Water? Or maybe some brandy?"

She must control this before it overwhelmed her again. She must find the strength. "Water, please." As he turned towards the ewer on the washstand, she loosened her grip on the post and wiped her nose on her sleeve.

After he handed her the mug he stood, looking down at her. "I'm afraid introductions are somewhat overdue. I am Thomas Chalmers, war artist. Although I am pleased to say I shall soon be without gainful employment."

"Thérèse Ruguel."

He bowed his head slightly before sitting down. "And how did you come to be in Quatre Bras? Do you live nearby?"

"I live nowhere. I followed the army. My brother..." She took a sip of water, her teeth chattering against the cup.

"Paul is your brother?"

She closed her eyes, willed herself to say it. "Yes, but he is dead." The words were a bare whisper.

"The rest of your family?"

She shook her head, her chest tight with the effort of keeping the double blow of grief inside her.

"No family?"

"My ... my father..." But it was too much. She collapsed onto the pillows, sobbing. She heard the rasp of the chair on the wooden boards as he stood.

"I will leave you for a while. Perhaps you will sleep again." With a click, the door closed behind him.

When Thérèse woke for the second time, there was no sense of disorientation, just the lead weight of grief resting over her heart. She remembered it from her father's passing at the turn of the year. He had wasted away in front of her, becoming his own shadow long before he closed his tired eyes for the last time. But Paul ... Paul ... he had been snatched away vigorous and young.

Fingering the locket around her neck, she stood at the window. Inside were a lock of hair from the mother she'd never known and one from her father. She had nothing of Paul; he'd laughed when she'd asked him, making a joke of it. He'd dodged the balls at Leipzig and Laon, what harm could come to him now?

The street below was full of soldiers, their red uniforms dusty and bedraggled. Some wore makeshift bandages, leaning on their comrades for support. The wounded were heading in the same direction, and she craned her neck to see a monstrous building with tall windows and a steeply pitched black roof. She supposed it to be a hospice of some sort. There would have been no such comfort for Paul.

How fast fortunes turned and turned about. After Napoleon's forced abdication the previous year, Paul had remained in the army, then gradually the soldiers had been dismissed. He'd returned to Roscoff just weeks after she had come home to nurse her father, but there was no work and his meagre savings dwindled away. He laboured a little in the fields at harvest time and sometimes on the fishing boats, increasingly angry his service to his country counted for nothing. Especially in Brittany, which had remained largely loyal to the Bourbon crown. At times it seemed it actually counted against him.

In early January their father had died. They spent what they had to bury him and Thérèse took in sewing and laundry, her job as a lady's maid in Rouen long since filled by someone else. Paul hated the inactivity and started to chop wood for a few sous, a scowl replacing his previously cheerful countenance, frustration at his inability to provide turning him bitter before his time.

In March, news reached them that Napoleon had returned and been accepted by troops at Grenoble. Overnight, Paul became his old self again: laughing, joking, ruffling Thérèse's hair. The emperor would need soldiers, and Paul would follow him to the ends of the earth.

Thérèse had been more cautious, in truth unnerved by the thought of being left in Roscoff on her own. Yes, Paul would send money; yes, with just one mouth to feed life would be easier … but it was the aloneness that scared her. Perhaps he would wait just a few more weeks until the army crept closer?

Almost before they'd reached a conclusion, Marshall Ney had pledged his support to Napoleon at Lyon. Now the thing was certain. When he heard Thérèse crying in the scullery, Paul suggested she join him; plenty of women followed the army, and with her skills as a seamstress she would have ample opportunity to earn money. And, of course, they would be together.

They arrived in Paris too late to see the triumphant entry of the eagle banners to the city, but straight away Paul was able to rejoin the remains of his unit. Soldiers were in high demand —

France's old enemies were threatening their borders and the army needed to be ready.

In mid-May, they began to march towards the Vendée to help quell an uprising. Thérèse was disturbed there should be fighting amongst her own countrymen, but in the end it came to nothing, a squall contained by local troops, and after two days they returned to Paris.

The expedition gave Thérèse a taste of life on the road. Paul entrusted her to the care of an elderly cantinière called Marie-Louise who he knew well, and with the other women they had set out, the last of a dusty train of wagons, the beat of the marching drums a distant echo ahead. Behind them rattled pans for making coffee and tin cups for serving it, while the heady mix of cheese and salt meat made Thérèse's stomach churn as the cart pitched and tossed on the rutted road.

She was relieved when they set up camp for the night, but there was no prospect of rest. She carried water for Marie-Louise to make coffee for those who couldn't afford the rough brandy or wine, then helped her to set up a table for their wares. As the sky darkened above them, she cut bread, cheese, and saucisson in the light of the flickering lamps, all the time keeping her eyes down as Paul had instructed. But even so, one soldier asked if she had favours to sell. She'd shaken her head mutely.

Paul had come across her towards nine o'clock, when the air was full of tobacco and song. His face was flushed and his eyes shining. "How do you like the march?" he'd asked her.

She hadn't known how to answer so as not to disappoint him. "Marie-Louise is kind. She has given me food in return for helping her."

"That is as it should be. I am letting it be known you are a seamstress. Soon you will be earning money for yourself, but I would counsel you to stay in Marie-Louise's protection."

She'd looked up at him and nodded. "Yes. I understand."

Thinking of Paul was too hard, and Thérèse brought herself back to the present. Only pain reached her — for the rest, she felt empty. Not even afraid. She had told the truth when she'd said she had no home. She could not go back to Roscoff; there were too many memories, and she couldn't bear the thought of her neighbours of so many years turning their backs on her as they had done Paul.

As she watched the shifting crowds of men outside, she spied the artist. Thomas Chalmers stood out from the soldiers in his broad-brimmed brown hat and voluminous white shirt, which trailed over his breeches. What sort of man was he? So far, he had been kind — exceedingly kind — but could she trust him? Everybody wanted something, after all. What did he want from her?

She bowed her head. What he wanted was of no matter. He could not hurt her because it was impossible for her soul to contain any more hurt. Already she was exhausted by it. After tonight, he might abandon her. Well, so be it. Tomorrow ... but she could not even think of tomorrow. Her knuckles were white as she clutched the windowsill.

It would be as well if tomorrow never came.

CHAPTER ELEVEN

It was an unusually hot day, even for London in late August, and Thomas stood back from the canvas to mop his brow. The picture needed colour. Much more colour. And something about the balance was wrong. But all the same, the essence of the aftermath of battle was there. The waste. The grief. There was to be a whole room for Waterloo paintings in next year's exhibition at the Royal Academy, and he wanted his to stand out. Another military portrait or fighting scene would not do.

With a start, he realised Thérèse was still in her pose, her cheek resting against the plaster pillar and her arms wrapped around it, in just the same position as they had been when he'd first set eyes on her all those weeks before. "I'm sorry, you can rest." He spoke in French.

"Thank you, Thomas." She stepped backwards, rubbing her elbows, and took off her cloak before walking over to the small table and pouring a cup of water from the jug. "For you, too?" she asked.

He shook his head. "I'm thinking."

But all the same, he found himself watching as she settled on the window seat with her sewing. His mother had given her an old mourning dress, and she was taking in the seams. The dark material flowed around her legs and onto the floor, and Thomas reached for his graphite. He saw grace in everything Thérèse did.

Not one to seek the company of young women, never before had he had the opportunity to study one so closely. Although he hadn't looked for it, now it presented itself it fascinated him. His sketchbooks were full of Thérèse threading a needle,

Thérèse sipping a cup of chocolate, Thérèse looking out of the window. He'd had enough of painting death and destruction, enough of the triumphalism of victory. This slight young woman was his inspiration now.

Since he'd brought Thérèse to London, his creativity had known no bounds. Despite her grumbling, his mother had taken Thérèse into their home and given her the visiting maid's room at the back of the house. She took her meals with the housekeeper, Mrs Taylor, which irritated Thomas, but his mother had drawn a firm line at Thérèse joining them in the dining room.

He looked up again, biting his lip as the almost liquid nature of the dress fabric eluded his graphite. Eyes narrowing, he tried again. This time, it was almost perfect and he let out a sigh, causing Thérèse to lift her head. The pallor of grief was still upon her, but the deep blackness beneath her eyes was fading. It was over a week since he had last seen her silent tears, and her recovery pleased him. It was a glorious day and the fresh air would do her good. He smiled at her. "This afternoon, we shall take your English lesson in the park."

The unfamiliar straw bonnet chafed Thérèse's cheeks as she tied the wide ribbon under her chin, but Mrs Taylor had insisted she wear it. She hadn't understood why, but the older woman's expression had been stern as she'd laid it on top of the borrowed shawl. Thérèse had been in no doubt at all about what she was expected to do.

A door slammed above and she heard Thomas's footsteps on the back stairs. "Mama has suggested we leave by the mews, so I will show you the stables."

They spent a few minutes admiring the horses then passed along the cobbled alley, following a carriage pulled by four great black beasts onto the main street. This was the view from the window of Thomas's studio high above them, and Thérèse was familiar with the stone porticos and gleaming white steps, but from pavement level they loomed large and forbidding. An enormous front door was opened by a footman and a woman stepped out, wearing an elegant brown dress with an elaborately braided front and cuffs that matched the trim on her silk bonnet. Thomas doffed his hat and she nodded to him, eyeing Thérèse with curiosity before being helped into the carriage.

Thomas muttered something under his breath before lengthening his stride, leaving Thérèse struggling to keep up. He only slowed when they reached the wrought iron gates of a park. "It will be pleasant to walk here, and I will teach you the words for flowers and trees."

"Thank you, Thomas. My head is becoming full of names for things, and that is good, but as yet I have no means of making them into useful sentences."

He stopped and looked at her, aghast. "Thérèse — you are right, and I did not even think of it. Tomorrow we will begin to draw your words together, but for today we will enjoy the sunshine."

As they strolled beneath the trees he explained the park belonged to the king, but as he now resided at Kew the gardens were open to the public. "Here the handsome people come to walk, dressed in their finery; men as well as women. It is the fashionable thing to do. Not that fashion concerns me, but beauty does."

Thérèse eyed the sumptuous outfits worn by ladies passing in the opposite direction: brightly coloured dresses peeped from silk coats buttoned only at the breast and edged with wide swathes of patterned silk. Chequerboard competed with brocade; blues and pinks and yellows. Matching bonnets danced with plumes or tightly ruched bows, everywhere a blaze of colour.

She had never expected to stand out in her plain straw hat and grey dress and shawl, although she knew she was of a different class, more akin to the maids who walked several paces behind the women. But no-one dressed like her was alone in the company of a man. Was she breaking some rule she didn't even understand?

There were men walking alone, though, and one of them stopped to speak to Thomas. He bowed low in front of Thérèse and kissed her hand, laughter in his eyes, but turned away without lingering to continue his conversation. He was dressed in extravagant fashion, his breeches so tight she flushed and averted her gaze. His tail coat was a deep pink and his boots gleamed almost as darkly as the silk of his tall hat.

Standing slightly away from them, she was able to observe Thomas as they talked. Their words flowed over her, but Thomas's laugh was unfamiliar, high pitched. They stood inches away from each other, closer than she had seen men before, unless they were drunk or brawling, but perhaps it was simply the way here. Then she saw Thomas's eyes and realised it was not.

Now she understood why he hadn't taken her when he'd had the chance. It had not simply been his gentlemanly nature. She smiled to herself. When Thomas said he wanted to paint her, that really was all he desired. She was as safe with him as she had been with Paul. Except ... what happened when the paintings were finished, or when he found another muse?

Eventually Thomas turned to her, his face glowing. "Thérèse, we should return home. The park is becoming a little too crowded, and I promised Mama our excursion would be a short one."

She nodded and followed a few steps behind the men as they continued to talk until their paths diverged. She watched Thomas watch him go, aware of his silence as they completed their journey home.

When she woke in the night, Thérèse still wept, the silky darkness the only witness to her helpless tears. Her father was gone, Paul was gone, leaving her in a strange country, dependant on a man she barely knew.

Sometimes there were nightmares about the battlefield, the search for Paul she'd been too cowardly to complete. Now she would never know how he'd died, or even if she could have saved him. At times, the regret was almost too much to bear.

There were tears the night after her walk in the park. Once her sobs subsided, she lit her candle, pulled her old woollen shawl around her shoulders and padded across the landing to Thomas's studio. His last Waterloo canvasses were wrapped ready for delivery to the City guild who had commissioned them. His sketches had been sold to newspapers — he had shown her one in the *Morning Chronicle*. For him, the battle was over. For her, it would never end.

In the flickering light, she made her way to his easel in the centre of the floor. She had barely looked at the painting he was working on, but now she stood in front of it, a mirror to her grief. He had captured her despair perfectly, the moment he found her clinging to the tree, unable to move for the weight of desolation. It was heavy on her now. She raised the candle to every corner of the picture, studying it minutely. If it hadn't been for Thomas, who knew what would have become of her?

From the window she looked down on the silent street. A light glimmered in the basement of the house opposite, and in the distance a church clock chimed the quarter hour. The candle spluttered, then the room was in darkness. Extinguished without rhyme, reason or warning. Like Paul. But the same hadn't happened to her. Her heart was beating. Her life went on.

The shapes in this room had become familiar, but deep inside she knew this place was a beginning, not an end. Thomas would tire of painting her. Maybe there would be another war and he would have to leave again. She needed to forge a path of her own, but how? Who would employ a French woman when their countries had been enemies for so long?

Paul would have told her she was making difficulties where none existed, would have laughed away her fears. But Paul would have been wrong. She whispered a silent apology to him for her cowardice as she wrapped her shawl more tightly around her shoulders and returned to bed.

CHAPTER TWELVE

Thomas was conscious of his mother eyeing him across the breakfast table. He pushed his plate to one side and pretended interest in his newspaper, folding it deliberately as if to study an article more minutely. But when she put down her lorgnette and coughed discreetly, he knew there was no escape.

"Thomas, we need to speak about Thérèse."

He barely looked up. "What about her?"

"Is she your mistress?"

"Good lord, no."

"Then even more reason to have care for her reputation."

He threw the *Morning Chronicle* a little too carelessly onto the table. "I'm not sure I know what you mean, Mama."

Margaret Chalmers sighed. "From any other man I would not believe it, but from you it is entirely possible. Your head is always in the clouds. I warned you against promenading with her in the park, and now people are talking."

"Well, let them. Their gossip is no business of mine. Or yours, for that matter."

"But Thomas, it is. You have a responsibility towards Thérèse; you need to think of her future."

He leant back, an amused smile on his thin lips. "Are you suggesting I marry her?"

"You know very well I suggest no such thing. Yes, it is time you were married, but to someone of your own class."

"I was teasing you, Mama. Taking a wife — any wife — would sap my creativity. Even Thérèse, who sits so quietly while I paint, would doubtless become demanding."

75

This was a well-worn battleground between them, but this time as a diversion tactic it failed.

"And if Thérèse becomes demanding anyway, or when you become bored of painting her, what then? The girl has nothing that isn't in your gift."

"I would not see her starve, or go without a roof over her head. What do you take me for?"

His mother reached across to pat his hand. "I know. You are not cruel, merely thoughtless. But I fear the harm to her reputation has already been done, and it may be difficult to find her a place in Kensington."

"A place?"

"Mrs Taylor tells me she worked as a lady's maid, and French maids are highly sought after."

"But if she was in another household, I would not be able to paint her."

"Quite so. But the present situation cannot continue." Mrs Chalmers stood up.

"I will not be without her, Mama."

She stopped halfway to the door. "I take it you're not in love with her?"

"What a ridiculous notion. But I need to paint her, surely you see that?" He looked at her with as much defiance as he could muster.

"Then I would advise you to complete your sketches quickly, because fortune may be about to favour that poor young woman and it would be most unkind of you to stand in her way."

Mrs Taylor tapped Thérèse on the shoulder, causing her to look up from her darning with a start. She spoke slowly. "Mrs Chalmers would like to see you in the drawing room. She has company."

"Company?" Thérèse repeated the unfamiliar word.

"A guest."

Still Thérèse didn't understand, but she set the stockings to one side and stood. Mrs Taylor took her gently by the shoulders, removed her shawl and straightened her mob cap. From these gestures Thérèse realised the interview was important, and she began to feel a little scared. For the last few days Thomas had been withdrawn, taking his walks in the park alone, and this morning she had sensed a change in the household, a supressed excitement she could not comprehend.

By the time she knocked on the drawing room door, she was almost shaking with fear. The handle slipped in her fingers, and she kept her eyes low as she entered.

"Ah, Thérèse, I would like you to meet my cousin, Mrs Elizabeth Daniell." Mrs Chalmers spoke in French and her voice was kindly.

Thérèse bobbed low then looked at the woman sitting on the sofa. She was wearing a light brown carriage dress, its seams stretching a little around her generous figure. Her feathered hat was beside her, revealing a cap with a matching ribbon perched on greying hair. She smiled at Thérèse, her pink cheeks flushed with pleasure.

"*Enchantée*, I'm sure."

Thérèse bobbed again, then Mrs Chalmers continued. "Mrs Daniell is travelling without a maid. I understand you worked as a lady's maid before your unfortunate bereavements, and it would be most kind if you could look after Mrs Daniell while she is here."

"Of course, Madame. It would be a pleasure," Thérèse stammered. Was that all? Her heart still hammering in her chest, she permitted herself a deep breath.

"Then it's settled. Perhaps you could start by unpacking Mrs Daniell's trunks. She is to stay in the blue bedroom."

Thérèse nodded and turned to leave, but Mrs Daniell spoke, her French perfect though heavily accented. "Thank you, Thérèse. I am very grateful."

Mrs Daniell's luggage was already in the blue room and Thérèse set to work immediately, thankful for having some small way to repay Mrs Chalmers' kindness. First she unpacked the heavy silver hairbrush and mirror and set them on the dressing table. There was a soft clothes brush in the same design as well as a button hook, a glove stretcher and three small round boxes. She rearranged them until they looked perfect, then turned her attention to the clothes.

These, too, were of the finest quality. The hems of the linen petticoats were richly embroidered and the ribbons in the chemises the softest silk. The outer garments were not of the highest fashion but beautifully made, and the evening dresses in the trunk shimmered like gossamer in the afternoon sunlight.

Some of the petticoats had become creased during their journey, so Thérèse took them downstairs to the housekeeper's room to press them. As she spread the thick blanket over the table and waited for the iron to warm by the fire, she found she was humming to herself. She stopped, wondering if it was disrespectful to hum when you were in mourning, then shrugged and carried on. Moments of contentment were rare enough, after all.

Although she was well used to the duties of a lady's maid, Thérèse was nervous as she knocked on the door of the blue room to dress Mrs Daniell for dinner. Mrs Chalmers had arranged a small supper party, so she knew the visitor would want to look her best, but she had no idea at all of the type of assistance she required; would she choose her own outfit, or expect Thérèse to do it? And what of her jewellery? Most importantly — if they were to communicate at all — how good was her French?

On that question Thérèse found she had no cause for concern. As soon as she entered the room Mrs Daniell started to chat, telling her how kind it was of her to help and how well she had laid everything out. Together they selected a dress and gloves before Thérèse helped Mrs Daniell from her travelling costume, ready to arrange her hair.

She was shocked to see how raw the skin on the lady's shoulders was, red with scaly patches flaking away. She pressed her cool hands onto it and asked, "What is wrong, Madame?"

"My own vanity, I'm afraid," Mrs Daniell answered. "I was tempted to use a vile concoction called Bloom of Ninon to whiten my shoulders. I am only thankful I did not use it on my face."

"This evening I will prepare a mask of honey and oats to soothe your poor skin. It is best used under your nightdress, Madame, as it is a little sticky, but I will launder it in the morning so it is fresh for you tomorrow night."

Mrs Daniell turned and looked at her. "And where did you learn such things, Thérèse?"

Afraid she had spoken out of turn, Thérèse stammered. "F-from the cook at the house where I worked in Rouen, Madame. Sh-she was very skilled in the use of such remedies."

"Then I shall be happy to try it. My skin itches so, and of course a lady must not scratch — in public, at least."

"You should not scratch it at all, Madame, you will make it worse. Now, how shall we dress your hair?"

"How would you have dressed it for your last mistress?"

Thérèse bit her lip. Her mistress in Rouen had been young and newly married, with a heart-shaped face quite unlike Mrs Daniell's round one. But perhaps such honesty was not the best policy. Instead, she clapped her hands together. "Madame, with your beautiful jewelled headband I know just the thing."

By the third morning of Mrs Daniell's stay, Thérèse was becoming accustomed to her new routine. At six o'clock she would take a tray of tea to the blue bedroom before returning to the kitchen to warm the water for the guest to wash. She had already learnt to overheat it, because Mrs Daniell liked to talk while she sipped her tea and Thérèse laid out her clothes for the day.

This morning, Mrs Daniell's opening gambit surprised her. "So, Thérèse, do you like London?"

Thérèse was cleaning the hairbrush and paused. "I have not thought about it, Madame."

"It is larger than Rouen, I would think."

Thérèse smiled, surprised Mrs Daniell remembered the city where she had worked. "I suppose, Madame. But Rouen seemed big to me because I knew more of it. Here, I am almost always in the house, so I do not know."

"You grew up in a smaller place?"

"Yes, Madame. The port of Roscoff in Brittany."

"Do you miss the sea?"

Thérèse thought for a moment. "I find the sea has many moods, Madame. But it is a wonderful thing when it glistens in the sunlight."

"We can see the sea from our house at Trelissick. It is some distance, down the river and beyond Falmouth, but we can see the shimmer you speak of all the same."

"Mrs Taylor said you live a good many days' journey away?"

"Yes, in the county of Cornwall, to the west. I am told it is very much like Brittany in aspect, so I think you might like it. Now, Thérèse, the pale green dress for this morning, if you please. And the gauze fichu. My shoulders are so much better I feel able to wear it again."

"Yes, Madame." Thérèse was glad to turn away to the closet, her eyes suddenly filling with tears at the thought of home. But as she brushed the dress then threaded the matching ribbon into Mrs Daniell's bonnet, her equilibrium returned. Being busy was a good thing because she had no time for her grief, and the hard work tired her so much that last night she had not woken until the housemaid had tapped on her door.

Once she had assisted Mrs Daniell with her toilette, she went upstairs to Thomas's studio. He was already at his easel, and his smile was thin when she entered the room.

"I am losing you, Thérèse."

"I am sorry, Thomas, but I must repay your mother's kindness as well as your own."

He nodded. "Of course." There was a long silence while she watched him choose a colour from his palette, then he said, "You must not feel beholden to me, Thérèse. When it is time for you to leave, you must. You are a free woman. Do you understand?"

Thérèse nodded, but her heart filled with fear. Had he tired of her so soon? Her throat was so constricted she could not speak. Her emotions must have shown in her face, because he put down his paintbrush and turned to her.

"I do not mean it unkindly, my dear, and you know that wherever you are, if you need a friend or wise counsel, you can look to me." He turned back to his easel. "Now, this morning I would like to sketch you on the window seat. The light is perfect, and I think we will begin with you looking up at the sky."

His words did little to calm her fears. For the first two poses he said nothing, and the only sound in the room was his graphite scratching across the paper. She paid little attention to the street below, even when instructed to look down. Inside her head was turmoil. Where could she go? How would she live? In the end, her tears spilled over.

The scratching stopped and she heard Thomas's footsteps on the bare boards. "What is wrong, Thérèse?"

"You want me to go and I have nowhere…"

"Then you mistake my words. I want you to stay, but I must think of your future."

She could not look at him. "I have no future."

"You have. And you must not make the wrong choice out of loyalty to me."

"Choice?"

"Mrs Daniell is to offer you a position. My cousin Gertrude is in a delicate condition, and her mother's maid has stayed with her to give what comfort she can. You are, of course, free to accept or reject Mrs Daniell's offer, and if you choose the latter you may remain here as long as you wish. It would please me inestimably if you stayed, but I fear my mother may have a different view."

Thérèse nodded. "My place here is … unusual."

A smile drifted onto Thomas's lips. "She fears for your reputation. That it would be difficult for you to find a place nearby in Kensington because we have been remarked upon promenading together."

"My reputation is safe with you, Thomas. I have seen it when we were walking in the gardens; you look at women only with an artist's eye. In other matters … your interest lies elsewhere."

Thomas gave her a hard look then turned and strode back to his sketchbook. The pages rustled as he picked it up, but he did not look at her. "It is best you leave, Thérèse. I have finished my sketches and Mrs Daniell has need of you."

"For today, or do you mean…?"

He paused for a moment before answering. "When you observe — or think you observe — something, it is often best to keep your own counsel. Especially in a country you do not understand." His voice was formal but held a sharp edge of anger.

Thérèse bobbed a small curtsey as she left the room. In her heart of hearts, she knew they would never speak again.

CHAPTER THIRTEEN

Thérèse braced against her seat as the carriage descended the steep hill, but opposite her Mrs Daniell did not seem in the least perturbed. Indeed, she craned forwards to look out of the window.

"We are almost at Truro, Thérèse. I can see the chapel of Saint Mary Portell through the trees." She sounded as excited as a young girl, and Thérèse could not help but smile wanly back.

She felt less sick when the horses slowed to a walk as the road levelled out. Now there were houses on either side, and they crossed a bridge over a small river. At the confluence of several roads, the carriage paused and Thérèse caught sight of a low looking inn and next to it a grocer's shop. After a sharp right turn, which caused her to clutch the edge of her seat, they came into a road of fine houses and stopped.

A footman in dark green livery emerged from a similarly painted front door, flanked by pillars and topped with a classical portal. The house was solid and square, four storeys high and dressed in a beautiful pale golden stone that seemed to glow in the sun. The footman ran down at least a dozen steps and opened the carriage door with a low bow.

"Welcome home, Mrs Daniell."

"No ceremony, Matthew. I know it looks well in the street, but stand straight and help me down, do."

He offered his arm and Mrs Daniell descended the carriage, Thérèse following behind.

Inside the house was no less grand and Thérèse gazed about her in awe. A vestibule with arched recesses led to a domed ante-hall, and from the main hall itself rose a staircase with the most beautiful wrought iron balustrade she had ever seen.

Mrs Daniell turned to Matthew and Thérèse strained to comprehend the words, being able to pick out just a few of them. "This is Thérèse, my new maid. She has very little English, so you need to use simple words and speak slowly while she learns. Please take her to Mrs Leigh so she can be shown the house." Then she turned to Thérèse and addressed her in French. "The family are at Trelissick, so we have but a small staff here. Mr Daniell has business in Truro, so we will sup here tonight then in the morning continue our journey. I will take a dish of tea now, so you may rest too and come to my room in an hour."

Thérèse thanked her and followed Matthew down a wooden staircase and into a spacious kitchen, where he spoke rapidly to a round-faced woman who was preparing a pie. The woman looked up at Thérèse and smiling, pointed to herself.

"Mrs Leigh. Housekeeper."

"Thérèse Ruguel, lady maid."

Mrs Leigh shook her head. "*Mam'selle* Thérèse. That is the way here."

Thérèse nodded. "Thank you." She hated using that word. It embarrassed her that the 'th' came out as 's', but hard as she practised she could not seem to get it right.

Mrs Leigh finished crimping the pie and put it into an oven on one side of the open range before dusting her hands on her apron. She took a plain china jug from a shelf and indicated Thérèse should fill it from a tap on the range, making a face-washing motion with her hands. Thérèse nodded, then, with the jug in her hand, followed Mrs Leigh up the back stairs. On the first floor she showed her Mrs Daniell's bedroom, then they climbed further to the servants' quarters.

Thérèse's was a narrow room at the front of the house. As well as a bed, there was a washstand and a small pine wardrobe with a deep drawer below. Best of all was the wide windowsill, and once she had washed and changed into a fresh dress, she allowed herself a few minutes to gaze onto the street below. Two fashionably attired men rode past on fine horses and a boy rolled a barrel from the building opposite. Her line of vision followed him past a terrace of well-proportioned houses, significantly smaller than the Daniells' but certainly well-to-do. At the other end of the short road was a much older stone building with mean windows and nothing in the way of decoration.

So this was to be her new home. Or one of them, at least. Mrs Daniell had explained the family lived in their manor at Trelissick for much of the year, but spent more time in town in the winter when assemblies and other social gatherings were held. Thérèse shivered, suddenly close to tears. It was all so strange, and she understood so little. Still, it would not do to sit here dwelling on it, and Mrs Leigh had seemed a kindly soul, for which she was profoundly grateful.

She ran down the stairs and, straightening her dress, knocked on the door of Mrs Daniell's room. There was no reply, but rather than wait she peeped around. Finding her mistress wasn't there, she started to unpack the small travelling case of items she would require tonight. A mahogany wardrobe almost filled the wall opposite the bed, and in it Thérèse found an array of dresses. The chemises and other undergarments were in a chest of drawers nearby.

The washstand was set to one side of a vast bay window, which overlooked a walled garden with a small orchard at the far end. But there was no time to gawp, and taking the jug Mrs

Leigh had given her she ran down the back stairs to fetch hot water.

When she returned, Mrs Daniell was sitting in a chair near the window, removing her bonnet and cap. Thérèse put down the jug and helped her, smoothing her hair back into place with gentle fingers.

"Ah, Thérèse, you are a good girl, and a quick one too. I see you have already laid out my toilette. Now massage my temples a little more, then we will select a gown for tonight."

Thérèse was buttoning Mrs Daniell into her dress when they heard a male voice in the hall below. Mrs Daniell clapped her hands in delight. "Oh, my dearest Ralph is home. Let us hurry, as I have been without him for so long and have so much to tell him." Despite her excitement she stood perfectly still, allowing Thérèse to finish her task then fix a heavy emerald drop necklace around her neck.

"*Et voilà!*" she said and Mrs Daniell smiled.

"Accompany me downstairs, Thérèse. I would like you to meet Mr Daniell, then you can take your supper in the kitchen."

Ralph Daniell stood when his wife entered the drawing room, setting his wineglass on a small table and crossing the carpet to embrace her. "My darling girl," he smiled. "Such a tonic to have you home, and looking so beautiful."

Embarrassed by this open display of affection, Thérèse looked at her boots.

"Ralph, dearest, I would like you to meet my new maid, Thérèse. As I wrote to tell you, cousin Thomas rescued her after Waterloo. Too awful, poor child, but she is excellent about her work and it will be an advantage for the children to be able to speak French to her."

"Indeed. Now our two countries are at peace, there will, I hope, be many opportunities for trade and social discourse."

Thérèse looked up to see a tall man with a ruddy complexion. He was of an age where he clung to the fashion for wigs, and his powdered rolls framed a face with heavy jowls, a small mouth and kind eyes. She bobbed a curtsey. He nodded again. "*Enchanté*, Mam'selle."

Mrs Daniell turned to her. "Thank you, Thérèse. You may go. Please tell Mrs Leigh we will sup in half an hour."

Thérèse had expected to continue their journey by carriage, so she was surprised the next morning to look down from Mrs Daniell's window to see Matthew carrying the trunks and boxes through the garden.

"Is the luggage to be loaded in the stables?" she asked.

"No, Thérèse, we will travel by boat. Dear Ralph's associate, Mr Vivian, has a sloop bound for Falmouth on this morning's tide, and it is of little matter to stop at Trelissick on the way."

The day was bright with a warm breeze. Mr Daniell accompanied them through the garden and onto the wharf beyond, where Thérèse was taken aback by the sudden hustle and bustle around her. There were several ships at anchor and men were unloading timber from two of them, smoke and noise from a foundry on the opposite bank filling the air.

She resisted the temptation to cover her ears with her hands and instead followed the Daniells closely. All around her people jostled and whirled, and being unable to understand their shouted words, she found herself trembling with fright. But really, was this so very different to the harbour at Roscoff? She shook herself. She must think of Paul and try to be even half as brave.

They were offered the hospitality of the captain's cabin, and when the ship was due to sail Mr Daniell kissed his wife's hand, promising he would ride to Trelissick the next day. Thérèse sat very still at Mrs Daniell's side on a small overstuffed sofa, and she was pleased when she suggested they take a breath of air on deck.

The ship had already left the town behind and was on a broad reach of water with steeply rising woods on their left and rolling farmland on their right. Mrs Daniell pointed out the hamlet of Mopus Passage where two rivers joined, then the banks closed in on either side, the trees stretching from hilltops to water.

"All this land belongs to our neighbour, Lord Falmouth," Mrs Daniell explained with a sweep of her left hand. "But on this side the land is ours. My dear Ralph can ride from Truro to Trelissick and never need use a path he does not own."

Thérèse gazed in wonder while the banks slipped past. There was a quiet beauty to the river as it wound through the woodland, occasionally punctuated by landing stages and tributaries that were broad, shallow creeks. Birdsong filled the air, and once they watched as a heron fished from the mud at the river's edge.

The captain pressed them to take a nuncheon of cold meats and fruit, and soon afterwards the sloop moored at Trelissick's quay. A gig awaited them and while the trunks and boxes were loaded onto a cart, a liveried groom drove them along a creek then up a steep slope before turning into open parkland. Ahead of them a wide expanse of water glistened in the sunshine while deer grazed between the track and the water's edge.

On top of a rise the house came into view, a plain grey stone building with tall windows, commanding all before it. The gig drew to a halt outside a modest portico and the groom helped Mrs Daniell down. The moment he turned to assist Thérèse, the door opened and two girls flew out, ringlets and skirts flying, to greet their mama. They were followed by a woman with a stern face in an unfashionable navy dress, and a boy of slightly older years.

In the hullabaloo Thérèse was completely forgotten and she stood by the carriage, clutching her reticule. This large, boisterous family was nothing like her own had been, but watching them together opened wounds she had thought were just beginning to heal. Had this all been a terrible mistake? But what choice had she had, really?

The groom nudged her. His words were unintelligible and she looked at him, shaking her head. With a shrug he gathered the horse's reins, leaving Thérèse to trail after the family into the hall.

CHAPTER FOURTEEN

She would never tire of this view, Mrs Daniell thought as she sat at her writing desk in the morning room, looking over the parkland. The mist hung in vast cobwebs above the river, the woodland to the left of the house stretching out towards it like a green arm.

Ralph had ridden for Truro an hour before, leaving her to her correspondence. He had come to her last night — as he still often did, even after thirty years of marriage — and the thought filled her with a warm glow. Theirs was indeed a love match, and she wanted the same for her daughters; a kind and clever man of good standing with whom they could share a lifelong partnership.

With Gertrude so far away she dearly hoped her marriage was such, but she had her doubts. Lieutenant Colonel Gosset had been quite a catch, and the children were coming along regularly enough, but her daughter's letters lacked her normal verve for life. Maybe it was her latest pregnancy, but it seemed to date from her husband's return from the Barbary States the year before. At least when he'd been away Gertrude and the children had been able to return to Cornwall, but now he insisted his family remain in London, even through the heat and stench of the summer months.

Her eldest daughter, Lizzie, was a different matter. By rights she should have been married years ago, but even her mother had to admit her looks were against her. In her mid-twenties she had seemed an increasingly sour old maid, but now she was courting a widowed naval captain. Her sallow skin had taken on an almost healthy glow, and her eyes became bright at the mention of his name. Mrs Daniell found William Wooldridge perfectly stuffy, but all the same she was exceptionally keen to see the match concluded.

She had waited ten years for another girl to live beyond infancy. Her first Mary had died at seven months, but her namesake was a flourishing young woman, soon to turn sixteen. Still, you never knew... Mrs Daniell shuddered. Henry had been sixteen when he'd died, cruelly taken in a hunting accident. In the three long years since, not a day went by when she didn't miss him. Resolutely she pushed her grief aside. Mary had to be her priority now.

She had no doubt Mary was ready to come out into society, despite one of her older sisters being unmarried. It was not the girl's fault, and Lizzie had had sufficient opportunity. Mary was pretty as a newly ripened peach, with huge brown eyes and a rosebud mouth. Mrs Daniell desperately hoped her penchant for schoolroom mischief would be calmed by the far more exciting prospect of finding a husband.

There was a knock at the door and, reluctantly, Mrs Daniell tore herself away from her musings, turning to see Mrs Passmore the housekeeper hovering on the threshold.

"I have the menu for tomorrow's supper party, Madam." She stepped forward, proffering a sheet of paper.

This was a daily formality. Mrs Daniell would read the list of dishes, make suitably appreciative noises, then Mrs Passmore would be on her way, but today she hung back, looking a little uncertain.

"Is there something else you wish to speak to me about?" Mrs Daniell asked.

Mrs Passmore jutted out her chin. "There is, Madam, but it pains me to have to raise it."

"But clearly you think you should."

"I regret, Madam, that your new maid may not be suitable."

Mrs Daniell frowned. "Not suitable? Why?"

"She ... she ... makes herbal potions ... and has other ungodly behaviours..."

"If you mean she does not go to church, she was brought up differently to how she might have been in England, that is all. And her herbal potions, as you call them, are in fact cures, made up for me and on my instruction."

"But all the same, the other servants are nervous of her."

"Then you must explain there is nothing — I repeat, nothing — to fear. And you are to make her welcome. Do you understand?"

Mrs Daniell picked up her pen, indicating the interview was at an end, and returned to the far more pleasurable occupation of planning Mary's entrée into society. The queen's continuing ill health meant there could be no question of a court presentation, so if a beau could be found locally it would save Mrs Daniell the rigours of a London season. But if she had to do it for her daughter, she would. Although it was more than tempting to wait for a year until Anne too would be sixteen and they could be introduced to society in the capital together.

In the meantime, she would make the most of the opportunities available in Cornwall. Perhaps a dinner with a little dancing afterwards to celebrate the birthday itself. Just the family and some of the more important neighbours: the Vivians, of course, and the Stackhouses, as well as their dearest friends the Lemons. Nothing ostentatious, certainly nothing that warranted having to invite Lord and Lady Falmouth, just enough to signal Mary was out in society.

Once this was done, she could attend the monthly assemblies in Truro and accompany Mrs Daniell on morning calls. Mrs Daniell was not enamoured of this ritual, preferring to spend her time with family or close friends, but Mary would need to make a good impression on the influential mothers in the county in order to stand a chance with their sons. Naturally her father's fortune played in her favour, but it also meant a certain amount of caution needed to be exercised in her choice of suitor.

There were preparations to be made, and quickly. She must write at once to engage the services of Mr Clements, the dancing master. Then there would be dresses, shoes, reticules, bonnets ... this Mrs Daniell did love, and the Misses Reed in St Mary's Street would be much occupied on her behalf. Next week she would return to Truro for a few days and take Mary with her to set her plans in motion. She had seen some of the latest fashions for herself while in London, but she would also consult the next edition of the *Ladies Monthly Museum*. And, of course, make the most of Thérèse's exquisite French taste.

Mrs Daniell smiled to herself. It would be quite an undertaking, and one she found she was looking forward to a great deal.

Thérèse stood in the kitchen corridor outside the servants' hall and took a deep breath. Inside was chatter and laughter she knew would stop the moment she walked into the room. All eyes would be upon her as she took her place between Mrs Passmore and Hannah, the chief housemaid. But she had to eat, so she had to face this daily ordeal.

She did not know what she had done to engender such bad feeling. Perhaps it was simply because their countries had been at war for so long. But Paul had doubtless been killed by a British soldier, and she could not hate an entire nation because of it. A wave of anguish ran through her, so strong it almost brought her to her knees, forcing her to grip the banister until it passed, then she climbed the four steps and opened the door. Silence fell, the only sound the slow and solid ticking of the clock and her hesitant footsteps across the floor. She bowed her head and whispered 'good evening' in her best English, then made her way to her seat. She knew now not to help herself to the food from the dishes until Mrs Passmore recited the usual prayer. It meant nothing to her — she had no time for religion — but she was beginning to understand how important it was to respect the customs of the place.

Her one ally amongst the servants was Miss Grafton, the governess, but she took her meals in the schoolroom with the older children. Thérèse had only just left its warmth, for every night before supper, once Mrs Daniell was dressed and had gone downstairs, she spent a brief but precious time in conversation with Mary, Anne and Edward to improve their French.

She waited, head bowed, while conversations began to flow around her. She strained to pick out a word here and there but knew too little to make any sense of it. Miss Grafton was helping her with her English, but as Mrs Daniell preferred to speak in French there was little opportunity to practice. Still, she needed to try, as however unwelcoming it seemed, her future could only be in this strange country. As Mrs Passmore said the prayer, Thérèse fought back her tears, some deep instinct telling her to hide her weakness. She had no option but to try to be strong.

CHAPTER FIFTEEN

Thérèse tied the straps of the plain grey bonnet in a large bow to one side of Mrs Daniell's chin and stood back. "*Et voilà*, Madame."

"Thank you, Thérèse. Now fetch your cloak, as I can hear the carriage being brought around and we must be away."

In deference to the warm morning they were to ride in the barouche, although its hood was up to protect them from the sun. On the seat opposite were large baskets full of bread, eggs, cheese and apples from the orchard. On the floor of the carriage was a leather chest containing the ingredients for barley water, herbs for poultices and thick glass bottles full of healing tinctures from the apothecary, which rattled as the horses broke into a trot.

They left the park on a high ridge of land with sweeping views down into a valley carved by one of the Fal's tributaries. Around them was all pasture, the fields separated by low walls partly covered with grass. Trees dotted the landscape, which had a soft beauty, and Thérèse was moved to tell her mistress what a pretty place Cornwall was.

Mrs Daniell shook her head. "Here, indeed, we are fortunate. But very soon you will see a change. Further north the land has a wildness to it, and it would be difficult to claim the mines are anything close to beautiful. However, they are essential, Thérèse. They bring work and with that food on the table. And great hardship when a mine closes." She shuddered.

Thérèse knew this was the business of their day. Mrs Daniell had explained her husband's mine had been closed more than a year before, and many were still suffering because of it. "It was not his choice, Thérèse, it was the landowners. They said the risk of further investment was too great; however, Ralph believes it was pure and simple jealousy of his success. But whatever the circumstances, it is our duty to help those who worked so hard for us."

Within half an hour of leaving Trelissick, the landscape did indeed change. The horses climbed towards moorland and the hedges on either side of the lane fell away. In the distance, Thérèse could see tall chimneys, smoke drifting upwards in the still morning air. And there were sounds, indistinct at first, but as they approached they heard a cacophony of hammering accompanied by the steady thud of what seemed to be an army of boots. It was all Thérèse could do to stop herself from putting her hands over her ears.

Groups of buildings dotted the landscape. Smoking chimneys, sturdy square towers, stone-built sheds and wooden lean-tos. On the flat surfaces around them women wearing long hoods that had once been white toiled, breaking lumps of rock with heavy mallets. But in some places the noise even from this was drowned by the rhythmic thudding issuing from buildings nearby.

The mines were stretched across the moor, some so close together they almost appeared as one, but when the barouche crossed a tract of open land the noise receded. Mrs Daniell explained the men worked underground, digging out the rocks, and the women on the surface broke them to reveal the tin ore. After that, some inexplicable alchemy took place in the stamping houses, which converted it into ingots.

"So you see, Thérèse, when a mine closes, a whole family can be without the means of scraping together a crust."

The journey across the moors seemed to last half a lifetime, but eventually the road wound itself through woods and into fields beyond. Even so, the distant sounds of the mines rang in Thérèse's ears, and before they had completely left her they began again ahead of them.

Here the landscape was different. The carriage began a slow descent into a valley, the chimneys in a straggling line along its slopes. Now the moorland was above them, gorse struggling yellow beneath the palls of smoke. The track twisted and turned until they rounded a corner, and in front of them was the rich azure of the sea.

Thérèse turned to Mrs Daniell. "I do not understand. We left the ocean behind us at Trelissick."

Mrs Daniell smiled. "Cornwall is surrounded by sea, Thérèse, on three of its four sides. Here the county is so narrow it is possible to cross it south to north in a few hours' ride. When we return, I will show you a map from Ralph's library."

In front of them was a triangle of flat land leading to the sea, and here the lane met a road following the coast. They took it and climbed steeply from the valley back into the sunlight. To Thérèse's left she could see cliffs rising some hundred or so yards away, while closer to hand an empty scar of land dipped below them, and at the top of the hill more mine buildings came into view, silent and abandoned.

"This is Wheal Nevek," Mrs Daniell told her. "See how quickly it decays with no-one to tend it. Already Ralph despairs of being able to open it again."

"So there is still tin there, Madame?"

"Not tin, but copper. And Ralph believes so, yes."

Beyond the mine was a hamlet of low housing centred around a coaching inn. In front of it was a strange granite stone in the shape of a horizontal cross about six foot long, which Mrs Daniell explained was for resting coffins on the long walk from the village to the nearest church in St Pirans. The barouche stopped next to it and a man came out of a stout wooden door in the centre of the tavern to welcome them. He bowed low to Mrs Daniell and helped her from the carriage before leading them into a small parlour at the front of the building. A fire was lit and there was bread, cheese and a bottle of canary wine on the table.

"Some refreshment after your journey?" The innkeeper spoke in a slow drawl and Thérèse was delighted to understand these few words. She arranged the cushions on the settle so Mrs Daniell was comfortable, then folded their cloaks before joining her mistress.

While they ate, the parlour became darker due to the press of people outside the window. The fire hissed and spat and Mrs Daniell pushed her plate away.

"They are waiting for us, Thérèse. We cannot eat while they are hungry."

Thérèse's heart swelled with admiration for the compassionate woman she was fortunate enough to serve. She stood and moved their meal to one side. "What shall I do, Madame?"

"Place the baskets on the other settle. Each person may take bread, and either eggs or cheese or apples. There appears to be quite a crowd, but the village is small so I am sure there will be enough. Meanwhile, I will dispense medicine to those in need."

It was mainly the women who came, some with children, others alone. It seemed they knew better than Thérèse what they should do, but when one small girl slipped an apple into her pocket when her mother had taken cheese, Thérèse said nothing. She had seen hunger in the child's eyes and she could remember how that felt.

The food was quickly gone. An old man walking with the aid of a roughhewn stick was the last into the room, but there was no more bread and Thérèse thought her heart would break for him. He was pale and thin, like her father had become in his last days, with a rattling cough that seemed to shake the windows. While Mrs Daniell dispensed a soothing tincture and some barley water, she told Thérèse to ask the innkeeper for another loaf, making her repeat the strange English words back to her to ensure she would be understood.

On the opposite side of the hall was a larger room, and she spied the innkeeper pouring ale from a barrel. She stood at the door, wondering how to attract his attention, but he was deep in conversation with a wigged gentleman in a dusty coat. Three more travellers had taken a table next to the fire and were finishing their meal, and two old men were sitting silently on a settle, tankards in hand.

Thérèse took a deep breath and stepped forward. "*Excusez-moi…*" She stopped in horror. Her carefully practised English words had deserted her in a moment of panic.

But then, like some miracle, there was a voice behind her in her own tongue. "You are French, Mam'selle? Perhaps I can be of assistance in translating your request."

She spun around to see a tall man she had not noticed before. He was leaning against the wall, a squat rummer of brandy folded into his strong hands. They were the hands of a working man, but his fingernails were neatly trimmed and the cuff protruding from his well-cut jacket was of the finest linen. In the dim light it was hard to see his features, but his luxuriant black hair was pulled back from his face, and he was smiling.

Recovering herself, Thérèse thanked him and told him she had a request for the innkeeper.

"And what is that request?" her champion asked.

"Mrs Daniell would like a loaf of bread to be brought to the parlour."

He raised his eyebrows. "Mrs Daniell, you say? Well, you go back to her, pretty French maid, and I will see it is done." All the same he did not move, and she felt his eyes burn into her back as she returned to her mistress.

PART THREE: 2015

CHAPTER SIXTEEN

In the middle of Tuesday afternoon, there's a knock on the front door of Nevek Cot. I've been restless today, moving from laptop to plans and back again. Until the planning certificate arrives, we can't do anything else on site and it's beginning to frustrate me.

I open the door to see Gun standing there. "You paid off my tab."

"Good afternoon, Sebastian, how are you?"

He has the good grace to smile. "Sorry. That was a little blunt, but I want to know why you did it."

"To thank you for putting out the fire. I could have sent flowers, but I don't know your address."

His grin widens. "Just as well you didn't — I don't like seeing those poor blooms cut off in their prime."

I open the door properly. "Coming in?"

"If you're not busy."

In a couple of steps he crosses the living room and starts to warm himself against the log burner. "I'm going to have to light mine soon, but I don't have much in the way of dry logs."

"Then take some of mine."

"No charity, Anna."

"Ah — is that why you jumped down my throat about your tab?"

"How are your hands?"

"You're changing the subject."

"Yes. Show me."

I hold them out for him to inspect and he bends over them then nods. "They've healed pretty well."

"Constitution of an ox, me."

"Without the horns and tail." We both laugh and the wariness leaves his eyes.

"Am I allowed to ask you something?" I say.

"That's a very odd question."

"Well, you seem a very private sort of person." He shrugs, so I carry on. "The guys in the pub said you make furniture — for your sister's shop. Before I fell out with the village, I was going to ask her if she'd like to supply some for Wheal Dream, but now I can ask you direct. Unless, of course, it would put you in a difficult position."

"Serena's my sister, not my keeper."

"Then you'll do it?"

"I'll consider it. Give me a list of what you want and I'll make some sketches. Then we'll see."

A dark red car pulls up in the lane outside and I realise it's Luke. I shake my head. "It never rains but it pours."

"And three's a crowd." Gun gathers his coat around him. "I'll leave you to it." He opens the door just as Luke is walking up the path, nods in his direction, then strides down the lane.

Luke steps to one side to let him pass. "Did I interrupt something?"

"No. Sebastian's a joiner and I was asking him about making some furniture for the yurts."

"Oh. Right."

I smile at him. "Are you coming in? Cup of tea?"

He nods. "That'd be good."

I wait in the kitchen while the kettle boils, rinsing out the teapot and finding some biscuits. It's just as well I'm not that busy today with all these visitors, but I'd be pleased to see Luke even if I was.

I make the tea and carry the tray to the living room. To my surprise, Luke is hunched on the sofa, head bowed and hands clasped in his lap. I put the tray on the floor and sit down next to him.

"Is something wrong?"

"It's seeing you with him. I know this is coming out all wrong and kind of weird, but I'd like to kiss you. Only I'm not sure you want me to."

"Isn't it a little soon for that?" I laugh, but all the same there's a warmth spreading through my stomach and a tingle of excitement chasing over my skin.

He shakes his head as he picks up a biscuit. "It's what you do to me, Anna Pritchard — I'm a gibbering wreck in your presence."

"I'm sure you aren't, not really, but either way I'm flattered." I bend to pour the tea. "Milk? Sugar?"

His voice is husky. "Just milk." I hand him his mug and he curls his fingers around it. I sit back next to him and nurse mine. We both stare at the flames licking around the logs in the burner.

Eventually he clears his throat. "I came because I have a meeting at East Pool on Friday. You were interested in the mine and I wondered if you'd like to come, take a look around."

"That's very thoughtful. There's no work on site at the moment, so I should be free. What time?"

"Meet you there at three?"

"Perfect."

He drains his mug and we both stand. "Anna ... where do we go from here?"

"East Pool?"

"That's not..."

I silence him with a quick kiss. His lips are firm and confident, and it's all I can do to pull myself away. "See you on Friday."

He sighs. "Anna ... you'll be the death of me. All right, Friday it is."

I don't watch him go but return to the kitchen to put the mugs in the dishwasher. Drizzle speckles the window, turning to rivulets as I gaze blankly into the middle distance. I like this feeling of control and I've come to value it. It's not about manipulating anyone else, just keeping my own emotions in check, although this time I'm aware I could be walking a precipice.

I'm also aware there's a corner of my life refusing to be brought into line, tamed, dealt with. A corner that's much too raw. I pick up my phone and read the last text again, my fingers hovering over the buttons to reply. But that's for another day.

When I arrive at East Pool, Luke is already parked on the grass beyond the granite gateposts, just past the 'closed for refurbishment' sign. It's a seriously disappointing place, tucked between a post-war council estate and some industrial units, a vast engine house towering above us. There's a flatbed lorry drawn up to one side and the yard reverberates to the clatter and clang of scaffolding being removed.

I swing my Peugeot next to Luke's car and he steps out. He's wearing chinos and a thick jumper, and kisses me on the cheek before grabbing his clipboard from the back seat. It's impossible to talk with the noise from the scaffolders, who are working with a gusto that can only mean they intend to finish before pub time. I glance across at Luke's profile as we walk, and when he looks down and catches me he winks.

The main hall serves as both museum and shop. It screams Victorian: heavy, serviceable, grim, even as the grey afternoon is chased away by largescale industrial lighting. Luke introduces me to the custodian, explaining I'm a Trelissick volunteer with an interest in mining, so he's roped me in to help him with the health and safety survey.

"Mining? Really?" The man looks eager, if somewhat surprised.

"Only to the extent I'm living and working in an old mining area and I'd like to know a bit more about it."

"Oh, right. It's just Luke never manages to recruit any pretty girls to help out here." Looking around me, I'm surprised he manages to recruit anyone, but I smile sweetly and pull on my gloves as Luke suggests we start the survey outside while there's still some daylight.

We follow a clinker track around the back of the buildings. Lumps of stone and abandoned machinery stud the grass, and Luke makes a note to buy some suitable signage to keep people from climbing on them. At the back of the complex is a room with high windows, empty inside, except for a rail of costumes and a dusty trestle table. Our footsteps tap across the wooden floor.

"What do you think?" Luke asks.

"Of what?"

"Of East Pool."

"Not much. It lacks the romance of the ruins on the north coast. Very industrial and grim."

Luke leans against the wall. "Those mines would have been grim too, especially for the men who went down them day after day and the women and children who spent their lives breaking ore."

"I know that, but it's their stories I'm interested in, their landscape. I guess I want to find out what my little valley would have been like, and I know it wouldn't have been like this."

Luke raises an eyebrow. "I'm sure there's a bal maiden costume somewhere." He levers himself off the wall and starts to rummage through the rail.

"A bal maiden?"

"A woman who worked on the surface of the mines. Here it is." He pulls out a shapeless brown dress and white hood. "Put it on and get closer to them."

"First a French maid and now a bal maiden. Do you have a thing about dressing up, Luke Hastings?"

"You wanted romance, Anna Pritchard."

I hold the dress in front of me. It smells of dry cleaning fluid, and I wrinkle my nose. "So what does romance mean to you? Putting on a mine captain outfit and giving the poor little bal maiden a good seeing to?"

The blush spreads from the base of his neck, right up into his cheeks. Because I'm right, or because I'm so off beam I've embarrassed him?

"Anyway, there's a fire extinguisher over there," I carry on. "Don't you need to tick that off your paperwork?"

He looks as though he's been seriously let off the hook, and I smile to myself. Sometimes the chase is the most thrilling part. But I actually like this man; he's kind, bright, and interesting. And liking him means I need to keep my physical feelings in check so I can be absolutely sure before taking this any further.

We leave the room through an arch into a brick-lined tunnel, stopping every now and then to check the emergency lighting. Towards the end, we pass underneath the mine's chimney and just before we emerge into the fading daylight Luke presses me against the wall and kisses me, the bricks cold and damp against my jeans as his tongue explores my mouth. My good intentions fade to nothing as the taste of him fills me and it's all too hard to pull away.

Outside are the ruins of a boiler house, and Luke tests the railings surrounding the pits. In one place a patch of rust has eaten deep into the iron and he makes a note of it. He tells me about the drying house that used to stand behind us, but neither of us mentions the kiss.

The yard is quiet now. The scaffolders must have finished and headed for the pub. We climb the steep outside staircase at the back of the engine house and Luke pushes open one of the double doors. Inside smells musty and damp, and I pull my jacket more firmly around me.

The whole place is dominated by the engine, which thrusts its way through the floorboards from one level to the next, brass levers and gauges gleaming in the harsh electric light. Our footsteps echo as we walk around it and Luke leads me to the top floor, where we gaze out of the window over the streetlights coming on below us. Row after row of 1950s housing leading to the sulphurous yellow of the higher lamps over the main road.

Luke turns and grasps my shoulders. "I want to kiss you again. More than kiss you, but I figure this might not be romantic enough for your taste. My apologies, I forgot the rose petals and scented candles, but I didn't dare hope I'd need them."

I trace my finger down the side of his cheek, the roughness of his stubble scraping and tingling where my skin isn't completely healed from the fire. "You don't. Not now, anyway."

"Because?"

"Because I like you as a slow burn." This time I initiate the kiss, pulling him to me with my hands beneath his jumper. His shirt is damp with sweat. Oh yes, he wants this. So do I.

It's when he starts to unbutton my jacket I move away. Away from him and away from the window. After a few paces, I turn to face him. "Why don't you bring that dog of yours over for a walk on Sunday?"

He shakes his head. "I can't. I'm at a conference next week in Crawley, and I'm visiting my folks for the weekend on the way." He looks at his watch. "But it's still early… Perhaps we could head back to your place and…"

I shake my head. "Sorry. Not tonight. Travel safely, Luke. I'll see you when you get back." I'm tempted to kiss him again, but that would be a seriously bad idea. As I walk down the steps and around the engine house to my car, I wonder just how long I can bear to keep him at arm's length.

CHAPTER SEVENTEEN

After a weekend of horizontal rain, during which I battle through a shift at an almost deserted Trelissick and a more sociable afternoon at The Tinners, Monday dawns crisp and clear. As I sit in my office, phone glued to my ear, the low sun stretches its beams into the valley and I long to be outside. After being on hold nearly forever, I reach the right person at the power company and progress of sorts is made.

I wander over to the patio doors and am about to slide them open when my phone bursts into life. A voicemail. I step outside to listen to it, trying not to hope it will be from Luke. There isn't even the slightest breeze, and the sun is enough to warm my shoulders. A rare day for November, even in Cornwall, I'd wager.

The message connects. Roland Tresawl. Some of the locals have asked the council about appealing the decision, but even though there's no way for them to do it their questions have delayed the all-important certificate by a few days. I curse under my breath. The groundworks contractors are ready to go and despite today's aberration, winter is fast closing in.

A bubble of anger bursts through the vague discontent of the last few days. I go back inside and power down my laptop before packing a bar of chocolate and some water in my rucksack. Whatever new frustrations the morning has to throw at me, I'm not interested. Monday or not, I'm damned if I'm going to waste the sunshine.

I cross the field behind the farmhouse and hop over the wall onto the path running along the back of the cliffs. Beyond Wheal Catharine the sea is sparkling; not the glorious turquoise

111

of early autumn, but a silvery blue. The gorse is still studded with pinpricks of gold, luminous amongst the brown of the stems and the decaying ferns. A robin sits on a branch, almost close enough to touch, and finally I smile.

As I stride towards the cliff edge, inevitably my mind turns to Luke. What will be my next move? What will be his? I try to shake the feeling that this time it matters, that I might just be falling for him in a way I haven't fallen for anyone for quite a while. Which is a very good reason to be cautious.

There's a high promontory overlooking the valley separating Wheal Catharine and Wheal Clare, and I scramble to the top and look out over the sea. The tide is low and the sand stretches to the headland, the couple walking below matchstick people, their dog no more than a white blur circling around them. This has to be one of the most beautiful places in the world; so beautiful it brings tears to my eyes. I stand and stare at it for a very long time.

"Anna!" The voice startles me from my reverie, and I turn to see Gun on the track below.

"Oh, hello." I retrace my steps to join him. "Glorious day, isn't it?"

"Too good to be indoors. I'm walking the coastal path to St Pirans — fancy coming? I could buy you a pint and a bowl of cheesy chips in the Sloop Inn."

"That absolutely sounds like an offer I can't refuse."

He smiles down at me. "Good."

Gun is undemanding company. Once we cross the valley and climb the other side, the path is too narrow for us to walk side by side anyway. We pass the ruins of Wheal Clare and walk on to the high downland at Tubman's Head, where we stop and share my chocolate and he tells me about the archaeological dig here that found evidence of an Iron Age settlement. Before we move on, he checks I have a head for heights and as the path dips it becomes evident why.

We thread our way through the gorse, closer and closer to the cliff edge. Here the land curves its shoulder down towards the sea, twinkling far below us. We clamber over a wall topped with vegetation, which Gun explains is called a Cornish hedge, and I follow him along a narrow track, the drop to our left becoming steeper with almost every step. In the distance a sandy beach of epic proportions fades into the haze.

Now our path turns inland through a run of stubby oak trees, but we emerge onto another headland with a grassy dip on the seaward side. To my amazement, there are two Clwyd Caps covering old mining shafts and I ask Gun about them.

"Even here, Anna. They put shafts every last place they could."

"My God — it must have been terrifying working somewhere like this."

"It was. But the miners had to eat."

We round another corner and an old harbour appears ahead of us. I stop at the top of a long flight of steps to take a photo on my phone, while Gun strides down them two at a time. I call that I'll catch him up and he waves in acknowledgement.

My descent is slower, and in places I need to grip the rail. There's a retaining wall at the bottom, and I lean on it to take a few more shots and check my messages before tucking my phone back in my pocket. Gun is sitting on a bench above the harbour wall, his long legs stretched out in front of him. He is facing away from me, and for a moment I think he's talking to someone but then I see he is alone.

I am about twenty yards away when I realise I was right the first time and I am witnessing one half of a conversation. It looks like his talking to ghosts nonsense again, and the hairs on the back of my neck stand on end. I remember Ray's words: 'Take no notice, Gun's shot away.' Is he really? I crouch to tie my shoelace.

"It's all right, Anna, Edith's gone."

I unfold myself slowly. "Edith?"

"She was telling me she comes here every day. Her son drowned saving another boy, but they never found his body and she's still waiting for him to be washed ashore."

"What absolute rot!"

"No, it's true. I can show you — there's a plaque on the harbour wall."

So that's where he got the story from. "You still couldn't have been talking to her."

He takes a step towards me. "It's up to you what you believe, Anna, but I ask you to let me be. Come on, I'm thirsty."

I trail after him, uncertain of what to say. He's right, it is up to me what I believe. And up to him what he believes too. He waits for me outside the pub, his shoulders hunched. As I approach, I can see his eyes are clouded.

"I'm sorry, Sebastian. It just freaked me out, that's all."

"There's no need. It's not frightening. The poor souls are trapped, you see, they can't move on, so I guess sometimes they need to talk."

"You're still freaking me out."

He nods. "They're just like us, you know — very often they're troubled because they need to move beyond something to find some peace. Now come on, that pint's definitely calling."

CHAPTER EIGHTEEN

Now it's come to it, I feel strangely nervous about putting on my lady's maid uniform. I arrive at Trelissick early for my shift, the crisp morning air making the tip of my nose tingle as I walk from the staff car park. I slip into the house through the side door, greeted by the sound of hoovering and the heady aroma of cinnamon and oranges.

Last time I came to Trelissick, the decorations hadn't been put up and I'm keen to see what a Regency Christmas looks like. I stow my bag and coat in my locker then make my way down the kitchen corridor to the main hall to take a peep. The central table is covered with a huge arrangement of hothouse roses and the doors are swagged with spruce and ivy garlands studded with slices of dried orange and golden ribbons. There is nothing restrained about it and I can't help but smile.

I missed the volunteer evening making the decorations because I had a date with Luke. He took me to a quaint old cinema in Redruth to see *The Lady in the Van* and we held hands and shared popcorn like a couple of teenagers. I drove myself there. I wasn't quite ready for him to take me home.

I have a feeling that's about to change. He turned up on Tuesday lunchtime with a schematic drawing of where the shafts of Wheal Nevek mine used to be. We stood on the patio of the cottage for ages, trying to pinpoint each one in the modern landscape. They started far closer to the village than I expected and extended all along the ridge that now carries the main road above the valley.

Afterwards I warmed some soup and made cheese sandwiches, which we ate on the sofa in front of the wood burner. A touch of our hands became a caress, the caress dissolved into kisses, the kisses into something altogether more intimate. If I hadn't had a meeting with the groundworks contractor, who knows where it would have led?

Actually I do know, and I was sorry it hadn't. I like Luke a lot; he's sexy and fun, kind and considerate, so it's definitely time to take the plunge. He says he has a surprise planned for me tonight, and I'm ready to take full advantage of whatever it is.

My reverie is interrupted by Liz appearing behind me.

"Haven't you changed yet? I expected you to be in full costume, ready to curtsey and bob and help me into my dress."

I grin at her. "Yes, milady. No, milady."

She laughs. "The Daniells were never elevated to the peerage. Mrs Elizabeth will do very nicely."

I wink at her. "Oui, Madame Elizabeth." After all, the maid was meant to be French.

For most of our shift we are doing our normal jobs as room guides but also explaining how our characters would have fitted into the household. I am stationed in the room next to the orangery with the best view of the park, along with another volunteer dressed as a governess. Thankfully it's her job to entertain the children with the Christmas games on display, although it's more fun than I thought it would be standing in for her when she goes on her lunch break.

The main event of the day is scheduled for four o'clock. About half an hour beforehand, Luke appears and leads Liz and me to the staffroom to run through what will happen one last time. We've already agreed no-one at Trelissick should know we're seeing each other — he's worried it would look unprofessional on his part. I think he's being overcautious but it's no skin off my nose, so I go along with it. Even so, he

116

takes the opportunity to pat my bottom as we pass through the darker recesses of the kitchen corridor.

By the time he's finished the briefing we can hear the horses being led from the stables, their slow hoofbeats competing with the squeaking wheels of the carriage. Liz and I disappear up the stairs to the costume room. Liz has an empire line navy coat, the same colour as her dress, with a high fur collar and cuffs. Her matching bonnet is trimmed with fur too but mine is plain grey, as is the simple cloak I wrap around me.

Putting on our outdoor clothes is an act of transformation. We fall silent and look at each other, for the first time conscious of the murmur of people waiting in the hall below. Liz puts her hand over her mouth. "Bloody hell."

"Come on," I tell her, "let's get this over with." But as I glance in the mirror before leaving the room, for a split second the face peering back at me from under the bonnet is not my own. I step away, almost falling over my skirt, but Liz is already ahead of me and I turn on my heel and stride after her.

I walk down the steps two paces behind her, carrying her muff and navy reticule. A sea of upturned faces falls silent and my heart thuds in my chest. At the bottom of the stairs, a footman waits.

"The parcels are in the carriage as you instructed, ma'am," he says. "Cook has made calves' foot jelly and plum pudding. There are cheeses from the dairy, loaves of bread and draughts from the apothecary. Everything needed to give good cheer to the poor of Porthnevek."

"Thank you." Liz turns to me. "It is a good and Christian deed we do today, Thérèse."

"Indeed it is, Madame." The words feel thick on my tongue.

"Come, let us go."

The crush of people around the porch is even heavier. The groom is showing some children how to pet the horses and the open carriage is resplendent, lined with faux fur rugs. The footman helps us both with the step, and I make a great show of tucking Liz under the covers before the groom jumps up in front of us and instructs the horses to walk on.

It is dusk and the lights hanging from the trees and studding the bushes make the whole experience magical. The brass buckles on the reins shimmer and the path is lined with people, many of them taking photographs. Liz waves regally and I begin to relax into my role and join in. We round the stables and pass the small sensory garden and the shop before heading towards the main gate, at the last minute veering right into the staff car park and out of sight of the crowds.

Luke is there to welcome us, slightly out of breath. "I had to run around the back way, there were so many people," he says. "It's amazing — one of our biggest days yet. Well done." As I jump down, he presses a piece of paper into my hand and I tuck it into my glove. "For later," he whispers, then turns to help Liz from the carriage.

It is a while before I am able to read his note. I slip the paper from my glove and tuck it into my bra as Liz and I change, retrieving it in the privacy of the staff toilet. *Come to Quay Cottage. 4769.* Quay Cottage is a National Trust holiday let a short walk away near Trelissick's pontoon, so I guess the number must be the key code.

The Christmas lights illuminate the path as I make my way past the shop. It's closed, but two assistants are inside cashing up, and there are still a few cars about. I feel almost furtive as I glance behind me before slipping out of the gate and into the lane. I pull my hood around my face and scuttle down the hill towards the river.

Only the fairy lights over the porch and a faint glow from behind the curtains give away the cottage is occupied. The key box is next to the door and wrapped around the key is a note. *Only use this if you're ready.* I finger it for a moment. Am I? I could get seriously hurt if this goes wrong. And if it goes right? What would happen come July? Luke could work anywhere but he loves Cornwall, loves his job. Hell! I'm running much too far ahead of myself. Just get in there, Anna, and give it a go.

The flickering light from candles and an open fire guide me to the living room. Luke is sitting on one of the squashy sofas, red wine in hand. He stands to greet me. "You came." He gestures the glass. "Consolation, in case you didn't."

"There's no need. It takes me a while, but I'm ready to trust you."

He turns away and pours me a drink, our arms entwining as he hands it to me. "To us," he whispers. We raise our glasses, our arms still locked together, the front of my coat brushing his shirt. He puts down his wine. "Here, let me." His fingers shake a little with the first button, but gain confidence.

My coat slips to the floor, then he takes my drink and pulls my jumper over my head, before tracing the outline of my bra and running his fingers downwards towards my jeans. He's fast and slow at the same time, his touch trailing like feathers. Almost before I know it, we are naked on the soft fur of the rug in front of the fire, the candles blurring his features, his desire matching my own.

CHAPTER NINETEEN

Desire is what it's all about, but that's the same in the early stage of any relationship. Luke turns up at the cottage late on Tuesday morning, saying he's between meetings, and wastes no time in taking me to bed. On a workday it feels like a guilty pleasure and that adds to the thrill, although sex with him hardly needs any embellishment.

Then I don't see him for almost a week; he's working at a property in the far east of the county and can't even make it at the weekend. Not that I have a lot of time either, between work and shifts at Trelissick. He sends me flowers, and frequent steamy texts to make sure I know I haven't been forgotten. And I'm enjoying myself rather more than I have done in a very long time; I don't think I've ever felt so completely wanted by a man.

He manages a whole afternoon off on Monday, and our plans to walk on the cliffs come to precisely nothing. Darkness has already fallen beyond my bedroom curtains when we remember. I want to make him supper but he isn't able to stay; his diary seems full of parties at various properties this week.

The Trelissick party is on Saturday night, and he promises me we'll be together afterwards. I have my fingers crossed it will be all night — already I'd love to watch him sleep and wake up with him at my side. Maybe after Christmas life will be easier for him; at the moment, he's working almost every minute God gives.

Not on Friday, though. There's a knock on the door at about three o'clock, and before I've even opened it properly he's slipped past me, grabbed me by the waist and begun hauling me up the stairs. We're kissing and giggling, then undressing and exploring, finally lying sated in each other's arms.

I turn to kiss him. "I'm going to the Christmas market at St Pirans later. Come with me?"

"God, I wish I could."

I sit up and wrap the duvet around me, pretending to pout. "Whose party is it this time?"

"No-one's. It's just Kelly…" He frowns.

"And what does she have that I haven't? Cute ears and a glossy coat?" I laugh and after a moment he does too.

"To be honest, it's more to do with the limits of her bladder. Look, tell you what, why don't I drop you over to St Pirans and join you later when she's had her walk?"

"That sounds like an excellent idea. Maybe we could grab some supper too?"

He kisses me before rolling away and climbing out of bed. "Maybe we could."

Some time alone at least gives me time to buy Luke a present. The guys in The Tinners have told me the market is quite a big event, drawing stallholders from across the county, so I should be able to find something. It's the only Christmas gift I have to buy this year, so it shouldn't be that hard.

When I get there, I see the main street has been closed and stalls snake around the churchyard and spill into the tiny square in front of the greengrocer. The smell of roasting chestnuts fills the dusk and I let my nose lead me to the seller and treat myself. The paper twist is red hot in my hands, but I still can't resist nibbling the first one, and with carols playing over the loudspeaker it really feels as though Christmas has begun.

I weave my way through the stalls, buying more for myself than for Luke. Local smoked duck, a half bottle of Cornish sloe gin, a few packets of olives and a homemade Christmas cake from the WI stand. My rucksack's already feeling pretty weighed down. Some Cornish wine for Luke, perhaps? Maybe. But English red isn't normally that great. Or a scarf? There's a soft cashmere one in royal blue that would look fantastic on him. I can't decide, so I remove myself to the Miners Institute for a cup of tea.

There are no free seats in the café, so I buy a takeout and browse the stands in the main hall, where I strike gold. The local museum has a bookstall, and amongst the shiny new titles are several second-hand tomes, one a social history of Cornish mining. There are also some walking books, and one called *In the Footsteps of Cornish Writers* will probably interest him — and give us some ideas about where to take Kelly when he finally brings her to meet me.

It is as I'm making my way back outside my phone rings. It's Luke, and he's arrived home to find Kelly's been sick on the carpet, so he doesn't want to leave her in case she's ill again. That's fair enough and I try to shrug off my disappointment, especially when he promises to make it up to me tomorrow night.

It's completely dark now and getting pretty crowded, so I make my way past the brightly lit stalls towards the bus stop. I can always drown my sorrows by hopping off outside The Tinners for a quick one. It is Friday, after all — and I haven't been in there for a while.

Suddenly, there's a hand on my shoulder and a hiss in my ear. "Don't think it's over, because it isn't."

I spin around to see Serena next to me. We are nose to nose, her sea green eyes, Gun's eyes, glaring into mine.

"Of course it's not over," I say smoothly. "We've only just started. And as we have planning permission, there's nothing you can do."

"If you think there's nothing, then you're wrong. All that expensive equipment your bloody turncoat contractors leave there overnight, all the..."

"Are you threatening vandalism? Or should I say, more vandalism? Because at least now I'll know where to send the police if anything else happens."

"No point. You won't be able to prove it." She tries to sound confident, but her voice is just a tiny bit shaky. It's time to call her bluff.

"You'd be surprised, Serena, very surprised what I know." I step away and continue towards the bus stop without a backward glance.

CHAPTER TWENTY

When I return to my locker after changing out of my maid's outfit at the end of my next shift, I get a text. *Popping home to check on Kelly. Should give us more time later xx.* How much more? Time for another tumble in front of the fire at one of the holiday lets? Or time enough to stay all night? As Liz and I start to unpack mini mince pies from their boxes and load them onto plates, my whole body is tingling with anticipation.

The Trelissick Christmas party is held in the drawing room and entrance hall. I change out of my French maid's costume and into a new red top I've bought specially, silky at the front with rows of tiny ribbons at the back. Not so much for the party — more for my date with Luke afterwards.

A barber's shop quartet sing festive songs and Christmas lights sparkle from every polished surface. Luke and Julie are working the rooms, making sure they talk to everybody, and I follow his progress from my vantage point next to one of the huge sash windows, willing the party to be over.

It would be too obvious — and too sad — to stand on my own, and anyway, my fellow volunteers are a friendly bunch. I find myself chatting to Pauline and Suzy, two of the most experienced members of the team. When Julie and Luke join us, I try not to look at him, suddenly nervous something will give us away, but he is his normal charming and slightly cheeky self, just as though there is nothing to hide.

Pauline watches him walk away. "It's so terribly sad, isn't it? And he's being so very brave."

I try to stop my head from shooting up when Suzy continues. "And to think, only last year Kelly was here, the life and soul of the party…"

"Kelly?"

Suzy turns to me. "Oh, didn't you know? I hope we haven't spoken out of turn."

"Well, how would Anna know?" Pauline replies. "She's new." She lowers her voice to a whisper. "Kelly is Luke's wife. She's got one of those awful debilitating diseases with initials … ME or something."

I am still trying to make sense of her words when Suzy chimes in. "She's proper poorly with it too — has been since last spring. She's had to give up work and everything — such a strain on them both. I bumped into her in Sainsburys on Monday. She could hardly drag herself around, but the poor girl was determined to buy a special ready meal for their anniversary."

I try my hardest to make a sympathetic noise, but my throat feels too full to speak. The singers launch into 'Have Yourself a Merry Little Christmas' and I fix a smile on my face and murmur, "One of my favourites," before taking a few steps away and pretending to listen.

I'm aware my reaction will seem callous and strange, but I don't care. As the melody mingles with the chatter and the clink of glasses, I try to process the fact Luke is married, and that his wife is ill. Almost the biggest affront of all is he's given her name to a presumably non-existent dog, and I begin to tremble with anger. I see the volunteer who plays the footman making his way towards me, so I slide into the next room and close the door behind me.

Only the safety lighting is on, casting dark shadows into cabinets full of china. I move through to the dining room and into the hall near the bottom of the stairs, intent on getting back to the staffroom unnoticed to collect my bag and get the hell out of here. But as I approach I hear voices and the clatter of washing up, so I dive up the four steps to the café.

I am close to tears. Red hot angry tears. At Luke for being such an absolute shit — and at myself for believing him. My feet echo across the floorboards as I weave through the tables to sit on one of the wide windowsills, a streak of moonlight showing me the way. I pull my feet up and curl myself into a ball, my forehead resting on my knees. This is beginning to hurt. Big time.

The chatter from the staffroom fades. Outside, the moon is full. There is a single lamp over the door of the gardener's cottage across the yard, but I spotted him in the hall an hour ago, necking his pint, so he may well need it to guide him home. A shadow moves, low to the ground, as a fox crosses my field of vision. An owl calls three times.

The sorrow pressing down on me feels more than just my own. It is the sadness of generations; of women lied to and cheated on — women who believed a man and paid the price. It cloaks me in greyness, and I am aware of sobbing. For a moment I think it's my own, but then I realise it isn't. I sit up straight but the sound has gone, leaving just the faintest of echoes. I begin to tremble from head to toe, then, gathering my courage, I slide off the windowsill and race for the bright light of the corridor outside.

CHAPTER TWENTY-ONE

I sleep late on Christmas morning then spend quite some time wondering if it's worth fighting the urge to stay under the bedclothes indefinitely. This week has been manic — right up until yesterday afternoon. The groundworks guys have made good use of the fine weather and the site has been levelled, their equipment safely taken away. Indoors I've been finalising the contract for the build and checking out Cornish interior designers. I haven't given myself time to think.

There is nothing to stop me from working today but it feels counterintuitive, somehow. Maybe a duvet day is in order, although on the other hand I'd been planning to roast a duck, with spiced red cabbage, cherry sauce and Hasselback potatoes. The perfect Christmas dinner for one.

I was always going to be on my own. Luke told me he had to visit his parents, but now I know the truth.

He texted me on Saturday evening to ask where I was. I pulled into a layby, heart thudding and eyes red hot with angry tears. I told him to go home to his wife, and I've heard nothing since. Part of me hurts all the more because I haven't — I must have really just been a shag he couldn't get at home. So much for all that sweettalk. He's such an accomplished liar, it's no wonder I fell for it.

I choke back a little sob and burrow into my pillows. Do I allow myself to give up, just for today, or do I fight this? I turn on my back and stare at the ceiling, following the crack from the lightshade to the wall above the window. Daylight is creeping around the curtains and the birds are beginning to chirp. I close my eyes again.

I don't know how much later it is when my phone bleeps. Is the text from Luke? I should have blocked the bastard, and I resolve to do it today. More likely it's a friend sending festive wishes, or maybe it could be a greeting in response to the card I agonised over sending, but finally popped into the letterbox five long days ago.

I was right. And I was wrong. *It's no use sending a card. You should be here. Like you weren't last year.*

I throw my phone across the room, not caring if it shatters into a million pieces. I'm not giving in. Not to anyone, and certainly not to my sister. She's been bullying me mercilessly with her texts for months and now this. At Christmas. How dare she try to foist the blame onto me? Driven by my fury, I head for the shower then make myself tea and toast with peanut butter. Then it's on with my coat and walking boots to tramp the cliffs until The Tinners opens at twelve.

When I push on the door at seven minutes past, I've never seen the pub so full. The owner dispenses mulled cider and the pool table is covered with plates of things on sticks and mince pies. There must be people from Porthnevek here and the muscles in my shoulders tense, but then I spot Ray and Tim squeezed into a corner by the bar. I push through the crowd to join them.

Other regulars come and go, and I feel protected in our little enclave. I don't see Serena, but some of her cronies are here and I keep myself in the centre of the group. Keith shows up with his daughter and son-in-law, and towards the end of the party Gun appears, his hair somewhat windblown as though he, too, has enjoyed a clifftop walk.

At two o'clock sharp, time is called and the owner wastes not a second ushering us all out. He and his staff have their own plans for Christmas. As I cross the road outside the pub, Gun falls into step beside me. We stop and wave as Ray drives past, the fresh air slapping me around the face and making my head spin just a little.

"What are you up to today?" Gun asks.

I shake my head. "Not much. How about you? Going to Serena's?"

"I was asked, but I'm not. Things are a little tense between us at the moment, and I don't want to spend the whole afternoon being nagged."

"It's not to do with the furniture for the yurts, is it?"

He stops and looks at me. "Some and some. But she's my sister, not my keeper, and I'll do business how I see fit."

"My sister's bossy as well."

"I didn't know you had one."

"No reason you should. We're at loggerheads — as usual — so she doesn't exactly crop up in conversation."

"Pains, aren't they?" There's a sparkle in his eyes and despite my misery, he cheers me.

"Fancy sharing a duck for Christmas lunch?"

He resumes walking. "Sounds better than an omelette. I can nip home and get some chocolates for pud. I keep an eye on old Clemo, so his daughter bought them for me. They look fairly posh."

"It's a deal. You fetch them while I put the oven on."

A few hours later, the duck is nothing but a carcass and I'm curled at one end of the sofa in front of the wood burner. The last of the second bottle of wine glows in its light and Gun's long legs stretch towards the warmth. For the first time, I notice one of his thick socks is navy blue and the other red and grey stripes.

I point at them. "They're odd."

He raises an eyebrow. "I'm odd. And I live alone. Generally nobody sees them."

"Fair enough. Being single has its advantages, doesn't it?"

He shifts on the sofa so he's facing me. "I thought the qualified first aider guy was your boyfriend."

"He was. Until I found out he was married."

"I thought there was something shifty about him."

"I saw absolutely nothing except this really nice, caring man. I was duped hook, line and sinker. And what's worse is his wife has ME. And what's really worse is that he made up a dog called Kelly as an excuse to go home, and that's her name." My voice is breaking, but Gun starts to giggle. "It's not funny." I throw a cushion at him and he catches it, looking contrite.

"I'm sorry, Anna. I didn't mean to laugh if you're hurting."

For a while the only sound is the soft pop of the firewood. I pick up my wineglass, swirling the liquid around to catch the light. "It's made me feel I'm a poor judge of character."

Gun shrugs. "Then don't judge."

"What do you mean? All the time we're assessing people, working out what they're like. It's human nature."

"But you don't have to judge them. You never see the whole. Take Serena. Irritating as she can be, she has a heart of pure gold, and she's hauled me through more rough times than I can remember. All you've seen is a hellcat."

"No, that's not quite true. When we first met, before she knew why I was here, she was absolutely lovely. Really welcoming. I thought we were going to be friends, but there you go — wrong again."

"I bet your sister's not all bad either."

I close my eyes. "Helen's always told me what to do, right from when we were small. I arrived the day before her second birthday, so she probably thought I was her present. Of course, when you're little you comply. And when I was a bit bigger, it was cool my elder sister wanted me to hang out with her."

"So what happened? Did you grow out of it?"

"In part. But when I was twelve, Dad left. She'd always been a daddy's girl, but then she muscled in on Mum. Of course, my mother was brilliantly even-handed, but it was as if scales had fallen from my eyes. I wanted to be everything Helen wasn't, so I stopped being her shadow and forged my own life. A life away…" My throat feels full again so I take another slug of wine. "Come on, let's do the dishes, then we can get stuck into the chocolates."

I'm decidedly unsteady on my feet, but I make it to the kitchen with Gun two steps behind me. I squirt washing up liquid into the bowl with some ferocity, watching as the foam billows on the rising water.

Gun leans next to the draining board, tea towel in hand. "Your mother's passed, hasn't she?"

I turn on him. "God, I hate that word. Pussyfooting around the subject. She's dead."

"Sorry. I'm not too keen on passed either. And it's not strictly accurate, but people generally think it's tactful. Like 'gone to a better place' or 'at rest'."

"Dead is dead is dead, whichever way you look at it."

"I can't argue with that."

I grip the edge of the sink. "I'll never see her again … and last Christmas, last Christmas … I didn't go … because neither of them told me…" I feel myself start to sway and the pan I'm holding slips into the water, releasing a tidal wave of greasy suds all over me. Then Gun's arm is around my shoulder and I bury my face in his jumper, the darkness a welcome cloak.

PART FOUR: 1815

CHAPTER TWENTY-TWO

Mrs Daniell pursed her lips as she watched Mary whirl around the drawing room floor of their Truro mansion with Mr Clements, the dancing master. This new fashion for waltzing seemed too intimate, somehow, especially for a girl newly out in society. Especially as that girl's face was flushed with pleasure, even in the grasp of a mincing middle-aged man.

She clapped her hands. "Mr Clements, I feel my daughter is a little young for such a dance. Perhaps we would be better advised to direct our attentions to the quadrille."

"But Mama," Mary protested, "Annabelle Lemon was waltzing at the last assembly."

"Annabelle Lemon is almost nineteen."

"If I may suggest, Mrs Daniell," Mr Clements interrupted, "there is a variation of the waltz where the lady keeps the gentleman at a … um … more respectable distance…"

"Then may I suggest that would have been the variation, as you call it, to teach my daughter. On reflection the lesson has gone on long enough for today, so I bid you good morning."

Mr Clements bowed and left, but the instant the door was closed behind him Mary sank to the floor at her mother's feet. "Oh, Mama, why were you so horrid? He may not even come back, and he is quite the best dancing master in Truro."

"He will come back, Mary, for fear other families would hear I had dismissed him. And get up, child. You make yourself ridiculous."

Mary did as she was told, but her petulance was clear in her voice. "Why are you such a crosspatch today?"

Mrs Daniell passed her hand over her forehead. "Because, Mary, watching you perform that obscene dance has left me with quite a headache. Please fetch Thérèse and ask her to bring my salts."

Only then did Mary's eyes slide to the floor. "Yes, Mama. I'm sorry."

Mrs Daniell lifted her feet onto the sofa and closed her eyes. Mary was proving to be a worry; on the surface she was a biddable and respectful young woman, but underneath such a wilful child. And yet at her first two assemblies she had behaved impeccably, filling only half her card, and that with the old country dances, and last time modestly turning down an invitation to join a most handsome army officer at the supper table. The trouble was, she never quite knew what Mary would do next.

The door opened and closed with a soft click. "Madame, Mary tells me you have a headache? Here, let me plump the cushions for you. Shall I massage your temples while you rest your eyes?"

Mrs Daniell sighed. "You are such a good girl, Thérèse, so clever and kind with such magic in your fingers. Already I do not know what I would do without you. I hope you are happy here."

"Of course I am, Madame."

Thérèse's touch was soft on Mrs Daniell's forehead, and soon the scent of lavender was seeping into her very being. She opened her eyes briefly to see an affectionate look on her maid's face. "I think I shall rest for a while, my dear. Please stay with me and tell me wonderful stories about your life in France."

"Well, my life was very simple when I was a child, but when I moved to Rouen for Mam'selle to marry Monsieur Logier, all that changed. The wedding itself was quite beyond my wildest dreams … shall I describe the dress for you?"

Already Mrs Daniell's head was easing, all thoughts of Mary's petulance forgotten. She smiled at Thérèse and nodded.

The return to Trelissick was, unusually for Mrs Daniell, not a happy one. Ever the consummate hostess, she forced herself to watch from the morning room window as the hunt gathered. Her two daughters in law, Lucy and Sarah, were at her side, although in due course they would follow the sport across the countryside, squeezed together in her eldest son Thomas's curricle. She could not wait for them to be gone.

It was not the fault of the young ladies. Lucy was pleasant enough, although a little embittered by nine years of childlessness, and Sarah was a dear, dear girl. But simply to see the hunt gather brought Mrs Daniell a pain so sharp it was almost too much to bear.

The chill air was reason enough for her to stay indoors. The hunt servants, standing with the hounds, stamped and wrapped their arms around their coats while footmen served warmed wine and wafers to the riders. Ralph looked so handsome in his dark blue coat and buckskin breeches, talking to Thomas, who at twenty-nine was already too heavy-jowled for his mother's liking. Young Ralph, however, was more like his father. He was in earnest conversation with Stephen Vivian but kept looking towards the window to steal a glance at Sarah, his bride of just one year.

It seemed to take forever for the hunt to be ready to move. Mrs Daniell tried to concentrate on the tiniest details of Lucy's latest trip to Bath to take the waters. Society gossip was of little interest to her, but she fixed a smile on her face and nodded at frequent intervals, while all the time her head thumped more and more relentlessly.

The horn sounded and the girls took their leave. Mrs Daniell stood at the window to wave to Ralph and her sons, cold dread settling into her heart. Only when they were out of sight did she collapse onto the chaise longue and allow herself to weep.

"Madame, what ails you?" She had forgotten Thérèse was in the room, quietly sewing in the corner next to the fireplace.

Mrs Daniell tried to control her sobs. "I am sorry, Thérèse, I am being so foolish, but seeing the hunt leave always makes me think of Henry."

"But, Madame, he was your son. Of course you think of him."

Mrs Daniell sniffed. "It was a morning just like this one, bright and chill with frost. And he was so excited and happy. He loved all gentlemanly sport; shooting and riding to hounds. He never saw any danger … none of us did… You heard of accidents, of course you did, but Henry was such a good horseman, although it counted for nothing in the end."

Thérèse was kneeling on the floor beside the chaise. "Do you wish to tell me what happened, Madame, or is it too painful?"

"They were giving chase through the woods near Feock. I can only suppose Henry chose the shortest route and a tree was half down across the path. He was turning to call to Young Ralph, so he did not see it and it knocked him from his horse." She gulped. "They say his neck was broke straight through."

Mrs Daniell closed her eyes, seeing only the nightmare that had haunted her for three long years. Thérèse's hand crept into hers and she squeezed it.

"You are such a comfort, my dear," she murmured. A comfort ... could she also be a confidante? The clock on the mantel seemed to tick more loudly. "They brought him back to the house." Her voice trembled. "Back to his home, to his mother. There was no mark on him, save for a red wheal on his cheek. I wanted to wash him, wrap him, give him one last kiss, but when I touched him, he was so cold... I could not do it. Thérèse, I failed my son."

There were no answering words of comfort, and Mrs Daniell opened her eyes to find silent tears streaming down Thérèse's face. "Oh, Madame," Thérèse gulped, "I understand. More than you know, I understand."

"Tell me." Mrs Daniell held Thérèse's gaze in hers.

"I wanted ... wanted ... to do the same for my brother after Waterloo. One of his comrades told me he had fallen, so I went to find him. But my courage failed me too. It was so ... so many awful things I saw ... and I have always wondered since. Was he still alive? Did anyone bury the dead with proper ceremony?" She paused and wiped her eyes on her sleeve. "But this is my sorrow, Madame. You have enough of your own to bear, and I have been thoughtless to burden you."

"You did so with the best of intentions, Thérèse. You were wise enough to know that sharing our sadness will make us feel less alone. Certainly it is a comfort to me to know you can understand the very nature of my secret grief. Even Ralph I could not tell, I was so ashamed."

Thérèse looked down. "Shame is a terrible burden."

Mrs Daniell squeezed her hand. "A burden we share, my dear, and although we shall not speak of it again, we will know."

"I am flattered by your trust, Madame, but for now I will make you a tisane of valerian, with just a little St John's Wort, for I am sure I spied some in the herb garden. There is little better for melancholy in my experience, and I would do everything in my power to ease your suffering."

CHAPTER TWENTY-THREE

Although the Christmas season was not quite upon them, the December dance at the Assembly Rooms was greatly anticipated. A number of officers from the town's barracks had been given leave to attend, which was a cause for added excitement for the young ladies of Truro and a source of worry for their mothers.

In the hours leading up to the family's departure for the ball Thérèse was kept busy, running from Mrs Daniell's room to Lizzie's and Mary's, teasing hair into curls, fitting gloves and selecting the finest jewellery to complement their gowns. Mrs Daniell's was a sumptuous creation in royal blue silk with a paler organdie overdress, while her daughters' dresses were more fashionable with narrower skirts dropping from their breasts. While Lizzie's was gold, with a line of bows on the bodice and a richly embroidered hem, Mary's was ivory with a more modest neckline and decorated with rosebuds.

When the carriage was brought to the front of the house, Thérèse accompanied the family party outside to arrange the ladies' skirts properly around them. She was quite affected by the way Ralph murmured to his wife how beautiful she looked and had to hide a happy tear as she ran back up the steps after Matthew and into the hall.

The house closed quietly around her. She was exhausted, but also hungry, and here she knew there would be a welcome in the kitchen. The aroma of spices drifted up the stairs, and as she opened the door the warmth from the range rushed to meet her. She smiled at Mrs Leigh and took her place at the table. After supper, she would fetch her sewing and stay here until the dancers returned. It was a stark contrast to her life at Trelissick, where she took a solitary candle to her room as soon as she could.

It was only a little while after the plates were cleared away when the bell at the kitchen door rang. With a show of reluctance, Mr Leigh shrugged on his butler's jacket and left his spot next to the range to shuffle down the corridor. He returned a few minutes later to say there was a boy with the message that Mrs Daniell would like Thérèse to take her a warmer wrap.

"I will prepare a lantern while you fetch it," he said.

Thérèse wrapped her cloak around her against the cold. The boy was poorly dressed and shivering. She had a penny in her pocket; she would give it to him once their short journey was complete. She held the lantern high to illuminate the alley leading to Princes Street.

"We go," she told him, and he scampered a few feet ahead of her, oblivious to the shadows.

The town was quiet, and even a few streets away she could hear strains of music from the Assembly Rooms, punctuated by raucous laughter from the Seven Stars. The boy paused in front of the colonnade leading to the market hall, and from between the pillars a man emerged.

"We meet again, Mam'selle." The words, in her own tongue, made her start, but she recognised the voice as belonging to the man she had met at the inn at Porthnevek.

"Indeed we do, Monsieur."

"Such a happy coincidence merits proper introductions. John Coates at your service, Mam'selle." He raised his old-fashioned cocked hat and bowed in her direction. The colour rose in her cheeks.

"Merci."

"But now you have me at a disadvantage. I know you are maid to Mrs Daniell, but not your name."

"It's Mam'selle Thérèse … Thérèse Ruguel."

"Your name is more Breton than French."

"That it is, Monsieur. But how do you know, as you are clearly English?"

He shook his head but there was a glint in his dark eyes. "Not English, Cornish. And I know because I have business interests in Brittany. What brings you out on such a chill night?"

"Mrs Daniell requires a warmer wrap, so I'm taking it to the Assembly Rooms."

"Alone?"

"I have this boy for company. The town is not dangerous."

"I would prefer to ensure your safety myself." He pressed a coin into the boy's hand. "You may go. Buy yourself a hot pie."

It was true Thérèse felt more comfortable with Coates by her side. He was tall and muscular, having a physical presence that would make any man think twice before tackling him. He took the lantern from her and they crossed the street to cut through St Mary's Ope. He wasted no words and she kept close to his heels as they skirted the churchyard to come into High Cross.

Here light and music streamed from the Assembly Rooms. Carriages waited, the horses' breath misting the air, while grooms huddled together near the door or made their way to and from the Unicorn Inn with tankards in their hands.

Coates stopped near the Daniells' carriage. "I will wait here then accompany you home." He pulled an enamelled snuff box from his pocket and turned away from her.

The liveried doormen presented a problem for Thérèse, but she did not wish to seek further help from Coates to make herself understood. Instead she repeatedly pointed to the cloak and said Mrs Daniell's name, until one of them allowed her to pass. Immediately she was engulfed by music and the heady aroma of spiced wine. Some soldiers in their bright red uniforms lingered near the entrance, and the sight of them caused her to shrink away, shivering.

She stood next to a fluted column to take in her surroundings. It was probable Mrs Daniell was in the ballroom. She could see Lizzie dancing what appeared to be a cotillion, with Mary in another eight where the men were all soldiers. She could only imagine how dashing they appeared to the young girl, but to her they brought nothing but terror.

Enough. Grasping the shawl tighter, she edged into the room and was relieved to see Mrs Daniell in close conversation with Mrs Lemon just a few yards from the door. Her mistress looked up and saw her, then frowned. "Thérèse, is everything all right?"

"Why, yes, Madame, I have brought the heavier wrap as you asked."

"As I asked?"

Thérèse faltered. "There was a boy ... with a message..."

Mrs Daniell's face cleared. "I suspect the message was from Captain Wooldridge. He has spoken to Ralph and is taking Lizzie onto the terrace after supper. How very considerate of him to send for a warmer shawl. I, for one, will be delighted if we have a happy announcement to make afterwards."

"Oh, Madame, that would be wonderful."

"Indeed it would. Now, if you could take my wrap to the cloakroom, I will ensure Captain Wooldridge knows of its whereabouts."

"Thank you, Madame." Aware of the formality of the situation, Thérèse curtseyed, then did as she was told.

Outside, Coates was deep in conversation with the Daniells' groom, Kitto, but when he saw Thérèse he broke off and walked briskly towards her. "Your errand was accomplished in a satisfactory manner?"

"There was a small misunderstanding on the part of the boy, but it was of little matter."

He raised an eyebrow. "Oh?"

"He mistook the request to be from Mrs Elizabeth Daniell, but it was on behalf of Miss Elizabeth Daniell, so I'm afraid the young lady in question will be forced to wear her mother's wrap."

Coates laughed. "I'd wager boys have been flogged for less. Come, let me escort you home."

He strode off with Thérèse following a few steps behind, but as they were passing the churchyard wall he stopped. "I am sorry. That was perhaps unkind. How can a house in Cornwall be home when you are in a foreign country?"

"But it must be home, Monsieur, for I have no other."

"No relatives at all in … where did you say you came from? Forgive me, my memory fails me. I seem doomed to be ungallant tonight, but I can assure you that is far from my intention. Perhaps we should put it down to my poor command of your language."

Thérèse shifted from foot to foot. "Not at all, Monsieur —
you speak it very well, almost with a Breton accent, in fact.
And since you ask, I am from Roscoff."

"Roscoff! My business in Brittany is there, and I sail from St
Pirans within the week. Is there no-one to whom I could take a
message?"

"No-one. My father died at the turn of the year, and my
brother ... he was in the army ... at Waterloo." She shivered in
the chill of the evening, as well as at the shock of seeing the
soldiers... She wrapped her cloak more firmly around her.
"Come, it is too cold to stand and talk."

But although he followed her closely, Coates did not desist.
"Then perhaps, Mam'selle, I can at least pay my respects at a
family grave or light a candle in the church?"

"No! I have no truck with religion, and when the dead are
dead they exist only to haunt our memories."

"Then we are, at least, at one on that subject. And I too,
have a dead brother. When I saw his battered corpse, I
swore..."

Despite herself, Thérèse choked back a sob. Oh, the shame
of it. Crying in the street in front of a man she did not know.

He lowered the light so no-one passing could see her face. "I
apologise, Mam'selle Ruguel. I did not mean to cause you such
distress with my coarse words."

"It was not the nature of your words."

He was standing close enough for her to feel his heat. "Then
what..."

"I never saw my brother's body. After the battle, I was too
cowardly to search for him."

"Come, do not chide yourself so. A battlefield is no place for
a woman. You could have done no more."

144

"But what if..."

"No, Mam'selle Ruguel. No 'what if.'" He touched her cheek and she jumped away. He hung his head. "Again, I must apologise. I meant it only as a gesture of friendship." He raised the lantern to look at her, his features sharpened by the angle of the light.

Thérèse bowed her head. "I take no offence, Monsieur. You have been very kind, and I am flattered you consider me a friend."

Finally he smiled. "My travels will be all the happier because of it."

When Coates left Thérèse at the kitchen door, she did not watch him go, although she listened as his footsteps receded in the direction of the harbour. After returning the lantern to the scullery, she climbed the back stairs to Mrs Daniell's bedroom. The heavy curtains were drawn against the chill of the night, but she slipped between them, hugging her arms around her.

She could just make out the flares that lit the quay beyond the orchard, the masts of the ships disappearing into the darkness above the quivering glow. Coates had said he would be sailing for Roscoff soon and part of her longed to go with him, although to what end she did not know. There was nothing for her there.

Nothing except memories. She pictured the narrow streets of the town, granite and slate houses rising to the church that perched on top of the hill. She had lived in its shadow, but of course they had never gone there, her father having eschewed all religion when his young wife had died. Instead, he had given his energies over to his work as a merchant's clerk, and to teaching his children their letters and numbers, and most importantly, to think, so they too could better themselves.

She knew he had been proud of her rapid progress from laundry maid to lady's maid in a good family. Apart from marriage, what more had there been for a girl of her class to aspire to? Despite fate's black hand in her life over the last year, she was as content as she could be in Mrs Daniell's service, and grateful for it.

But all the same, her conversation with Coates had dredged up her guilt and grief. How odd to have confided in a stranger like that, because for all he had said they were friends, she knew him not at all. Yes, she had felt safe at his side, but still she sensed a danger about him, in a way she could not quite understand. She turned away from the window and set about banking the fire. Only fate would decide if their paths would cross again.

CHAPTER TWENTY-FOUR

Although she had no love for the house, Thérèse had to admit the grey walls of Trelissick were brought to life by the preparations for the festive season. There were many reasons for the family to celebrate this year, not least the twin joys of Lizzie's engagement and the news that the Daniells' third son, Will, would have leave from the navy in early January. All talk was of the ball Mrs Daniell was planning to mark both occasions.

But Christmas was also a time to think of the poor, and on the twenty-second of December, Thérèse and Mrs Daniell set out for Porthnevek. A farm cart had preceded them, loaded with supplies. The innkeeper had been persuaded to put his kitchens to use preparing a warming stew made from vegetables and mutton provided by the Daniells, and a tankard of ale for all.

Thérèse had visited Porthnevek three times and was becoming accustomed to the noise of the mines that accompanied much of their journey. Now the days were short, and they would need to make haste to return to Trelissick before nightfall.

The villagers gathered in the main room of the inn, women and the elderly squeezed around tables, men standing with bowls of stew or their ale in their hands, children weaving between the groups. Bread, cheese and cabbages waited in the parlour to be collected after the festivities, but even so a steady trickle of sick and infirm appeared at the door to receive their poultices and tinctures.

Thérèse noticed the slow old man with the stick was not among them. She asked leave of Mrs Daniell to try to find him in the main room, but when she peeped around the door and could not see him she became concerned.

"You are a kind soul, Thérèse," Mrs Daniell told her, "but why does it worry you so?"

"I do not wish for a man in so much need to go hungry, Madame." She looked down. "And besides, there is something about him that makes me think of my father in his last months."

Mrs Daniell put a hand on her arm. "Old William has perhaps already passed to a better place. Fetch the innkeeper and I will ask."

The innkeeper thought the man was still alive but went to enquire of his neighbour. "She says his cough is worse and he is too addle-pated to rightly know the few yards up the hill, but she will take his bread if Mrs Daniell permits it."

"Addle-pated, you say?"

"I am afraid his mind is failing him, Mrs Daniell. It is a sad and sorry thing in one so proud."

"Perhaps the loss of his son weighs more heavily on him with his increasing years. It was a terrible thing."

Thérèse understood little of the conversation but noted the frown on Mrs Daniell's face. "The old man is ill, Madame?" she asked.

"Yes, I'm afraid he is."

"Then permit me to take him some stew and the tincture for his cough."

Mrs Daniell smiled at her. "If you wish, Thérèse, but find Kitto to go with you. The innkeeper will show you the way."

Kitto was called from his ale, and after fetching the stew the innkeeper accompanied them to the door and pointed out the cottage. It was no more than a hundred yards away but the slope was steep, and Thérèse struggled not to slip on the mixture of mud and wet leaves beneath her feet.

The cottage was low and dark, its roof badly in need of patching. The door had swollen in the wet weather and was ajar, but nevertheless Thérèse knocked.

The old man spoke, then coughed, so she went in, taking a slant of the grey daylight with her. Old William was in a chair next to a mean fire, more smoke than flame, but his eyes lit up when he saw Thérèse and he spoke again.

She crossed the room and put the bowl of stew in his hands, casting around for a spoon. To her surprise, the old man spoke sharply to her and she looked around at Kitto, who was standing by the door. He replied to Old William with equal force and the man indicated a shelf cut into the wall, where Thérèse found a spoon and handed it to him.

He smiled at her and started to eat the stew with shaking hands. There was fresh wood stacked by the door, so she took a log and put it on the fire before showing him the bottle of tincture and putting it on the table. He reached out and grabbed her wrist so tightly she almost screamed, but then he stroked her hand more gently with his stubby fingers, before stretching up towards her bodice.

Kitto was across the room in two steps and pulled Thérèse away. He spoke to Old William again then ushered Thérèse from the cottage, looking more than a little shaken, and before he went to fetch the carriage he exchanged a few words with Mrs Daniell.

Once the horses began to trot down the hill away from the inn, Mrs Daniell turned to her. "Are you quite all right, my dear? Kitto tells me Old William mistook you for his wife, and she's been gone many a year."

"I ... I did not understand that, and now his behaviour makes sense. But he did not seem to have a fever..."

"It is not a fever, Thérèse. The innkeeper told me Old William is increasingly gripped by bouts of madness. He has lost both his sons, one way or another, the elder in a terrible accident in Wheal Nevek and the younger... Well, it would have been better if the younger one had never been born."

"The poor man..." began Thérèse, but her mistress had closed her eyes. Thérèse was left to look out of the window at the first signs of dusk gathering over the mines.

After a while, Mrs Daniell broke their silence. "Thérèse, I have such a headache."

Thérèse pulled her smelling salts from the folds of her cloak and administered them, then wrapped the rug more firmly around her mistress. Although the carriage jolted on the rutted road, she did her best to massage Mrs Daniell's temples. "Is there laudanum in the chest, Madame?"

Mrs Daniell nodded and Thérèse gave her a draught. "You are a kind girl, Thérèse, so thoughtful. And I almost let you walk into danger..."

"Nonsense, Madame. You made me take Kitto, so all was well. There is no need to blame yourself."

Mrs Daniell's eyes closed again, and Thérèse hoped she would sleep for the rest of the journey.

When Thérèse found the silver comb with its wreath of engraved leaves and pearl berries, she knew exactly what it meant. It was only because it caught the light of the flickering candle that she saw it at all, buried as it was in the folds of her second chemise, deep in the chest of drawers in her room.

She sank onto the bed and closed her eyes. What to do? Return it quietly to Lizzie's dressing table? But what if another valuable piece appeared in its stead? Tell Mrs Passmore? But it was beyond her grasp of the English language and anyway, she could not be sure the housekeeper had not put it there herself.

Taking the comb to Mrs Daniell was out of the question. After their long day at Porthnevek she had retired early to her room with a light supper, and Thérèse had already been dismissed for the night. But what else could she do?

She had one possible ally at Trelissick, one person outside the family who had shown her kindness. She just had to hope she would be believed.

Placing the comb into the pocket of her skirt, she made her way back down the narrow staircase from the servants' quarters towards the nursery corridor. At this hour of the night the children would most likely be in bed, and she hoped perhaps she would find Miss Grafton alone at her mending. Every step she took threatened discovery, and she was trembling by the time she turned the handle of the door.

Edward and Anne were in their nightshifts, kneeling in front of the hearth at their prayers. Thérèse made to leave but Miss Grafton beckoned her to stay, before putting her finger to her lips. Thérèse closed the door gently behind her and leant against it, heart pounding.

When the children had finished they scrambled to their feet, Thérèse staying in the shadows while Miss Grafton ushered them to their bedrooms. Thérèse stood rigid, gazing blankly at the nursing chair with the pretty heart-shaped back next to the fire. It seemed an age before Miss Grafton returned. Smiling, she asked Thérèse to sit down and join her in a cup of chocolate.

Thérèse propelled herself forwards into the light, holding the comb on the flat of her hand. "I found this. In my room. Someone must have put it there."

Miss Grafton looked at her, aghast, then turned to close the connecting door to the nursery. "Oh, my dear, how awful. You did right to come to me so we can consider what best to do."

Her understanding reduced Thérèse to tears, and she sank onto a footstool near the fireplace. "I know I am not liked, but I cannot countenance being hated so. It makes it hard for me to stay, and yet I have nowhere else to go."

Miss Grafton sat down opposite her. "You have no need to go anywhere. The Daniells are good employers and the family value your services. It is the person who did this dishonest thing who should have to leave."

Thérèse shook her head. "I do not want to make trouble. I just want to be left alone. I am accepted well enough by the staff at Truro because Mrs Leigh would not permit any unpleasantness, but here it is so very different."

Miss Grafton toyed with the comb in her hand. "Perhaps I should speak to Mrs Passmore."

"But what if this is her doing?"

"I think not, but perhaps … she may know of it. After all, she hasn't raised a finger in your defence."

"My defence?"

Miss Grafton shook her head. "No, that is the wrong word. I only mean… Thérèse, I believe there is a member of staff who thinks they have reason to dislike you, but I would not wish to cast doubt on their character without evidence."

"But what have I done? Perhaps if you could help me to apologise to them…"

"You have done nothing. Except take a job this person supposed their sister could be sure of."

"And I thought this was all because our countries have been at war." She gazed into the fire. "But if it is personal…"

"All the more reason to speak to Mrs Daniell."

"She has retired early with one of her headaches, and I would not wish to upset her further."

"I am sure you have not upset her at all."

"Not me, but there was an old miner who was so addled he thought I was his wife, and that caused Madame Daniell much distress."

"I understand. But you must tell her about this or worse could happen. Tomorrow, as long as she is well enough. In the meantime, we will vouch for each other in the matter of the comb and I will keep it in my sewing box here in the schoolroom. But you must be brave, Thérèse. Promise me. You must do it before the comb is missed."

CHAPTER TWENTY-FIVE

There was little chill in the breeze, but all the same Thérèse gathered her cloak around her as she walked through the park. It was Sunday so the family was in church, and she was able to be alone with her thoughts. It was also the day before Christmas, and she was bowed and overburdened by sorrow.

Last night she had dreamt of Paul. Or rather, it had seemed to be Paul. He had come to her on the quay at Roscoff, laughing and smiling, but then it had started to rain and his hair had darkened until it was quite black and his face became that of Monsieur Coates. And he'd asked her to dance, and they slipped and slid over the cobbles, with one turn becoming Paul and the next Coates. Coates and then Paul. And somehow she couldn't shake the feeling of his arms on hers.

She took the path in front of the house then along the promontory above the River Fal. The sun glinted on the distant harbour, white horses whipping at its gate. In front of her, the river opened into a wide estuary only to narrow again some miles away as it reached the sea, protected by a castle on either side. Protected from whom? The French, of course. Her countrymen. They were at peace, but peace was fragile — and here at Trelissick she at least seemed to be at war.

Despite the season there was some warmth in the sun. Later in the day she would accompany Mrs Daniell and the children to pick holly, ivy and mistletoe to decorate the house. It was an important tradition here and she would respect it. But she could not enjoy it. Her heart was too heavy with grief — and the knowledge that despite her promise to Miss Grafton, she had yet to tell her mistress about the comb.

154

Now there would be little opportunity. After the gathering of the greenery and the decorating, there was to be an elaborate supper. She could, of course, tell Mrs Daniell while she was dressing her for the evening. Could, and probably should. But she did not wish to spoil the occasion, especially as Young Ralph and Mr Thomas and their wives would be joining the rest of the family.

Perhaps it was best to wait until after Christmas. But here the celebrations stretched into January, and then there would be the ball... She looked into the distance, beyond the harbour, beyond the white horses, all the way to France. But there was nothing for her there either.

"Courage, ma petite soeur, courage." The breeze whispered the words from a long way off.

Choking back a sob, Thérèse turned towards the house.

As soon as Mrs Daniell opened the drawing room door, the scent of cinnamon and oranges stuck with cloves rushed out to meet her, mingled with the richness of burning oak. The fire crackled as the flames licked the yule log and the mantelshelf was topped with holly, its berries reflecting the light from the fire. All was as it should be, ready for the family to gather to listen to the wassailers on the terrace before Christmas dinner. And family was what was most important. In church this morning she had whispered a prayer for Henry, and for the babies who had not been long in this world, but now it was time to enjoy the living.

She climbed the staircase with an easy tread to find Thérèse laying out her costume for the evening. She had chosen a rich blue with gold embroidery and a gold overdress, which fastened just below her breast. On the dressing table Thérèse had set a selection of gold jewellery, but she knew exactly which piece she was going to wear.

Thérèse helped Mrs Daniell out of her day dress and in the warmth of the fire began to brush her hair.

"I will wear the cameo necklace, I think, Thérèse. It may be a little heavy, but it was a gift from Ralph so it will please him." It was indeed beautiful, set with a dozen small images of the god of love, each edged with fine filigree work.

Thérèse nodded and continued to brush.

There was a knock on the door.

"Mama, I cannot find my silver comb. Thérèse, have you perhaps seen it? I am sure it was brought from Truro."

Thérèse stared blankly at Lizzie, her hands gripping the hairbrush.

"Thérèse?"

"Sorry, Madame. I was thinking. I remember placing it in Mam'selle Elizabeth's jewellery box after the last assembly."

Mrs Daniell laughed. "Unlike my heavy shawl, which everyone seemed to forget about. I suppose it was all the excitement of Lizzie's betrothal." She turned to Thérèse. "As you put the comb away, it must be here at Trelissick. Lizzie, perhaps Mary has borrowed it without thinking to ask, or little Janetta, even. She has such a passion for dressing up. Last week Miss Grafton had to return two pairs of my best calfskin gloves."

"Thank you, Mama. I will ask them. I so want to wear it tonight."

Mrs Daniell smiled at her daughter. "When Thérèse has finished here, she will come to dress your hair. Hopefully by then the comb will be found. Now, Thérèse, let us continue my toilette at the dressing table." But Thérèse's hands were fumbling and when Mrs Daniell saw her in the mirror, her face was white. She turned around. "What is it child, are you ill?" Thérèse shook her head. "No, Madame. Let us continue or you will be late."

"No, Thérèse. You are not yourself and you must explain." Her voice was almost a whisper. "I know where the comb is."

"Then why did you not say?"

"Because ... because ... it is such a story, Madame, and I did not want to concern you with it at Christmas, especially now when we have so little time." She stifled a sob, before stiffening her back and walking across the room to fetch Mrs Daniell's dress.

"Very well, Thérèse. We will make a bargain. I will not trouble you further now, but once I am dressed you will collect the comb and take it to Lizzie. If she asks, tell her it was in my jewellery box all along. But tonight, when you come to help me prepare for bed, you must tell me everything. Is that understood?"

Head bent, Thérèse dropped a curtsey. "Yes, Madame."

Try as she might, Mrs Daniell found it hard to put Thérèse's strange words and behaviour out of her mind. Had she judged the young woman wrongly? Was there a thread of dishonesty through her? She brushed the thought away — had she not proved her care and loyalty time and again?

After some wine Mrs Daniell began to enjoy herself with her family around her, although it was hard to forget Thérèse completely when the silvery glint in Lizzie's hair reminded her of the matter at every nod and turn. She retired as early as was polite and found Thérèse waiting for her. Usually the girl was busy about some task, but now she sat outside the circle of the lamp, hands clasped so tightly in her lap her fingers were quite white. "Well, Thérèse?" Thérèse stood and Mrs Daniell noticed the blotches of red on her cheeks. She softened her voice. "Do not be scared. Just tell me the truth."

Haltingly, Thérèse began her tale. Mrs Daniell sat on the end of the bed and watched her face through every agonised phrase, refraining from interrupting until she had finished. Her final words were almost a whisper. "You must, of course, ask Miss Grafton to tell her story when she returns from her family."

"There will be no need for that, Thérèse. I believe you." Clearly Mrs Passmore had done nothing to stop the ill will of the other servants. Mrs Daniell was angry.

"Oh, Madame, Madame, thank you." Thérèse dropped to her knees at her feet. ·

Mrs Daniell reached out and put her hand on her head, her mob cap as fresh and crisp as it had been this morning. Thérèse was a good girl and an excellent maid. It would not do to lose her. "Get up, Thérèse, you will dirty your dress on the floor. What you have said concerns me greatly, but I will need to speak to Ralph. His steward has overall management of the household and must be consulted."

"I want no trouble on my behalf, Madame. It is best not to wake the sleeping cat."

Mrs Daniell could not help but smile. "In English it is a sleeping dog. The dog has a bigger bite, but perhaps in this case ... the cat could be more spiteful. You must trust me, Thérèse, to speak to Ralph and we will do what he thinks best. But promise you will tell me of any more unpleasantness straight away."

"Yes, Madame." It was barely a mumble, and Mrs Daniell was not at all sure she meant it.

PART FIVE: 2016

CHAPTER TWENTY-SIX

I lean on the gate at the top of the valley. It's three months since I first arrived here, and it's time to take stock and write a report my boss, Cecile, can deliver to the board of directors. The hard core that's been laid for the road and car park glistens after this morning's rain, but the levelled area where the main circle of yurts will stand is a muddy scar.

There are voices in the lane behind me, breaking through the hum of traffic from the road and the distant crash of the waves in the cove. There's a rustle of anorak and a man says, "What on earth's happening here?"

I turn to see a couple in their sixties wearing head to toe hiking gear. I smile at them. "We're building a glamping site."

"Looks a bloody mess to me."

He's spot on, and viewing the valley from above makes it a hundred times worse. I glue my smile into place. "It won't be like this for long. By April most of the work will be done and we can start greening up the site again."

"So what's going to be built down there?"

"A single-storey facilities building and about thirty yurts. Most of them will be on the levelled area in the middle of the valley, but there will be some dotted around the edges for people who want a less communal holiday."

"We've never stayed in a yurt," the woman pipes up. "What are they like?"

"Ours are good, thick canvas. They're each built on their own deck so they have wooden floors and proper furniture and log burners for the winter. Some even have en suites in mini-yurts attached to the back, but there's one big kitchen in the facilities block for everyone. We try to strike a balance between luxury and back to nature."

"Looks like the nature down there has taken quite a hit," says the man.

"We've done our best, but it is hard during the build." I point to the floor of the valley to my left. "See that band of vegetation? It's a wildlife corridor, though judging by some of the disturbance in the gorse, something a bit bigger than a fox or rabbit's been going through there."

"Any deer about?" the woman asks hopefully.

"The tracks look more like a two-legged creature to me. Well, enjoy your walk."

I open the gate and make my way down the rubble surface that will soon be a road. Already it's strong enough to take heavy equipment, and the portacabin that will be my office is arriving later today. I'd like it to be high up, where I'll have the tiniest view of the sea, but practicality dictates it will be put at the Nankathes end of the site. I can't help thinking it might be more vulnerable down there.

Serena and her gang have been very quiet over Christmas, and I'm hoping it's more than just a seasonal truce. I'm sure I saw a spark of genuine fear in her eyes when I mentioned the police, so maybe it was enough to make them think again.

Gun has been conspicuous by his absence too, and it's making me uneasy about what may or may not have passed between us at Christmas, when I woke late in the evening on the sofa, tucked under a blanket but only wearing part of my clothing. In my heart of hearts, I know it was nothing — when I picked up my jeans and jumper they were greasy and damp, so there was every reason to take them off — but for now as I glance towards Nankathes I'm biting my lip. I'm pretty sure his is one of the unpainted houses, but what would I say if I plucked up the courage to knock on the door? And if any of his neighbours saw me, would that make things difficult for him?

I'm making excuses. Maybe I just don't want to know. After all, Gun's shown no concern at all about what people think, even Serena. But that isn't quite right either. The night of the fire he let slip how much he hates his nickname. So now I tell myself off for using it, even just in my head.

I continue down through the valley. It's soaking underfoot and the lorry bringing the portacabin is going to churn things up even more. I look around me, wondering if this build really is the right thing to do. The coastline is so wild and beautiful... I square my shoulders. Glamping means more people will be able to enjoy it. Small scale, low impact. The perfect development.

Half hoping to see Gun, I run the gauntlet of Nankathes and out onto the cliff path. The sea is gunmetal beneath the heavy sky, clouds churning above the cliffs, but in the distance the sunshine is glinting on St Ives. The wind whips in from the west and its bitterness rams home how sheltered Wheal Dream's valley is. Again, it's the perfect place for yurts.

I almost sound as though I'm convincing myself. I stop and hug my arms around me. Everything seems so uncertain at the moment; shifting, reshaping, and it's making me ill at ease. Apart from anything else, I'm on the rota at Trelissick later today. Should I go? Should I let what happened with Luke stop me? I was such a fool I can't bear the thought of actually seeing him.

I hunch my shoulders against the wind and walk on. It whips around my hat, pulling strands of hair across my face and making my cheeks sting. Even up here there's a hint of salt and spray, while below me the waves pound the cliffs, sending white plumes into the air. It's raw and elemental and entirely beautiful. So much so it makes me want to cry.

"Oh, Mum, you'd love this," I whisper. But of course she'll never see it, never feel it. Never know I'm here. How come it's starting to hurt so much after all this time? It's almost as though talking to Gun about her has opened some sort of Pandora's box inside my head.

I decide to keep my shift at Trelissick. When I arrive, I am stationed in the dining room, and to fill the time I ask Julie if there is any information I can read up on about the china and glass set out so beautifully on the table. The collection of Spode in the library is well documented, but that dates from the time the Copeland family owned the house and is fairly recent, but I do know this room is set in Georgian fashion.

Here Julie corrects me. "More properly, it's Regency. The Trust inherited the contents and they were brought here. Nothing actually remains from the Daniell family's time as far as we know."

"Was it because they bankrupted themselves doing up the house?"

She shrugs. "It could have been. The first exhibition we had after we opened to the public was all about their era, so I'll pop and get the file for you. There might be something about the dinner service in there."

I settle myself in a chair by the window, the heavy ring binder on my lap, and start to flick through it. I need to keep busy today to stop myself worrying whether Luke will show up, but his car wasn't in the car park and last night it occurred to me I'm a bigger risk to him than he is to me. The thought actually made me feel quite smug for a few moments, but coming here has put me well back into kicking myself mode.

The first document I come across is a potted history of the Daniell family. Luke said something about them being clogs to clogs in three generations, but that was another lie — apparently they were established in Cornish society long before Thomas Daniell Senior teamed up with his wife's rich uncle to buy the business interests that would make his fortune.

This Thomas, though, had nothing to do with Trelissick. He lavished his money on a mansion house in Truro, which apparently still exists. It was the last word in Georgian luxury and faced with Bath stone — the first in the town to use it. It took seven years to build and was completed just in time to welcome his son, Ralph Allen Daniell, into the world in 1762.

Now this Ralph is our man. It seems although he lived in the Truro house after his father's death, he rented Trelissick from about 1805 and bought it eight years later. I look down the list of his children with something close to awe — no wonder he needed a big property — when he first moved here he had eleven of them. His poor, poor wife.

But maybe riches made up for it. I smile to myself — maybe he was also a demon in bed. But whatever the case, she wouldn't have had much choice. And they married when she was just eighteen years old.

Over the next few pages, his connection with Wheal Nevek becomes clearer. In 1799 Ralph re-opened the derelict mine, and within a few years it was making him £20,000 per annum — a huge fortune. The workings expanded rapidly, and I find a copy of the schematic Luke brought to Nevek Cot. I can almost feel the warmth of his arm against mine as we tried to pinpoint the shafts in the modern landscape. I shake my head like a wet dog to rid myself of the image.

But in 1813 Wheal Nevek needed investment, and although Daniell wanted to carry on, the three owners of the land couldn't agree and it closed a year later. Was this, as well as the money spent on Trelissick, the start of the family's slide into ruin?

I am pondering it when Julie pops her head around the door to say the café in the courtyard's heaving and would I mind going over to clear tables. I grab the chance to be active, and somehow manage to spend the rest of my shift cheerfully collecting plates and cups, patting damp dogs and stacking the dishwasher.

CHAPTER TWENTY-SEVEN

The low cloud barely lifts from the horizon for almost a week. On Monday I spend all day setting up my office in the portacabin, running to and from the retail park with flat-packs and assembling desks and shelves. There's no phone signal and no landline installed yet, so I have to keep going back up to the cottage to check for messages and emails.

On Tuesday morning, I arrive to find a neat pile of dog shit on the step outside. Bloody great. And almost certainly deliberate. But it's trespass at worst, which is not a criminal offence. It makes me uncomfortable, but should I brazen it out? The mizzle drips from the hood of my anorak as I think about it. What's the point? I'd be better off in my dining room.

On Thursday afternoon, the rain begins to lift and I can see the valley clearly from the cottage window. The earth circle in the centre looks different, disturbed. My heart sinks. I set down my mug and grab my keys before pulling on my wellies and coat and heading for Wheal Dream. But even from the gate I can see the lines of light grey pebbles, presumably from the beach. It's a very simple message and it ends in 'off'. For the moment at least, I'll leave it where it is.

Instead of going home I turn towards The Tinners, but it's a bit too early in the day for Keith and his comforting crossword, so I head out onto the cliffs, the ruined tower of Wheal Catharine in my sights.

By now the rain has stopped and the clouds have lifted sufficiently for St Pirans Beacon to be visible for the first time in days. Maybe I'll loop past Wheal Clare then skirt its slopes before heading back for a well-earned pint.

The cliff edge path to the old mine workings is steep, the shale slippery underfoot. It takes my full attention, and it's not until I reach the plateau forged for the engine house I notice Gun sitting on a bench, looking out over the waves. Did he see me approach? Either way I can't ignore him, because whatever may or may not have happened or been said, that would be a line in the sand I'm not prepared to draw.

I sit down next to him. "Nice to be able to get out for a change."

"I always get out." His voice is dull, monotone.

"You must have got soaked this week."

"I dry."

"And all to see the sea." I try to laugh, make it sound like a joke.

"I hate the frigging sea."

The venom in his voice takes me aback. "Sebastian, are you all right?"

"No."

"Do you want to talk about it?"

"No."

We sit in silence, the dampness from the bench oozing into my trousers, my buttocks slowly becoming blocks of ice. Eventually I pluck up the courage to speak. "It wasn't Christmas, was it?"

Now he turns, a furrow deep in the centre of his forehead, his beard bushy and unkempt. "Christmas? No … Christmas is all right … it's afterwards, now…" His gaze is far, far over my right shoulder. Then he shakes his head.

"Sebastian." I touch his hand. "I'm listening."

"There's nothing to hear." He stands and plunges his fists into his pockets, before bidding me a terse goodbye and heading back along the cliff towards Porthnevek. When he is about fifty yards away, he turns. "Anna — go to see your sister. It's what your mother wants you to do."

Those words of Gun's are not ones I can easily forget. Not 'what your mother *would* want', but 'what your mother wants'. Coming from anyone else it'd be a slip of the tongue, but not from Gun. Am I beginning to believe his talking to ghosts malarkey?

His words whirl around my head throughout the tribulations of the next few days: the new telephone wire mysteriously detaching itself from the pole the very first night it's installed; the constantly changing words in the pebbles. Petty, insidious — nothing that's absolutely breaking the law. Cecile gives me a stern talking-to about my personal safety, but the police are too understaffed to visit the site. They will if things escalate when the build starts, but the valley is a muddy swamp and has even developed its own stream between the platform and the nature corridor. There's no way heavy equipment can get anywhere near it.

With the telephone reinstalled, I make a point of moving my office into the portacabin, but only during daylight hours. I'm not so busy I have to work late anyway. I've even put in the order for the yurts and briefed two designers on the shabby chic surfer vibe I want for the resort. So largely I'm twiddling my thumbs and thinking too much.

Every logical argument is in favour of picking up the phone to Helen and telling her I'm coming to visit. I picture the granny flat above her garage, musty and cold, a film of dust on the family photos on Mum's dressing table, her clothes hanging flat and empty in the wardrobe. No welcoming smell of homemade soup or a stew in the slow cooker. Everywhere reminders of the fact she isn't there.

For the first time I wonder how Helen lives with it day after day. The thought is enough to bring me to my knees so I push it firmly away, wind my scarf around my neck, and head for The Tinners.

It's early, so only Ray is at the bar. I perch on the stool next to him and order a pint of the guest ale. He raises an eyebrow. "Living dangerously?"

"Why, is it foul?"

He points at his habitual lager. "How would I know?"

Months ago his silence would have unnerved me, but not now. I exchange a few words with Rich but then he potters off to lay tables for supper. A sudden squall beats at the windows and Ray sighs.

"Endless, isn't it?"

"I know. We're totally stalled on site. Can't get the equipment in."

He sips his pint. "It'll be a while, even after it stops. The water table rises, see, and once it hits the old mine workings it's sodding everywhere."

"The valley must be riddled with them, the number of shafts they put down from the ridge over the years. I'm thinking of making our new stream a feature."

"You could do worse."

I am halfway down my pint when Tim breezes in. "Bloody hell," he says, "I didn't expect to be later than the working classes."

"There's nothing either of us can do at the moment," says Ray. "Sodding weather."

"And I can't get out onto the golf course," Tim tells us. "The wife's got me doing all sorts of jobs. Talking of which, anyone seen Gun recently?"

Ray snorts. "Not at this time of year."

169

"Why's that?" I ask.

"He gets depressed. January's bad for him."

"What, some kind of seasonal affective disorder?"

"Not really. Something happened, you see, when we were nippers..."

The door from the car park blows open and then slams again, rattling the glass. "Jesus, Tim — can't you shut it properly?" Ray jumps up to secure it, but before he's even regained his stool Keith arrives, newspaper slightly soggy under his arm. Tim and Ray start to bicker about the door, so I join Keith at the corner of the bar and get stuck into the crossword.

When I return home, Gun is still on my mind. Should I try to see him or not? At first, the thoughts tossing and turning around my head are a welcome relief from the constant conundrum about Helen, but somehow the two become linked and I find myself in a real pickle.

I sit at the dining room table, notepad and pencil in hand. I write 'Christmas' then draw a line under the word. What happened? My gut tells me nothing bad, but given there's a chunk of time I can't really remember maybe I said or did something to hurt Gun? No — be sensible — Ray said this was an annual thing. Maybe best leave him alone. After all, he really spooked me by saying that about Mum. How much did I tell him on Christmas Day? Could he have been twisting my words deliberately to freak me out?

No, no. He's kind. I've never seen him be anything other than kind. But I thought Luke was kind too, and I hardly know Gun at all. Is there a dark streak that runs alongside the depression? It's possible. Another reason not to go. But what sort of friend am I if I don't?

And what about Helen? I could easily take a long weekend, head up country, get the job done. But I just can't face doling out Mum's possessions one at a time. Can't face the thought of what's left of the life she gathered around her ending up in a charity shop or skip. I can't let that happen ... yet I have no room for any more stuff in my life as things stand. Nowhere to put it without a permanent home.

Come on, Anna, woman up about this. Or at least make a deal with yourself. Gun or Helen, one or the other. I almost flip a coin, but after another pointless hour of going around in circles, the bonds of blood lose out.

I can't visit Gun empty-handed, so I make an Irish stew and pour it into my biggest flask. At least I'll have something to leave if he doesn't open the door. I ponder taking some beer, but perhaps booze and depression don't mix terribly well.

I am still in two minds about which of the unpainted houses is Gun's, but one has a handrail next to the steps and is in total darkness, whereas light seeps from between the poorly drawn curtains of the chalet further up the slope. When I get closer, I can see the decking is made from offcuts of timber, but even so it's flat and tight. That nails it. This must be Gun's.

I'm wrong-footed when I hear voices inside, but after a moment the canned laughter makes me realise it's a television, so I take a deep breath and knock. I wait for over a minute, but there's no response. I try again, this time harder.

"There's no need to break the bloody door down."

I say nothing, listening to Gun shuffle across the floor. If it hadn't been for his voice, I'd have thought there was an old man in there.

The light from a lamp spills over the decking, and I can't make out his features as he says, "Oh, it's you." His voice is as flat as it was on the cliff.

I smile at him. "Ray said you probably weren't well, so I've brought you some stew."

"Oh yes, that's right. It's politically correct to call depression an illness now, isn't it? Well, let me tell you — it's not an illness, it's a curse."

I stand up straighter. "You can call it what you like, but it's bloody freezing out here. Are you going to let me in?"

"The place is a tip."

"I haven't come to see the place."

He allows me to pass then follows me into the room, turning off the radio on the windowsill next to the sink. The bowl is half full of dirty plates and mugs, and the air is stale.

I try not to look around as Gun slumps into a chair on one side of the wood burner, indicating its partner with a sweep of his hand. His coat is spread across it, so I fold it in half and place it on the floor. No more than a low glow comes from the burner and three thin tree branch cuts are spread in front of it, presumably to dry.

"Running low?"

"No charity, Anna," he growls.

"No charity, Sebastian. But my logs are already dry. I'll lend you some, then if it stops pissing down for half an hour at the weekend, we can go out and find some more to replace them."

"I'm no company. I'll go on my own."

I shrug. "Suit yourself. Do you want the stew, or is that charity too?"

"I'm not hungry."

"When did you last eat a hot meal?"

"If it's not charity then it's bloody well interfering."

"Oh, like you did the night of the fire? Saving me from third-degree burns? Interfering, was it? Charity, was it?"

He shakes his head, frowning. "Of course it wasn't."

I sit back and fold my arms. "Well then."

There is a long silence. "Maybe … you could leave the stew. I will eat it, I promise. I've just woken up — my body clock's all over the place. Some days I'm practically nocturnal."

"It hits you hard, doesn't it? Ray says…"

"And has Ray told you why?" He leans forwards, the palest of green sparks reflecting in his eyes.

"No." But I'm sure Ray had been going to say something.

"Good. You're a kind woman, Anna, and a true friend. I'd like to keep it that way."

"Yes, me too."

Somewhere underneath his wreck of a beard he smiles. "You'd best go now, though."

"I'm a good listener."

"And at the moment I'm a poor talker."

"Fair enough." I stand and gather my coat around me. "I'll put some logs in a trug in my porch tomorrow — you can pick them up when you're out walking. Leave the empty flask as well."

"We'll see."

"Okay."

He remains in his chair, and it's only as I'm opening the door that he speaks. "Have you been to see your sister yet?"

"I'll tell you at the weekend." I hope he'll laugh, or even swear, but he simply closes his eyes.

CHAPTER TWENTY-EIGHT

I try not to jump when the door of the portacabin crashes open the next morning and my heart starts thumping loudly when I see Serena.

"Mind the dog shit," I tell her, recovering myself. "But you probably already know it's there. No point cleaning it off when another pile arrives every morning."

Her emerald eyes bore into mine. "Stay away from my brother."

"Your brother?"

"Stop messing around. You know very well Sebastian's my brother."

"And just why should I stay away from him?"

"Because you don't know what you're dealing with, that's why."

I look back down at my computer screen and continue to type.

"Listen to me!" she snaps.

I fold my arms. "Have you ever listened to me? When I've tried to have a reasonable conversation about Wheal Dream? No. So why should I listen to you now?"

"You're a cold bitch, aren't you? Well, this makes it personal — do you understand? Stop using Sebastian to get at me or I'll make sure there's no way on God's earth you're here by the spring."

"Like to put that in writing? It'll be all the police need to move in. They're just waiting for you to slip up, you know. They know what you and your friends are up to."

The high spots of colour on her cheeks are all the more accentuated my her sudden pallor. Her mouth forms a small 'o' as she gazes at me, then she gathers herself. "Watch out for yourself, Anna. It may not be tomorrow, it may not be next week, but you'll never be safe as long as you're here. Never. And that I can promise you."

The site is quiet once the contractors leave for the day and all around me the development is beginning to take shape. The yurt platform in the centre of the valley is still a brown scar but the facilities building is going up and the tarmac on the new road will be laid later this week. We're still behind schedule and the marketing department is snapping at my heels, but there's just a chance we might be open for May half term. With good weather and a fair wind behind us.

Some of the delays have been down to Serena's tricks, and there are times I've had to employ a security guard to sit in the cabin overnight. That in itself was interesting — the next morning he showed me an envelope stuffed with ten pound notes someone had pushed under the door, with the suggestion he might like to fall asleep for a few hours.

I don't go near the village, but Tim tells me there are posters everywhere about stopping the site and discussions on the Facebook groups on how best to boycott the visitors when they start to arrive.

The clock on the computer tells me it's almost five, so I have an hour or so of daylight to inspect the day's work then head for The Tinners. I'm at Trelissick tomorrow, and so far Luke has avoided me with great aplomb. Every time I go there, his duplicity smarts a little less.

But for now I check the security camera then lock the cabin door. The jackdaws' calls echo across the valley and any hint of warmth has gone from the sun. The wooden frame of the facilities block rises skeletal against the slope but the curved roof is now in place and the cladding materials are stacked beneath it. Do I trust in the camera until the guard arrives in a couple of hours, or do I wait? I chew my lip.

I climb the short slope onto the yurt platform and to my surprise see Gun crouching between the end of the new road and the nature corridor. He is perfectly still, in what looks like an uncomfortable position, his long coat trailing on the ground behind him.

As I walk towards him he stands, but turning towards me puts his finger to his lips. I stop some yards away and listen. In the distance the sea, the cars on the road above, but nothing more. After a while he says, "I can't understand her."

"Understand who?"

"The woman." He frowns. "I can't see her either, but maybe that's not important. What she wants is to be heard." He looks down, shaking his head. "It's what they all want."

Not this again. I still don't entirely trust his mental state, so I play along and ask him how he knows she's there.

"Because she's talking to me. But the words … they're strange, I can't make them out. There's real anguish in her voice though — real pain."

I don't know what to say. A small, sad smile briefly appears from the depths of his beard. "There's no need to humour me, Anna."

I grin back. "Sorry. I'm off to The Tinners for a quick one. Fancy coming? If we talk about that furniture it could be a business expense."

"No. I'll stay here just a while longer, try to work things out."

At first, I don't know what's woken me. After running around like an idiot all day, I thought I'd sleep the sleep of the dead. But all of a sudden, I'm staring at the ceiling, the hairs on the back of my neck standing on end.

The sound's coming from outside. Scuffling. Whispering. My befuddled brain leaps off in the direction of Gun's mysterious voice and I grip the duvet. I take a deep breath then edge myself up on my pillows and listen harder. An owl hoots in the distance, making me jump. No. Whatever's out there is definitely earthly. Should I call the security guard? Or is that what this is all about, some sort of decoy so havoc can be wrought below? The doors and windows are locked. No-one can get in. Someone's trying to frighten you, Anna, that's all.

It's no good trying to sleep, so I turn on my iPad and read. But it's hard to concentrate, knowing there's someone outside. I consider some music, but all things considered it's better to be able to hear what's going on. I frown. It's gone quiet again. Is that good or bad? But then there's a different noise; not a cry, not a wail, something in between and almost unearthly. My iPad hits the floor as I leap out of bed.

The noise stops. There's a moment of quiet, then back to the whispering and shuffling. The clock on my phone tells me it's just gone three. This could prove to be a very long night indeed. Especially when I begin to wonder if Gun's little act earlier was the start of it.

CHAPTER TWENTY-NINE

The next day, Gun appears at the portacabin in the early afternoon, clutching two sheets of paper. He thrusts them in my direction. "What do you think?"

I'm not altogether happy with him but I need to put the job first, so I spread them flat on my desk to take a look. His designs are beautiful and rustic, narrow logs twisting this way and that to support rough-planked table tops and bench seats. They're amazing, but not for here.

I look up at him. "Didn't I say? We're going for the surfer chic look." I turn my computer screen around. "Grab a chair and I'll show you."

He is silent as I take him through the mood boards and designs for the yurt interiors. Eventually he mutters, "Then these won't do."

"The tops might…"

"You're humouring me again, Anna. Let me think."

I bite back a retort and instead ask if he wants a coffee. He nods and pulls a pencil from deep within his coat and starts to chew the end of it.

I collect two mugs before heading outside to fill the kettle from the standpipe and to ask if any of the workmen want a brew. I take my time, climbing the low slope to the platform and gazing at the spot where Gun was yesterday. In my heart I know he's a good man and I want to trust him, but can I trust my own judgment? I remember his words on judging people too.

By the time I return to the cabin, his pencil is flying over the back of a sheet of paper. Now both tables and benches are in the shape of surfboards, with sturdy A-frame legs holding them up.

He glances at me. "Bit too obvious?"

I can't help but grin. "Simply fabulous."

He taps his pencil against his teeth. "I thought … maybe use bleached pine … with some random pale blue planks?"

"Sounds good to me. Any idea how much?"

"About a hundred a table and fifty a bench. Bit more if you want some larger. Trouble is…" He's looking everywhere but at me.

"What is it?"

"I'll need some cash up front. For materials."

"That's not a problem. But are you sure you're charging enough?"

"It's the normal sort of price."

I fold my arms. "Not if I had to buy it elsewhere."

He grins at me. "Well, maybe a bit of danger money in case Serena finds out."

I turn away to make the coffee. "She's found a new way of plaguing me."

"A new way?"

While he's been ill I haven't told him what's been going on, and it seems Serena hasn't either. "Oh, it's all been small stuff, nothing illegal. She seems very scared of the police for some reason." I look over my shoulder, but his face gives no clues. He simply asks what she's doing.

I set his coffee on the desk in front of him and tell him about the night before. When I finish, he shakes his head. "Might not have been her."

179

"Maybe not directly, but one of her cronies…"

"I didn't mean that. I heard strange whispering too, remember?"

"Oh, so you're in on this too, are you, Gun?"

He stands up and wraps his coat around him. "Of course I'm bloody not. Why would I be? And don't call me Gun."

"I'm sorry I…"

But he's gone.

The noises in the night return. At almost exactly the same time, as far as I can tell. In a pool of cold sweat I listen to the whispering and the footsteps, but eventually I pluck up the courage to creep downstairs. As I stand in the chilly hall, the ululation starts. That's the only word I can think of for it. And then the blessed silence.

When the whispering and shuffling begin again, I realise whoever's doing it is staying on one side of the house. The side nearest the village with the windowless wall, so from inside I won't be able to see them. That seals it for me — it's definitely a diversionary tactic to make me call the night watchman away, but after tomorrow there will be no need to guard the site for a while; the cables and pipes will be safely underground, the building at a point where it can be secured.

The next morning, I need to go to Truro to see Roland Tresawl. There's been an attempt to appeal the development to the Secretary of State and although it got nowhere, we need to discuss the implications. Before I leave, I walk around to the blank wall of the house to see if there's any evidence of last night's visitor, but there's nothing, not even a footprint in the damp earth.

It's the first time I've been to Roland's office, but it doesn't surprise me to find it's in an imposing Georgian building near the Coinage Hall. A flight of stone steps sweeps up towards a dark green door, and the whole frontage is faced with pale golden Bath stone. Inside, the entrance hall is no less impressive with beautiful period plasterwork and the staircase has the most gorgeous cast iron banister I've ever seen, with flowers and vine leaves intertwining up its whole height.

A number of businesses have their offices here, and I'm shown into what I assume is a shared meeting room on the first floor. Its curved bay window looks out over Tinners Court, a narrow cut through from Princes Street to Lemon Quay, lined with shops. The view would have been so different when the house was built. I half close my eyes and imagine the masts of ships at the end of a walled garden, but my reverie is interrupted by Roland pushing open the door, a bundle of files in his arms.

After our meeting I wander around the shops, strangely reluctant to return to Porthnevek. I browse around Debenhams, only to find myself sprayed with my mother's favourite perfume by a pushy sales assistant. I run out onto the concrete expanse of Lemon Quay, great gulping sobs rising from nowhere.

I hurry past the bus station and away from the town centre to lean on a bridge, traffic thundering behind me while I gaze down at some old sluice gates. A black-headed gull bobs in a circle, round and round on the ebb of the tide in ever decreasing circles. Is that me? Creating my own vortex of grief by trying to brush it under the table? Maybe Helen's right. Maybe we both need closure. Before I change my mind, I type a text: *I'm coming to it, I promise. I just need a little more time.*

I stand there until my legs are stiff but there's no reply.

Just when I'm thinking things can't get any worse, I arrive back at Nevek Cot to find Serena lurking near the front door. She looks for all the world as though she was about to hide around the side of the cottage but realised I'd seen her, so I park across the gate to block her escape.

I take my time gathering my handbag and coat. She starts to edge between the rear bumper and the wall, so I pick that moment to climb out.

"Can I help you?" Icily polite. That's the way.

"Yes. You can piss off back where you came from."

"Not going to happen. That attempt at an appeal was a waste of time, wasn't it? Not to mention money."

"Nothing that puts a spoke in your wheel is a waste."

"So I gather."

We gaze at each other across the roof of the car. Neither of us blinks. Her eyes are so like Gun's, fiery emeralds set deep into tanned skin. How close are they? How much does he know? I force myself not to shudder.

It's almost as though she reads my mind. "Sebastian's not going to make your furniture, so you can stop hounding him. Stop pretending to be his friend."

I hitch my handbag further onto my shoulder and lock the car. "Was that his decision, or did you make it for him?"

"He's not capable at the moment, as you very well know…"

"Of course I'm capable." Gun is standing about twenty yards up the lane, shoulders hunched, hands in pockets.

Serena turns to him. "Sorry, hon, but you…"

"Don't you 'sorry hon' me. And don't you bloody interfere. I'm a grown man, Serena, and if I have a battle I'll fight it myself."

Oh, God — he really is mad at me. Serena is in my face. "See — you've upset him. I knew you would!"

"Serena — get out of here." But it isn't my voice, it's Sebastian's. "Now."

She stomps away in the direction of the village, leaving us looking at each other.

"I'm sorry about yesterday," I tell him.

"So am I. I should have realised you were more shaken up by it all than you were letting on. It's just it's taking me a while to get totally straight in my head. Serena was right about that, at least. Not that I'd give her the satisfaction."

"Then I'll need to be more patient."

"You've been nothing but patient. Better friend than some I've known for years. Didn't keep mithering at me to talk, just listened to my silence. You've no idea how much that helped."

I feel myself smiling. "I'm glad." He's looking at the ground, and so am I. "Look, I need to get back on site. See you later?"

He nods and carries on up the lane.

Later can mean any time with Gun, and I find myself a little disappointed when he isn't in The Tinners when I take myself up there for some company and supper. Walking home, I tell myself off. I need to start properly thinking of him as Sebastian. I don't want another slip of the tongue to upset him. As I approach my cottage, I begin to think about the whispering voices. What if there's someone there? Then I give myself a stern talking-to; it's only eight o'clock — far too early. But all the same, there's something in the air making me uneasy. Something in my head, more likely. I make a fist of my keys as I all but jog the last couple of hundred yards home.

Tonight there are no voices. I suspect I wake at three o'clock because there aren't, and of course it's hard to get back to sleep. Four nights on the trot, now silence. It almost makes me more uneasy. Moonlight streaks through a crack in the blinds and I edge them open a little more, scanning the field and the valley below. The silver casts its pale spell over the side of the facilities building and the portacabin windows gleam. I smile at its strange beauty and am about to drop the blind back down when one pane of glass shines brighter than the other. A reflection — but from where? A moment and it's gone.

Two lights dance along the nature corridor, appearing and disappearing, but I know they're there. My hand is on my phone to call the police, but what would they do? It's only trespassing — the buildings look secure, and there's nothing else to damage down there at the moment. With sweaty fingers I log onto the security camera to check it's working. If there is anything wrong tomorrow, we'll have them. I watch for the lights for another twenty minutes, but there is nothing more to see.

CHAPTER THIRTY

I stand at the window of the portacabin as the builders drive their truck around the yurt platform to the end of the road. Even though the weather's been kinder, they're churning up the earth something rotten — why the hell can't they walk down? I put my head in my hands. They're here over the Easter weekend when they could be with their families. I need to be nice to them, but I'm feeling too crabby for words.

Sleep deprivation, that's what it is. After two quiet nights, the voices outside returned — earlier this time — just as I was trying to drop off. In the end I resorted to ear plugs, but even so I can't say I slept very easily. Whoever's doing this to me must be bloody nocturnal. At least this time there was no strange screeching.

I'm watching the truck disappear towards the gates when I notice Sebastian sitting on a rock on the slope, about ten yards away from the Clywd Cap. I'm too knackered to be productive, so I lock the cabin and make my way through the mud towards him. His head is bent in concentration, and I wonder if he's hearing things again.

I approach silently and sit down next to him. He nods in acknowledgment and together we watch as the last rays of weak sunshine flee from the valley up the slope towards Nevek Cot. In the end, he sighs.

"It's no good, I can't make head nor tail of what she's saying."

"You're sure it's a she?"

He nods. "I've seen her now. A couple of times, but not today. Very slight with a long grey hooded cloak."

"Sounds like your typical wraith."

"There is something almost ethereal about her."

"Well, isn't that the thing with ghosts?"

"Are you mocking me?"

I shift into a more comfortable position. "No. I'm just tired. My night-time visitors are back. Can you ask your grey lady what the hell's going on? Or even better, ask your sister?"

"I can't ask the grey lady, as you call her, because I wouldn't understand her reply. It sounds like a load of gibberish to me." He passes his hand over his face. "But all the same, it's important. She was crying again yesterday."

I pick at an invisible thread on my coat. "I'm sorry, Sebastian, I just don't understand how this works."

"No, I don't either. But it happens, so I live with it."

"How long has it been going on?"

"Since I was a child, really. I think all children have a sixth sense of some sort, but it gets educated out of most of them when logic takes over. Certainly when Serena's youngest was small she could see what I saw. Thankfully not any longer."

"Thankfully?"

"You think it's a blessing? Well, let me tell you, it's not. People sometimes refer to it as my gift, like it's something I wanted, but I'd just as soon I wasn't this way. The trouble is, they need someone to talk to. And that someone is me."

"They can't ... you know ... talk to each other?"

"Search me. But sometimes ... I think ... there's some sort of release in telling their story. I mean, not always; look at George. He'll talk about anything, and he seems happy enough. Some of them are." A long shiver runs through me. Sebastian looks at me sideways. "If it bothers you, then don't believe me."

"I don't know what to think. I'm naturally sceptical, but all the same I don't have you down as a liar." I stand and stretch. "This is a seriously odd conversation. Fancy a bit of supper?"

He stands too. "No point hanging around here. What's on the menu?"

"Probably just some jacket potatos. Cheese and bacon suit you?"

"An absolute feast."

Together we walk up the valley then along the lane to Nevek Cot. The sunset glows red against its plastered walls, and I find myself smiling. "D'you know, this place really is beginning to feel like home. Which is rather a shame, given I'm going to have to leave in a few months."

"After all that's been happening, you'd actually want to stay?"

I shrug. "No point wanting what I can't have."

"Everyone has choices, Anna. You just have to be brave enough to make them."

"My choice now is to cook supper while you stack the wood burner."

"Fair enough."

And so I potter about in the kitchen, heating the oven and scrubbing potatoes. I consider opening some wine and am about to call through to Gun when he shouts he's going to the log pile to fill the basket. The back door closes behind him, and I find I'm humming to myself. Maybe I'll stick on a bit of background music. I'm reaching for my iPad when Gun reappears at the kitchen door, his face grim.

"Think I've found the answer to your midnight voices, Anna."

PART SIX: 1816

CHAPTER THIRTY-ONE

Mrs Daniell sat in bed, propped up by pillows and with her breakfast tray beside her while Mary curled into a chair near the fire. Thérèse was in the window seat, using the best of the light to darn a tear in Mary's best stockings with the tiniest of stitches.

"How ever did you do such a thing?" Mrs Daniell asked. "I have to say, I do not recall any unladylike behaviour on your part at our ball last night."

"I should hope not, Mama. Truly, I was an angel. I even danced with old Mr Stackhouse and Captain Davey's half-witted son."

"Do not be unkind, Mary. I do not think him half-witted, just rather shy."

"And a very poor dancer. His shoe buckle ripped my stocking during the Lancers' Quadrille. I should be pleased never to have to partner him again."

Mrs Daniell laughed. "So who would you care to partner?"

Mary screwed up her face. "Choosing between the men invited last night is difficult. The most dashing one was Will in his navy uniform, but it is hardly proper to dance continually with one's own brother."

"Quite so. And he was rather in demand, with Charlotte Boscawen especially. Although I was pleased he accompanied Annabelle Lemon to supper. It would be a most suitable match."

"You surprise me, Mama. I would have thought a viscount's daughter…"

"Lord Falmouth is an unprincipled prig whose intransigence is causing much needless suffering in Porthnevek. I consider his refusal to allow the mine to stay open a personal affront to your father. As was not coming to the ball himself last night and leaving his dreary aunt to chaperone poor Charlotte." Mrs Daniell took a sip of her tea. "You are not setting your cap at her brother, I take it?"

"Oh, Mama … *quel nez…*"

From the window seat Thérèse supressed a giggle. Mary leapt off her chair and ran to her, speaking in French. "Then you saw his nose too?"

"It was a little difficult not to. I was drawing the curtains when their coach arrived, and I have to admit to lingering to see who would alight from such a smart carriage."

"And did his nose alight first?" Mary was giggling too, her head close to Thérèse's, and Mrs Daniell smiled at them.

"You do appreciate, Mary, that this line of conversation is for the boudoir only. I know I don't have to tell Thérèse."

"You don't have to tell Thérèse anything, Mama. She sews like an angel, does my hair so beautifully and laces my corset to show my bosom to best advantage. And she is so clever with her tisanes and special oils… Thérèse, do you think you could make a potion so all the young men will fall in love with me?"

Thérèse laughed. "Oh, Mam'selle Mary, there is no need…"

Mrs Daniell shook her head in exasperation. "Don't, Thérèse, she has airs enough as it is. And Mary, Thérèse is not a witch, for heaven's sake, she simply knows how to make me feel better when I am out of sorts."

Thérèse bowed her head, her skin flushed deep pink. "Quite so, Madame. In France we have no witches, because under the law magic does not exist."

"Oh, but we do in Cornwall, I'm sure of it," Mary said. "And the servants say because you do not go to church…"

"Enough of this nonsense." Mrs Daniell cut across her daughter. "You should not be gossiping with the servants."

"Sorry, Mama."

After a long moment of stillness, Thérèse pulled the thread to her lips and bit the end to cut it, then turned the stocking inside out. "Et voila, Mam'selle Mary. As good as new." She set it to one side and stood. "Which dress today, Madame? The dark green, perhaps?"

Mrs Daniell stretched her legs under the coverlet. "I don't know, Thérèse. Perhaps I will rest in my room a little longer and attend to some correspondence while Mary reads an improving book. We can think about dresses later."

Finding herself with some free time, Thérèse opened the kitchen door as the church bells of Truro sounded all around her. Nearest were the rich tones of St Mary's, but if she listened carefully, she could pick out a softer peal from somewhere across the river. At first the variety of bells had surprised her, but then she realised the town was far larger than she had initially supposed. Not only that, but given the new houses springing up on the hillside opposite, its prosperity was causing it to grow at quite a rate.

In the early days of her employment, Mrs Daniell had explained the whereabouts of a catholic church, but Thérèse had bowed her head and told her religion did not interest her. Her father, normally the mildest of men, had eschewed it after his wife died so young and neither she nor Paul had been brought up to any faith. She wondered briefly if it would give her comfort if she could believe she would see her family

191

again, but it was too far beyond her comprehension to warrant much contemplation.

The garden was stark in its winter livery. Only the herbs flourished in the low-hedged bed closest to the house, and she ran her fingers over the lavender. She would pick some on her way back to make some more soothing oil for her mistress.

She had no clear idea of where she was going, but the rain that had been plaguing them for what seemed like weeks had finally ceased and she was determined to make the most of her few hours of leisure. A stable lad was sweeping the cobbles at the quay end of the garden and he stopped to doff his cap, so Thérèse smiled and bade him good morning in her best English.

Lemon Quay was quiet. She stopped for a moment, next to a schooner named for the town, its rigging neatly tied and its damp flags wrapping themselves around its tall rear mast. Behind it was a brig, a solitary sailor standing guard at the top of its gangplank, the pungent smell of his tobacco reaching her on the still morning air.

At the end of the quay she turned left and crossed the bridge which marked the point where the harbour ended and the River Kenwyn proper began. Following the other side of the water downstream, she quickly found herself at the edge of the town. Ahead of her the river was swelling with the tide, the muddy brown water rushing from the rain-soaked land to meet it. She stood for a moment, mesmerised by its churn, before setting off down the narrow lane bounding it. She knew something of the track because on the high ground to her right stood Mr Thomas's fine new house, which she had visited with Mrs Daniell.

"Mam'selle — Mam'selle Ruguel — please wait."

She spun around to see John Coates striding towards her, his coat flapping behind him and his boots glinting in the watery sunshine. She found herself smiling. "Monsieur, you have returned."

He gave a little bow. "Some days ago in fact, but I had no news of your whereabouts until this morning."

"News?"

He winked. "A businessman never reveals his sources. I am sure your Mr Daniell would concur."

"I will have to take your word for that, as I have very little discourse with him."

"Because he does not speak your tongue?"

"Because he would have nothing to say to his wife's maid beyond the usual courtesies."

Coates laughed. "No, I suppose not. I, on the other hand, have plenty to say to her. Will you permit me to accompany you on your walk?"

"I intend to go only a little further. I suspect the track will be muddy after so much rain."

"You are wise to be cautious. Further down it is much rutted by the carts going to and from the quarry at Newham. But I have a rather confidential matter to discuss, and I would not want to do so with ears flapping on the quay."

Thérèse looked up at him, her eyes fixed on his. "A confidential matter?"

"Indeed. As you know, I had business in Roscoff, although as events turned I did not stay in the town, merely passed through on my way to Morlaix. But I was there long enough to hear an interesting rumour."

Thérèse frowned. "And what was that rumour?"

"Mam'selle Thérèse, you may need your smelling salts at the ready."

Suddenly, her heart was thudding in her chest. "Why?" she gasped.

"You said you had not seen your brother's body. There is a rumour — and only a rumour — that he is alive."

At first Thérèse could not be sure she had understood his words correctly. Her knees felt weak and a sheen of sweat engulfed her. "You are sure?" she whispered.

He shook his head, dark eyes intent on hers. "There is no certainty, none at all. I had it from a man at the inn, who had it from a man who burns charcoal, that an injured soldier had returned to the town in search of his sister. He could not even be certain of the name, and by the time I returned from Morlaix to join my ship, I could not find him again."

"Then it could be anyone?"

"It could be but, Mam'selle Thérèse, how many soldiers from such a Bourbon stronghold fought for Napoleon?"

Tears pricked the back of her eyes. "Almost none. Indeed, when Paul returned to the town during Napoleon's exile, he was all but shunned because of it."

"Then you may, perhaps, permit yourself just a little hope."

"But what should I do? How can I find out? I cannot write to my neighbours because they are old and cannot read. Perhaps I could..."

He touched her briefly on the arm. "There is no need for you to do anything. I have an associate in Roscoff and have instructed him to make enquiries. I travel to Guernsey to meet him next month and pray there will be definite news."

Thérèse was dizzy with hope. "Monsieur Coates, how can I ever thank you?"

He put his head on one side as though weighing her up before he spoke. "By permitting me to walk with you sometimes? I am too often in the company of men, and your face is a rare tonic."

The heat from Thérèse's chest rose up her neck and into her cheeks. For a moment she thought Coates was about to laugh, but he became suddenly serious.

"Mam'selle, I have embarrassed you and I regret it. We should talk of other things while I escort you home."

Coates was good to his word, and on the walk back to the quay he told her amusing tales of his visit to Morlaix. Outside the stables he doffed his hat and bowed low, before disappearing towards the green. Thérèse watched him go, biting her lip. His long legs and muscular body were stirring something deep inside her, something long buried by grief. She shook her head and turned away. She had no business to be feeling such things. But at least she was feeling.

She stopped under a bare apple tree in the garden, her fingers tracing its gnarled bark; perhaps now she had just a little hope the long winter of her soul was beginning to end. But that hope was far too fragile. No, she could not even countenance it to be true, because if it proved false the pain would begin all over again. She needed to be patient and in the meantime take her comfort from serving Mrs Daniell as best she could.

CHAPTER THIRTY-TWO

A few days of pale sunshine had brought a feeling of spring to the air, but once again the wind was blowing from the northeast and Mrs Daniell snuggled more deeply into the fur rug Thérèse had wrapped around her. The gentle sway of the carriage normally made her sleep, but she was troubled about this visit to Porthnevek, in no small part because Ralph had insisted she bring Matthew, who was riding postilion with his rifle across his knees.

At least Ralph shared her sense of responsibility to the former miners and understood she had to go. It was the hungry time, when little grew on the strips of rough land they tended around their cottages. She was determined to once and for all cut off the Falmouths who had caused this unnecessary poverty. She did not care if Will was mooning over their daughter; he was back at sea now and would be for some time. There would be no match there.

The journey from Truro to Porthnevek was no shorter than from Trelissick but covered different ground. Outside the town they climbed onto a wide tract of rough farmland, the wind catching the carriage as the horses trotted along. There were no villages, just the odd cottage, and they passed only a single mine as they climbed to what felt like the very crest of the county. Everywhere around them looked windswept and forlorn.

Mrs Daniell shivered. She had travelled this way many a time, but there were rumours of a coach journeying from Bodmin to Truro being held up and its occupants told they would be taken for ransom. It was only the sudden appearance of a party of excise men that had saved them and the perpetrators had fled, but the rescuers swore one of them was a notorious smuggler. And if he was correct, the culprit had strong connections with Porthnevek.

"Madame, are you all right?" Thérèse herself looked grey, having never become fully accustomed to a closed coach, and Mrs Daniell nodded.

"The wind is a little cold, that is all, but the fire at the inn will be all the more welcoming for it. We must stay in the parlour today, Thérèse. If there are errands to be run, Matthew or Kitto can go."

"Matthew and his gun are making me nervous, Madame."

Mrs Daniell laughed. "The intention is quite the reverse. But there is nothing to worry about, simply rumours of gangs of footpads, most likely starving miners, and Ralph wanted to be sure of our safety." After their last visit to Porthnevek, it would not do to frighten Thérèse any further.

When they arrived there was already a small crowd waiting outside the inn, and Old William was among them. As the innkeeper ushered them inside, Mrs Daniell could not help but notice the way he looked at Thérèse. Her sense of foreboding deepened, so she called Matthew to accompany them into the parlour.

While Thérèse started to distribute the food, Mrs Daniell dispensed essence of clove to a young mother with a howling baby, who was clearly teething. The child was sickly and thin, and Mrs Daniell's heart bled for them. She whispered a silent prayer of thanks that her children would never know hunger.

Before long, Old William was standing before her, his cough a fierce rattle. Mrs Daniell composed her face into a smile.

"I have some more of the tincture. Does it soothe you?"

"Nothing soothes me now you have taken my wife as well as my son."

"But William," she said softly, "your wife has been gone many this long year."

"My wife is here." He pointed at Thérèse with a shaking hand. "You have stolen her from me and I will have her back." Mrs Daniell shifted uncomfortably in her seat. "You are mistaken. The young lady is my maid."

Old William thumped the table. "She is mine and I will have her!" Silence fell in the room and Matthew stepped forward.

"None of that, old man. Show some respect."

"Why should I when this evil woman has taken everyone I care about from me?"

Matthew grabbed him by the elbow but he struggled, trying to lunge for Thérèse, who was cowering behind the table. Then two of the older women in the queue stepped forward.

"Come now, William," one of them said, taking his arm. "Don't go on so. You know the maid t'aint your Wenna. We'll just take our vittles, then we'll all be going home."

Her companion turned to Mrs Daniell. "He isn't capable of apologising as he does not know he's done wrong. It is a sorry state to end his days like this, and although us neighbours care for him the best we can, it's not like family."

Mrs Daniell cleared her throat. "Then it is true ... his younger son ... he does not visit him?"

The woman looked down and muttered, "I've not seen him in the village these three months past."

"Do you think William would be better in the asylum?"

The woman shuddered. "I would not wish that on anyone, Mrs Daniell."

"They are not all cruel places..."

"We can look after our own in Porthnevek. After all, he's no real danger to anyone, except perhaps himself."

But Mrs Daniell was far from convinced.

CHAPTER THIRTY-THREE

As soon as the church bells started to ring, Thérèse slipped out of the kitchen door and through the garden to the stable entrance. Around her the buds of the narcissus were swelling and early crocuses pushed from beneath the trees in the small orchard.

As she stepped out onto the quay, she saw John Coates standing in front of the warehouse to her left. He raised his cocked hat in greeting.

"A fine morning, Mam'selle Thérèse. Are you perhaps intending to take a walk?"

Thérèse bowed her head, trying not to blush. "Indeed I am, Monsieur."

"Then might I accompany you? The path along the river to Truro Vean is quite dry at the moment and the valley most picturesque."

"Thank you, Monsieur, you are most kind. It will be a pleasure to see some countryside."

He started to walk towards Quay Street and she fell into step beside him. "So do you miss Trelissick?" he asked.

She shook her head. "The town suits me much better, but a change of air is always welcome."

"And when do the family plan to return to their country estate?"

"I do not rightly know. Now Mam'selle Mary is out in society, Madame wishes to give her every opportunity."

"I would have thought the house at Trelissick far more impressive if she's to catch a husband. I heard Ralph Daniell spent more than three thousand pounds on improving it last year. Three thousand pounds!"

Thérèse pursed her lips. "I do not know, Monsieur."

"Of course you do not, pretty Mam'selle, but you must know you work for the wealthiest man in Cornwall."

"It is not important to me. What matters is that I serve Madame Daniell well."

"Quite so. I understand she is a charming lady."

They crossed the new bridge, the river churned beneath it by the nearby mill. Thérèse stopped for a moment to watch the paddles on its wheel beat the waters, the fine spray misting her face like dew. "The mill works, even on a Sunday."

Coates winked. "Even Lord Falmouth would not be so ungodly, but the river runs when the river runs."

Embarrassed by her ignorance, Thérèse felt her cheeks colour. "I have no reason to think Lord Falmouth a particularly godly man. Madame says he is responsible for the starving miners at Porthnevek."

"Those starving miners are not helpless. The poor and hungry in your own country should have taught you that."

"I was not born when the revolution started, Monsieur, and as you know many in Brittany remained loyal to the crown."

"But not your brother Paul, nor you."

Thérèse turned to him. "Do you have more news?"

"I regret not, as my ship has been unable to sail due to the storms."

The path took them through a wooded valley. On the opposite side of the river, long gardens ran down to its banks from the houses on Pydar Street, but they walked beneath the budding branches of trees thronged with birds singing their welcome to the weak sunshine. Coates questioned her about her childhood in France, and then about her work, but carefully avoided any further mention of Paul. She was grateful for this, as even with the faint hope she carried, those memories brought nothing but pain.

They soon reached another, smaller mill and here Coates stopped. "This is Truro Vean, Mam'selle, and beyond it is the prison, which is somewhere I do not care to go."

"Nor should I, but I am pleased to see the willow trees because I have need of their bark."

"Their bark, Mam'selle?"

"It has healing qualities, and Madame Daniell can have such headaches. I must recall where the trees are and return when I have something to cut it with."

"Here, at least, I can be of some assistance." He pulled from his pocket a heavy silver knife, its blade tucked into its handle. He opened it for her. "Be careful, it is very sharp."

Thérèse crouched next to the forest of side shoots emerging from the bottom of the trunk and began to peel away the bark. Coates sank to his haunches beside her.

"You have knowledge of such things?"

"A little. But I am careful with it, because already the servants at Trelissick accuse me of witchcraft."

"Superstitious nonsense. I am surprised Mrs Daniell allows it."

"Servants' gossip is difficult to stop."

"Any gossip is difficult to stop." His voice was sharp.

Having collected enough bark, Thérèse returned the knife to him, the brush of their hands unexpectedly pleasurable. She stood. "We should start back or Madame Daniell will have returned from church and may ask for me."

"You are at her beck and call all the time?"

Thérèse shrugged. "I have nothing else to do. And I am very fond of Madame."

"You could, perhaps, walk out with me a little more often. But alas, I fear the Daniells would be most unhappy if they knew."

"Due to some custom of this country I know nothing about? In France, it is permitted for a maid to see who she chooses."

"No, more because of who I am. Or rather, how I make my living."

"But you said you were a man of business. Is not Monsieur Daniell the same?"

Coates laughed. "You mean the same, only more rich, more powerful, more influential than a miner's son could ever be."

"But surely..."

He turned and started to stroll towards Truro, Thérèse at his side. He looked down at her. "It is my line of business he would disapprove of. Not all of it, but some at least." She looked up at him, questioning. "I buy whatever I can profit from, Mam'selle. Being in business in a small way, my choices can be — shall we say — limited. And brandy has the highest profit of all, provided the excise men don't hear of it."

Thérèse nodded. She had grown up seeing barrels loaded onto the ships at Roscoff and knew they were often hidden beneath other cargoes. She knew it could be a hazardous trade, and during the war rumours had been rife of smugglers turning to spying for both sides. Sometimes the men involved had not returned home.

"Is it dangerous, Monsieur?"

"And do you care if I am in danger, Thérèse?"

"But of course..."

He stopped walking. "Only because I can bring you news of your brother?"

Thérèse bowed her head. "You try to trick me, Monsieur. That is not gentlemanly."

"But I am not a gentleman, am I? I have told you what I am."

"A smuggler."

He tilted her chin so she was looking him in the eye. "Yes. But I am no worse than that. Some vile rumours abound, Thérèse, that I am worse, but I swear they are put about by excise men and are not true. All the same, it would be best not to tell the Daniells you are friendly with me."

"What rumours?"

He shook his head slowly. "If you believe they are not true, you do not need to know them. Isn't that the case?" His black eyes bore into hers, but there was a hint of sadness in his smile, a barely perceptible droop in his shoulders.

"I believe you," she said.

CHAPTER THIRTY-FOUR

Thérèse waited patiently in the ante-hall as Mary straightened her gloves then studied her reflection in the ornate looking glass that hung above the marble side table. Finally, she set her bonnet on her head, its peach tone complementing her skin perfectly.

She turned to Thérèse. "Could you tie my ribbon, please? Slightly to one side — it looks so much prettier that way."

"But of course, Mam'selle. Then we must go. It will not do to keep Miss Reed waiting."

Matthew winked at Thérèse as he held the front door open for them, but she shrugged her shoulders in return. As far as she could see, girls of marriageable age should always take care of their appearance, but she did not expect men to understand such things.

A boy wheeling a barrel from the cooperage stopped to stare at Mary, and Thérèse hurried her past the sharp angle of Coinage Hall and into Duke Street. Mary dawdled, looking first in the window of the stationer's, then lingering outside the tailor to study a display of buckskin gloves.

"I may buy a pair as a gift for Papa," she explained to Thérèse. "He has been so generous, allowing me more new dresses than I ever expected."

"That is a kind thought, Mam'selle Mary." It didn't escape Thérèse's notice that the gloves would most certainly be put on Mr Daniell's account, but she decided not to comment further.

Just then, the shop bell rang and a soldier walked out, resplendent in a red jacket with gold braid at the shoulders and shining boots. Thérèse took a step back into the road, but to her surprise he approached Mary and gave a short bow. In return Mary inclined her head and bade the man good day. That much Thérèse understood, but when they started to talk in a hurried fashion there were very few words she could pick out and make sense of.

Thérèse knew she had to conquer her irrational fear of the red uniform to move closer to her young charge and if possible draw the conversation to an end. The two had clearly been introduced, but it was still most unseemly for a young lady to stand on a street corner talking to a man. It simply would not do.

One look at Mary's glowing face told Thérèse separating them would not be an easy task, and reminding her of their appointment with Miss Reed would likely not be enough to draw her away. Oh, how she wished Mrs Daniell or Miss Elizabeth was with them. They would stop this nonsense right away. But she had an uneasy feeling that if they had been, the soldier would not have made such a bold approach.

Her suspicions strengthened her resolve, and she stepped forward and spoke to Mary in a low voice. "Excuse me, Mam'selle, but I think perhaps we should continue to the dressmakers. In France, we believe a lady should always leave a gentleman yearning for a little more, yes?"

Mary turned and clapped her hands. "Yes! A thousand times yes," she replied in French, and with a scant farewell to the soldier swept Thérèse up St Mary Street without a backward glance. She did not pause until they were at the door of the shop. "Thank you, Thérèse, I was in danger of forgetting myself. But do you not think Captain Gilbert handsome?"

Luckily Thérèse did not have to reply as Miss Reed appeared on the step to greet them and usher them inside.

All evening Thérèse wrestled with whether to tell Mrs Daniell about the encounter and contrary to her normal habit while in Truro, climbed the stairs to her room straight after supper. Mrs Daniell would call for her later to help her to undress, and by then she needed to have made her decision. She was getting quite a headache worrying about it.

She sat on the windowsill and looked out over the roofs at the slate tiles glistening in the wake of a sudden shower that had poured down the windows and no doubt filled the gutters while she was in the kitchen. Light from the half-moon reached through the buildings, chasing long shadows, and in the lanterns' glow from Boscawen Street, she could see the tin ingots shimmer in the distance as people came and went.

Princes Street was quiet, but after a while a figure appeared from the direction of the market and knocked on the door of the cooper opposite. It was a figure she knew well; tall, muscular, with a cocked hat on his head. Of course, if Coates traded in brandy he would have need of barrels. Or perhaps he traded them for profit too.

Thérèse knew smuggling had its dangers, but she considered Coates a careful man. She could not help but worry for him just a little, though; after all, he was her only hope of news from Paul. But was it more than that? Somehow, since the day he had told her of the rumour, her feelings about the two matters had become confused. However hard she tried, she could not separate them.

But now she must return to considering Mary and Captain Gilbert. Except she suddenly found herself drawing an uncomfortable parallel between her secrecy regarding Coates and the dilemma now facing her. But Mary was young, and it had been just one conversation that carried on slightly longer than was wise. It could have been by chance that they met, after all. Thomas Chalmers' words about not meddling when she knew little of the country's customs still burned in her heart. She would never wish to draw such chilling wrath from Mrs Daniell.

She rested her head against the cool glass of the window. After a while, she became aware of raised voices somewhere below and craned towards Boscawen Street before she realised they were sufficiently muted to be coming from inside a building. In fact, when she listened carefully, it was just one man ranting, but the pauses meant he was listening to someone reply.

There was a muffled crack and a yelp of pain, then silence. A few moments later, Coates emerged from the cooper's, setting his hat straight upon his head. He glanced towards the house and instinct made Thérèse shrink back, although in her darkened room it was impossible for him to see her. Then he walked briskly away in the direction of Lander's Inn on the corner of Quay Street.

CHAPTER THIRTY-FIVE

"Please, Mama, it is such a fine morning. May I accompany Thérèse to the haberdashery? I am sure the air will do me good, and I could help select the lace."

Mrs Daniell looked up from her bureau. "But of course, Mary, as long as Thérèse does not mind you drawing out her errands."

Thérèse smiled. "It will be a pleasure to have company, Madame. And Mam'selle Mary could choose a new pair of gloves, as I am sorry to say I failed to remove the tea stain from her cream ones."

"Perhaps you have letters to post, Mama?"

Mrs Daniell nodded. "Yes, I am just finishing one to dearest Gertrude. By the time you have found your outdoor clothes, it will be ready. Thérèse, can you wait for it?"

Thérèse stood next to her mistress as Mrs Daniell's pen scratched over the paper. She knew how worried she was about her eldest daughter as her confinement neared. She watched as Mrs Daniell blew on the paper to dry the ink and turned up the top and bottom of the page, before folding it again then sealing it with wax. She sighed as she handed it to her.

"I do wish Gertrude was closer to home at this time, but I have to accept she has her own life now. And of course the best doctors are in London, should she need them."

"I hope it will not come to that, Madame."

"I hope so too. Now go, because Mary will be waiting for you and becoming impatient. You are so very tolerant of her wilful ways, but she is a dear girl really."

"I know that, Madame."

Mary was indeed waiting in the hall and together they made their way out into the February chill. The post office was next door to the Daniells' mansion, and Mary insisted on taking her mother's letter herself. Thérèse followed her to the counter, but Mary turned her back quite deliberately when she spoke to the postmaster. Out of the corner of her eye, Thérèse was sure two letters passed between them, the slim fold of Mrs Daniell's and the other a small, square packet.

At first Thérèse said nothing, but as they walked down Boscawen Street she was plagued by a nagging doubt.

"So you had a letter of your own to send, Mam'selle Mary?"

"No, I ... it was not a letter as such." Her cheeks were turning pink as she spoke, her eyes unable to meet Thérèse's. "It was a card. In celebration of Saint Valentine — you have that in France?"

"But Mam'selle — you have no beau!"

"So it could not have been mine, could it?" Mary bit her lip. "Oh, Thérèse, please don't tell, for these things are meant to be secret, but ... Lizzie gave it to me. And she is, after all, engaged to be married. I know Captain Wooldridge is ancient, but it's still very romantic, do you not think?"

"I think he would not be happy to be called old and you should not say such things, certainly not in the street."

"No-one will understand. We speak in French, after all."

"You would be surprised. This is a trading port and I have at times heard my native tongue."

Mary shrugged, the ribbons on her bonnet dancing prettily around her face. "Come, it's a cold day; let us hurry to Mrs Ferris's to be out of this wind."

But as they turned into King Street, Mary stopped in the middle of the pavement. "Why, if it isn't Captain Gilbert."

There were, in fact, three red-coated officers walking down the road, but Mary clearly had eyes only for the tall, fair one on the left. Thérèse supressed a shiver, as much from foreboding as her irrational fear of their uniforms. She dearly hoped Mary would not stop to speak to them and was relieved when she simply acknowledged their bows with a few words about the next evening's assembly and moved on.

On the day after the assembly, Mrs Daniell was seated on the sofa in the drawing room with Mary and Lizzie. Lizzie had spread the latest editions of *La Belle Assemblée* over the chaise longue to better view the illustrations of wedding dresses.

"My dear, is there anything to catch your eye?" Mrs Daniell asked her.

"It is all supposition about the dress Princess Charlotte might wear. Really, I will be better to wait until she is married in April and the style for the season set. If I decide now, my choice may prove unwise."

"Not if it is a dress that suits you."

"No, Mama. I intend to marry only once, and I will have the most fashionable of dresses. After the royal wedding is over, we can go to London to have one made — and, of course, to visit dear Gertrude and her baby."

"I do worry about Gertrude."

Mary looked up from where she was sewing with Thérèse. "You worry more about her than any of us. Just because she is ... enceinte."

Lizzie sniffed. "I can only hope when your turn comes..."

There was a knock on the door, and Matthew stepped into the room carrying a salver with a card on it.

"A Captain Gilbert has called to pay his respects, Mrs Daniell."

"Please tell him I am not at home, Matthew."

"But, Mama…" Mary started.

One look from her mother silenced Mary, at least until Matthew had left the room, when she leapt from her chair, almost upsetting Thérèse's workbox. "But why do you snub him? It's … it's cruel. And rude."

"It is no such thing. You may have danced twice with Captain Gilbert at the assembly, but you must not continue to encourage him. I certainly will not. Which is why we are not at home to him this morning."

"But it is right he calls the next morning when…"

"That does not mean it is right for me to receive him, and now at least he will know I do not approve of his attentions."

"It isn't you he wants to see." Mary stamped her foot.

"Enough. Go to your room now."

"You're treating me like a child!"

Mrs Daniell stood to face her. "Because you are behaving like one. You will stay in your room until supper time, when I will have had the opportunity to speak to your father about this."

As Mary slammed the door behind her, a tight band of pain gripped Mrs Daniell's forehead and she sank back onto the sofa. Both Lizzie and Thérèse jumped up.

"Madame, what is wrong?"

Two anxious faces leaned over her, and their concern brought tears to her eyes. "Oh, my dear girls, she has given me such a headache."

Lizzie asked Thérèse to fetch the lavender oil. Thérèse ran from the room while Lizzie moved the magazines from the chaise longue and settled Mrs Daniell there with a soft cushion behind her head.

"Mary's behaviour cannot be allowed to continue," she said. Mrs Daniell closed her eyes. "Not now, Lizzie, please. Let me rest."

"Sorry, Mama."

The door opened and closed softly as Thérèse returned, her skirts rustling as she walked past to take up her position close to Mrs Daniell's head. The scent of lavender enveloped Mrs Daniell as Thérèse gently massaged her temples and Lizzie knelt close by, holding her hand.

"My dear girls," Mrs Daniell murmured. "My dearest, dearest girls. What would I do without you?"

Lizzie squeezed her fingers. "I am so glad you will have Thérèse at your side after I am married," she said.

"It is my pleasure to serve Madame," Thérèse replied. "You can be sure of my care and devotion long after you have a home of your own."

CHAPTER THIRTY-SIX

The Cornish climate was much like Thérèse's native Brittany in its capriciousness, and she commented on the fact to Coates as they strolled along the eastern side of the river towards Mopus Passage. It seemed as if overnight the frequent storms had melted into the first breath of spring, and early primroses were beginning to flower on the grassy banks.

"If the winds stay as they are, it will be good for business. Despite the pleasure of your company I have been too long cooling my heels, but now my ship is being made ready at St Pirans and I can sail for Guernsey."

"And what will you trade there?"

"A small amount of tin, some bolts of cotton newly arrived from the Indies…"

Thérèse swallowed hard. The incident she had witnessed from her window had been playing on her mind, and now was her chance. "Not barrels?"

He stopped and looked down at her. "Why barrels?"

She felt herself redden. "I have seen you at the cooperage. It is, after all, opposite the house."

"Not in recent weeks. I will do no business with a man who is both a gossip and a fool. But more important, my dear Mam'selle, is what I shall bring back from St Peter Port."

"Brandy?"

"And news. I hope, after all this time, for word from Roscoff. And a definite answer, one way or the other."

A lump came into her throat and she cast her eyes down, before walking on.

"Mam'selle Thérèse ... I feel wretched in case I have given you false hope."

She could not look at him. "False hope is better than none, Monsieur. Come, let us continue our walk."

He fell into step beside her, and for a while they were silent. Around the bend in the river they came across a natural bay, flooded with sunlight, where a small harbour was under construction.

"Your Mr Daniell's doing," Coates commented. "At least, he is one of the partners in this venture."

"But why? Is the port in the town not more convenient?"

"The river is silting up, so this is their insurance. And the harbour dues will line their pockets well."

"Is that why you sail directly from the coast?"

He smiled at her. "One of the reasons. But I have to admire their adventurous spirit."

She nodded. "I suppose, when I think of it, so do I."

He was suddenly intense. "Would you ever want more for yourself, Thérèse? More than just being a maid?"

"My only wish at present is to serve Madame Daniell well." Her reply was pat; change was not something she had considered, and his reason for asking her made her feel a little unsettled. If, indeed, he had reason at all.

"Would it surprise you to know I once served the Daniells? But in such a small way they would doubtless hardly be aware of it."

"Really? Do tell."

"I come from low stock, Thérèse, and as a boy followed my father and older brother into one of their mines. The hardness of it, the suffering — and all to line their pockets. And then my brother died in an accident underground, and I was so angry I swore I would better myself, not work all my life for the profit of others."

"I have sometimes thought... Are you so very kind to me because you know what it is to lose a brother?"

He shook his head then turned away from her, clenching his hands into hard fists. "I suppose ... in part ... but more than anything I am glad you were spared seeing your brother's body. I saw mine and I wished I had not, so bloated and battered was he."

"What happened?"

"The men were instructed to dig near some old workings. They were against it, but the captain swore it was safe, as there was nothing untoward on the plans. He was wrong, though, and a great wall of water engulfed them, throwing them back down the levels. It was days before their bodies were even found."

"I am sorry, so sorry, Monsieur Coates."

Slowly he unfurled his fingers, which were perfectly white, and began to rub them. "Well, at very least, because of it I have made a better life for myself. I measure the risk of danger on my own account and I do not go hungry."

"Madame Daniell sees to it the miners do not go hungry either. Even at Porthnevek where..."

"I know about that." His voice was suddenly sharp. "Do you not remember it was where we first met?"

"She is a good woman, Monsieur Coates, and besides that she needs me." Thérèse jutted out her chin. "And will do so all the more after Mam'selle Elizabeth is married."

"You often say she needs you, but that is something I struggle to understand. Has she not more daughters at home?" He still sounded combative.

"Yes, but they are in the schoolroom at Trelissick. And Mam'selle Mary is not much comfort at present, truth be told."

"Why is that?"

Thérèse shook her head. "Already I have said too much."

He smoothed a stray leaf from her cloak. "Do you not trust me? Are we not friends? Perhaps … more than friends?"

She blushed even more, hoping he could not hear the thudding of her heart. "I do not know, Monsieur. Such things are not possible."

"So you only tolerate my company to learn news of your brother?" Was he teasing her now, or was he still serious? She did not understand these rapid changes of mood and decided to humour him.

"No! I enjoy our walks."

"Well then. But I have no wish to embarrass you with my affections if they are unwanted. You were telling me about Miss Mary?"

Thérèse closed her eyes. It went against her nature to talk of the family in this way, but she needed to show him a little faith. He had been good to her, and…

"It is but a small thing. Of no matter really, but to a young girl of sixteen…"

"Then it must be a dress or a man." Coates winked.

Thérèse laughed. "I fear it is the latter. An army captain who has been a little too familiar for Madame Daniell's taste."

"One who perhaps danced twice with Miss Mary at the assembly?"

"Oh … then it is all over the town."

"Perhaps not that bad. Remember I take an interest in the Daniell family because you are in their employ. But if the soldier concerned is a Captain Gilbert, then Madame Daniell is right. He is not even welcome at Lander's Inn anymore because of his behaviour towards one of the serving wenches, and they say his bastard will be born before the summer's out."

Thérèse shuddered. "He scares me so, with his red uniform. All the soldiers do. It makes me remember Waterloo."

"Then all the more reason to keep Miss Mary away from him. Just think how grateful her mother would be to the loyal maid who brought her the news of Gilbert's indiscretion."

"But ... but I cannot. How will I say I came by it?"

"That you overheard it?"

Thérèse shook her head. "My English..."

"Your English must be improving by now. And perhaps better to have half understood something and be seeking clarity from your mistress. I am sure at even the merest whiff of a rumour Mr Daniell would make his own enquiries."

"You are right, of course. It is my duty to protect Mam'selle Mary's reputation."

"Your sense of duty is strong, Thérèse. Would that I could win such loyalty."

Thérèse's heart lurched in her chest. There was something about him ... something good, and strong, and kind. Yet... She looked up at him and smiled. "I must return to those duties. But I wish you good travels, Monsieur Coates, and a safe return — with or without news of Paul."

CHAPTER THIRTY-SEVEN

Mrs Daniell looked across the carriage at Mary's scowling face. Already there had been an argument about what she should wear, and it had taken all of Thérèse's tact to persuade Mary her plain brown dress was the most appropriate for their trip to Porthnevek.

"But they know we are richer than they are, so why should we bother to hide it?" Mary had cried.

"Because it is kinder that way," Thérèse had explained. "And you know it is a good thing to be kind."

Even so, Mary was being less than gracious about the visit. Mrs Daniell was beginning to truly fear for her daughter. Neither Lizzie nor Gertrude had behaved like this, but they had come out some ten years before and life had seemed simpler then. Perhaps it would be better to send Mary to Ralph's sister in Hereford for a few months, but there was no knowing how the child would react to the strict discipline of a cathedral canon's household. Maybe a better answer was the distraction of a London season — and quickly — well away from avaricious army captains of dubious repute.

The coach slowed to cross a particularly muddy stretch of road, and Mrs Daniell was pleased at the thought of Matthew with his gun sitting next to Kitto. Rumours still abounded of kidnap threats — the latest relating to a doctor's housekeeper from Portreath, just along the coast. Ralph had heard a modest ransom had been paid and the woman restored to her employer, so Mrs Daniell fervently hoped the felon's success would not act as encouragement.

The normal knot of villagers was outside the inn awaiting their arrival. As she descended the carriage, Mrs Daniell cast her eye around for Old William, but he was not among them. All the same she wanted to keep Thérèse close at hand, so she whispered to her, "I think you should show Mary how to distribute the food, and I would ask you not to leave her side. She must learn to be gracious to those we are responsible for, and you must be my eyes and ears in that respect."

"Of course, Madame."

The innkeeper came out to greet them, bowing to Mrs Daniell and to Mary, before showing them into the parlour. Mary was charming to him and seemed excited by the prospect of visiting an inn, but the man was clearly preoccupied. While his serving maid helped the girls to set out the food, he took Mrs Daniell to one side.

"Mrs Daniell, I am pleased you have some protection, for I have worrying news — Old William has been missing these last days, and before that he was here at the inn, ranting about how he would steal his wife and son back from you."

Mrs Daniell shivered. "Oh, the poor man, such violence does not seem to be in his nature."

"Nor is it, Mrs Daniell, but his mind has quite gone. The villagers are afraid for him, and there is a party of unemployed miners searching for him now."

"I am sure they need no incentive, but there is a half sovereign and a flagon of ale for the man who finds him and delivers him up safely to the asylum."

The innkeeper nodded. "I fear you are right, Mrs Daniell, it has indeed come to that. Although it is a sorry way for anyone to end their days."

Later that evening, Thérèse left the convivial table and warm hearth of the kitchen to attend to a stained fichu soaking in lemon. She took a lamp from the dresser and made her way to the scullery, drawing her shawl around her shoulders. The tiny corridor at the back of the house was always cold, but tonight a draught from the open garden door added to the chill, so she closed it as she passed.

At the sink she rinsed the delicate fabric in cold water then held it to the flickering light. The strong lye soap was far too harsh to use, so she rubbed on a little more lemon, then rinsed again. This time the mark had vanished, and she nodded to herself before reaching up to hang the fichu on the line over the sink to drip.

A movement in the garden caught her eye. The blur of a lamp, as if held half hidden, partially lit a slight figure hurrying away from the house, but no sooner than she had seen it, it was gone. Her imagination? Or a spirit? She shivered, but there was something familiar about the trim of the cloak at least.

Thérèse closed her eyes. Surely, surely, even Mary would not be so brazen and so stupid? The family were at the supper table, but she had pleaded a headache after her dancing class and had taken to her bed. Thérèse's heart sank; she knew she should act, but what to do without exposing Mary's shame further?

She hurried back to the kitchen, where she told Mrs Leigh she was going to ask Mam'selle Mary if she would take a tisane. As she climbed the back stairs her heart grew heavier, but all the same she nursed a shred of hope Mary would still be in her room.

There was no answer when she knocked, so Thérèse pushed the door open to find an empty bed. A candle guttered low on the chest next to the window, where the curtain was undrawn. She padded across the room and looked out. At the far end of the garden, near the corner of the stable block, were two lights, close to each other. This was the very worst turn of events, and she knew she should go straight the dining room and alert Mr and Mrs Daniell, but there would be hell to pay for the girl if she did. Were there any other servants she could trust with the secret? It would need a man to confront the captain, and Mr Leigh and Matthew were serving supper. What could she do?

As she watched, the lights separated and one began to move towards the house. Thank heaven — Mary had not been outside long enough to come to any harm. Perhaps Thérèse could persuade her to see sense.

The wait seemed interminable, but eventually she heard footsteps scurrying along the landing and Mary slipped into the room with a deep sigh, which turned into a stifled squeal when she saw Thérèse.

"What are you doing here?"

Thérèse stood. "Waiting for you, Mam'selle."

"I … I needed some air, that is all."

"I saw you in the garden. I also saw a second lamp. Oh, Mam'selle Mary, please have a care for your reputation."

Mary's voice shook. "There was no second lamp. You must have imagined it. I merely walked around the herb bed and picked some lavender for my headache. Look." A single stalk lay crushed in her palm.

"It is a good ruse, but I know the truth, and I must surely tell your mother before you come to harm."

"Frederick would never harm me. He loves me and wants to marry me, if only Mama would receive him."

Thérèse was shocked by her use of his given name. This had already gone much too far. "I fear Madame Daniell is right. I understand Captain Gilbert has a certain reputation about the town."

"And how would you know? You understand nothing that isn't spoken to you in your own tongue. You're too stupid to even learn English." She stamped her foot.

"I understand enough, Mam'selle, and your mother must be told."

Mary pulled off her gloves, her slender frame shaking.

"Mam'selle … please … promise me you will give him up, and then I need say nothing."

Mary turned on her, eyes blazing. "You will say nothing, Mam'selle Thérèse," she cried, "or I will tell Mama your little secret — and then where would you be?"

Sweat dampened the back of Thérèse's dress, and she tried to keep the tremor from her voice when she answered. "I have no secrets from Madame." Only Coates … but how could Mary know?

Mary tossed her gloves on the bed. "Then she knows you are a thief? Albeit not a very clever one."

Thérèse exhaled. The comb. That was all; Lizzie's comb. "In the matter of the comb Madame Daniell knows the truth, and I have nothing to fear. Even if I had, I would still tell her because your reputation has a price above silver and pearls."

"My reputation is safe with Frederick. He loves me and I love him. We will be together … if I have to wait until I am twenty-one … or if we have to elope…" She flung herself on the bed, sobbing.

As quietly as she could, Thérèse left the room and went to wait for Mrs Daniell to come upstairs.

Time hung heavily as she prowled around the bedroom. She could not bear to look out into the darkness of the garden, and instead her eyes kept coming back to the clock on the mantelpiece, the gilded cupids flanking it seeming to mock her as the hands turned with agonising slowness. Whatever Thomas Chalmers had said all those months ago, she knew she had to speak — and probably should have done so long ago.

By the time her mistress arrived, her courage had almost left her. Her hands shook as she hung Mrs Daniell's dress in the wardrobe then wrapped her shawl around her shoulders, ready to brush her hair in front of the fire.

"Thérèse, whatever is wrong?" Mrs Daniell spoke at the same moment as Thérèse said, "Madame, I have something to tell you."

Mrs Daniell grasped her hand. "You are not leaving me, are you?"

Thérèse smiled down at her. "Never, Madame. As long as you want me, I am here. But there is something of great importance you need to know."

"Well?"

"I went to Mary's room while you were at supper to ask if she would take a tisane, but she wasn't there. Madame, I saw two lights in the garden and I have reason to think she was meeting Captain Gilbert."

"No!" Mrs Daniell went deathly pale.

"Your salts, Madame?"

She waved the bottle away. "Just tell me ... tell me..."

"I do not think she was outside for very long. I begged her to give up the captain, but she will not hear of it. She even spoke of elopement. Madame, you must do something."

"I certainly will. I shall have Ralph speak to the garrison's commanding officer and have Captain Gilbert sent away, but tomorrow we shall remove ourselves to Trelissick. I will have to pray it is far enough to keep them apart until he leaves."

"Monsieur Daniell's words will be enough to ensure that, as I fear when Captain Gilbert realises the match is so vehemently opposed he will quickly turn his attentions elsewhere. But Mam'selle Mary's heart will surely be broken."

"Then, Thérèse, it is her own fault. But we must be sure she can make no rash move tonight. I will have Ralph ask Mr Leigh to make the house doubly secure. He can mention rumours of robbery or some such. Now, brush my hair quickly and fetch my dressing gown. Then if you would be so kind as to bring Ralph from the library, I will break the news to him."

CHAPTER THIRTY-EIGHT

The grey walls of Trelissick looked even more grim to Thérèse through the drizzle. The morning had been a storm of tears, recriminations and hasty packing. Mary had even feigned hysterics and faints, but in the end had walked to the carriage with her head held high when Mrs Daniell had threatened she would tell Matthew to carry her if necessary.

Now Mary sat in the corner opposite her mother, as far away from Thérèse as she could manage. Lizzie would be staying in Truro to fulfil their social obligations, including hosting a supper before the last assembly of the season. She would also let it be known Mary was suffering from croup and had been taken to Trelissick, where the country air would aid her recovery.

The carriage rumbled to a halt outside the porch, and the footman opened the door. Inside, Miss Grafton waited with the children, but Mary fled straight to her room. The governess raised a quizzical eyebrow as Mrs Daniell hugged her youngest, Charlotte, and Thérèse whispered she would tell her later.

No quarter was given to Mary's weeping and wailing by her mother, but when Thérèse tried to take her a tray of tea and sweetmeats a plate was thrown at her, making her flee without a word. Even worse, in the corridor outside, the nursery maid spat in her face and called her a witch, causing her to shed some tears of her own in the linen cupboard. Thérèse knew what heartbreak was, and to be the catalyst for Mary's desolation cut her to the core.

After enduring a silent supper in the servants' hall, Thérèse was glad to escape to the schoolroom. She could hear Miss Grafton next door, ushering Anne to bed, so she sat on the stool by the fireplace and waited, watching the flames. She was beginning to truly hate this house, and sadness seemed to seep from its every wall.

Miss Grafton did not sit down, and when she spoke her words were harsh. "So it is you who has caused all this upset, Mam'selle Ruguel."

Thérèse got to her feet. "It would be a simple defence to say it is of Mary's own making, but I do feel some responsibility, yes."

"She is saying you are a witch who has stolen her mother's affections and lied to her to sully her reputation. And she is telling all and sundry you are a thief."

"You know that, at least, is not true. But of the rest, I wish I had told Madame Daniell of my fears earlier so things might never have gone this far and Mam'selle Mary's reputation would be perfectly safe. I acted only in her best interests, Miss Grafton, I swear."

The governess's face softened. "I did not want to believe ill of you, but Mary was in my care for many years and I cannot bear to see her laid so low."

"Me neither. I, too, have become fond of her over the last months. But love is a fickle friend, especially in one so young, and she believes herself to be in love."

"Then she is a silly goose. I shall make us a cup of chocolate and you can tell me all."

"Perhaps if I do you will be able to help Mam'selle Mary, as I clearly cannot. She sees I have taken sides against her and does not want me near."

So Thérèse told Miss Grafton about the captain and about the previous night. She listened with some sympathy for all concerned then asked, "You said you did not act quickly enough, but that I do not understand."

"There were two things, the second making the first seem more important, but still I said nothing and now I know that was wrong."

"And what were those things?"

"There was an occasion when I was walking with Mam'selle Mary and we met Captain Gilbert. Although I could not understand their conversation it seemed a little too long, but I managed to plead lateness for an appointment to draw Mam'selle away. Afterwards I could not decide whether the meeting was by chance or had been arranged."

"It seems that was little enough to trouble Mrs Daniell. Mary is naturally talkative, although you were right to have concerns about her behaving in such a manner in the street. What was the second?"

Thérèse paused. How much should she say? "I heard bad things about Captain Gilbert's reputation ... that ... he had an unfortunate liaison with a serving maid in Lander's Inn."

Miss Grafton put her hand over her mouth. "That is just too, too awful. That he could have sullied himself so while courting our Miss Mary."

"You see, I should have told Mrs Daniell."

"But, Thérèse, it is hard. I take it what you heard was no more than gossip?"

Thérèse's mouth went dry. What would she say if Miss Grafton pressed her further? "I … I overheard it when I was out walking, and of course my English… I could not be sure…"

"Well then. Do not blame yourself. And in any event, you had to tell Mrs Daniell what you witnessed last night, although I have to admit to being shocked by Mary's behaviour."

Thérèse shifted in her chair. "Perhaps she has shocked herself. Perhaps that is why she seeks to blame me and to pretend the fault is not hers. Maybe it is better for her that way."

Miss Grafton put out her hand and covered hers. "You are such a kind and charitable soul, Thérèse. Thank you for confiding in me. I will do all I can to distract Mam'selle Mary as her poor heart mends."

Thérèse watched the carriage disappear in the direction of Feock church before beginning her walk. She felt herself drawn to the river with its views past Falmouth to the open seas, so she set off through the parkland in front of the house. The ground was soft after the days of drizzle and even now the deer sheltered under the trees, as if fearing more rain.

She was tired, having slept only fitfully since returning to Trelissick, and her soul was restless for reasons she did not wish to examine too closely. But in the quiet of a Sunday morning, with the toll of the bells reaching her over the creek, she had to admit to missing Coates. His tales of his travels, his easy laughter, his respectful solicitousness. Yes, there was an emptiness in her life without them, and she was awaiting his return for more reason than news of Paul.

There would be no news, she was sure of that. He had been chasing a rumour on her behalf — the soldier could have been anyone. Her brother was lost. All the same, the tiny seed of hope itched in an uncomfortable manner, with every fibre of her body telling her it was safer not to believe.

It was safer not to believe in Coates in any manner at all. Certainly not her own confusing feelings. She could not love — could not permit herself to. Despite his alluring words, hers would be a life in service. Mrs Daniell was a good woman, and she was fortunate to have secured such a position in a strange land. A land she must somehow make her own.

But what if Paul lived? That could change everything. Then what should she do? But he would likely marry in time, and if she returned to France she would have no real home, and perhaps new positions were scarce in a country scarred by revolution and war. How could she give up all she had? But how could she not? The notion it may be better if he were dead came half-formed to her mind, and she bowed her head in shame.

Again her thoughts returned to Coates. He had hinted ... no, more than hinted ... of his esteem for her. Something deep in her body stirred at the thought of his strong arms around her, but she pushed the thought away. It would not happen, could not happen. But why? He was a successful trader ... but then he was a smuggler too, and whatever the morals of the question, it was outside the law and he could very easily be put in jail. Better stay safe ... better just to walk out with him on Sundays ... or better to avoid a broken heart like Miss Mary's and not to see him at all.

Almost without realising, she had taken the low path along the river towards the ferry. A schooner in full sail passed her, so close she could make out it was the Truro, no doubt bound for London. A small child on the deck waved at her and she waved back, a smile lighting her face for the first time in days.

Rounding the corner, she saw a man waiting beneath the trees. He was tall and wearing a long cloak, and for half a moment she thought it was Coates. There was something familiar about him, though, so perhaps he was a worker from the estate.

"Mademoiselle Thérèse." He spat out the words as she approached.

"C-Captain Gilbert." There was no smart red uniform today, and his sideburns looked untrimmed. She made to hurry past him, but he blocked her path.

"You will take a message." His French was laboured and heavily accented.

She replied in English. "No." Despite trembling inside, she looked at him defiantly.

"I repeat. You will take a message."

"Let me pass."

He did not move.

She turned on her heel to go back the way she'd come, but he grabbed her by the shoulder, pulling her towards him. She screamed.

"Listen, you stupid woman. You will tell Mary I am waiting for her. Here. She will come."

"No. She will not."

"If she does not, I will tell of your liaison."

"I have no liaison…" Thérèse found her voice shaking.

"Ha! You give yourself away, Mademoiselle."

"Let me go!"

"Give her the message."

"No!"

"Then I will tell the excise men where to find that scoundrel Coates on a Sunday morning. The stable lad is mighty obliging to all gentleman callers, I'll be bound. But I think he will find I pay better than most." He pushed her away.

So he did know. Her secret was out. But she could not risk Mary's reputation. Could not and would not. Trying to hide the trembling in her voice, she repeated her request to pass. Reluctantly, he stood to one side.

"Think on it as you walk. I am sure you will come to your senses and deliver the message."

She straightened her back and strode away from him, head held high, but with a river of silent tears streaming down her face.

PART SEVEN: 2016

CHAPTER THIRTY-NINE

As I step out of the car after my shift at Trelissick, I spy a lone figure walking below in the valley. My shoulders relax when I realise it's Sebastian. There's no mistaking his height or his gait. He must be paying a visit to his grey lady.

Having debunked my whispering voices as particularly earthy, he's still chasing shadows with her. The evening last week when he found a black cylinder in a plastic bag in the log pile both solved the riddle and meant I could sleep at night. A Bluetooth speaker with a range of about a hundred metres, easily controllable from Nankathes. I wondered how a technophobe like him even knew what it was, but he said his nephew had been given one just like it for his birthday.

Sebastian doesn't even have a phone. If he did, I'd call him and ask if he fancied a drink at The Tinners. He may well end up there later anyway. He's started on the furniture, and I paid him more than he asked for in advance. For once he didn't mutter about charity, and it's good to see him with a bit of money in his pocket. It's not my business if he spends more on beer and weed than he does on food and logs.

The lights in the valley showed up on the security camera last week. At the very edge of its reach you could just see them bobbing about, but there have been no more petty acts of vandalism. It could just be someone using Wheal Dream as a shortcut or to walk their dog; they go up towards The Tinners, disappear for half an hour or so, then come back, so it's the right sort of pattern. It's just a strange time to do it.

I showed the footage to my boss Cecile when she came on a site visit. We wound it backwards and forwards but agreed that without actual damage, there was nothing that warranted bothering the police.

She was worried for my safety, though. Over lunch in a smart hotel just outside St Pirans, she told me she'd gone into Porthnevek and had been surprised to see the strength of the campaign against Wheal Dream.

"Normally they give up once we've got planning," she said.

"The Sussex tree huggers didn't."

"They did when we started to build."

"Only because things turned a bit nasty and the police got involved. You know, somehow their not-so-peaceful protests were easier to deal with. Here it's more insidious. They're not stepping outside the law, just making a nuisance of themselves."

"I'm worried about what might happen when our visitors start to arrive. It won't exactly be a relaxing holiday if the village is openly hostile."

"I have my fingers crossed the place will be so packed our guests will blend in with everyone else. And whatever they say now, those businesses in Porthnevek need tourists to survive. Even the ringleader's dependent on them."

"Who is he?"

I took a sip of my mineral water. "She. She owns the furniture and gift shop near the village store."

"I went in there and bought some gorgeous scented candles. You're right, she must make a bomb in the summer."

I twisted linguine around my fork. "Do you still expect Wheal Dream to open in time for May half term? With a fair wind from here on in I reckon we can do it, but I wouldn't start taking bookings just yet. Give me until the end of the month and things will be clearer."

"Honestly, Anna, you never let me down — you must be the best project manager I've ever had the pleasure of working with." She looked at me. "Do you fancy a different sort of challenge for next year? We're expanding into Europe, buying some land near the national park just outside Genoa in Italy."

It's a chance I should jump at, and I'm not really sure why I didn't. "Can I think about it?"

She looked slightly taken aback. "You're not planning to leave us, are you?"

"Of course not. I'm just a bit preoccupied with everything here at the moment, that's all."

Once Cecile left, I took a long walk over the cliffs. The sea sparkled in the spring sunshine, white horses dancing as the tide receded. I headed past Wheal Clare, its engine house tower glowing the softest of reds, and on to Tubman's Head. Here the ocean was all around me, the western tip of Wales and Ireland beyond the far horizon. I felt like I was at the end of the world. My world. I wanted to go no further.

How did that happen? I'm probably working in the place that's been the most hostile to me, but all the same it's got under my skin. I've made friends, though, real friends. Liz at Trelissick, Keith and Ray and Tim — and, of course, Sebastian. Outside Porthnevek itself, the people are warm and welcoming. They were the same in Porthnevek until they knew why I was here.

I stood for so long on the headland pondering this realisation that the light started to fade, so I ended up half running along the path back towards The Tinners. I took a shortcut through the gorse, no more than a rabbit track weaving between a family of Clwyd Caps, fervently hoping all the old shafts had been blocked off. In retrospect, it was a stupid risk — the last thing I need right now is a twisted ankle. I need to get this job finished, then I can consider my future.

Several days later, the Clwyd Caps come to mind again. I'm sitting with Sebastian on his rock while he listens to his grey lady. It's a good vantage point for the valley, so locking the portacabin when I finish work and climbing up to join him is becoming something of a habit. We sit together in silence as he strains to understand the gibberish only he can hear, and I survey the day's work.

The cap is just below us, hunkered down in the gorse. The low branches have twisted and straggled through one side of the wire mesh, their tiny bright flowers glowing in the late afternoon sun. A Red Admiral alights on a bud, and I nudge Sebastian and point. It's the first one I've seen this year.

"Souls of the dead," he murmurs. "Have you been to see your sister yet?"

"I'm working up to it."

He nods.

I continue to watch the butterfly as it flits in and out of the cap. Beneath the tendrils of gorse is the loose shale typical of the valley, but it's unusually flat. I frown. I'm sure the caps I jogged past the other day covered quite distinct dips. I ask Sebastian, but he just shrugs.

"Probably plugged."

I'll get no more out of him while he's listening, so I head back across the valley to Nevek Cot.

I sit in front of the wood burner with a glass of wine and my iPad, to see what I can find out about capping mines. Thinking about it, there must be different ways. I hunt around for the Wheal Nevek shaft plan Luke brought me. I almost saw him at

237

Trelissick the other day, but he veered off into the shop. Cowardly shit, running away like that.

Eleven shafts but only two visible caps; the one in the valley and the other in the field next to the main road. There might be a smaller one close to the village, but I can't quite remember. So how do you block off a shaft when you need to?

The answer seems to depend on when and where. If it's well out of the way of the public, you just pop a Clwyd Cap over it, stick up a danger sign, and you're done. For environmentalists it's the preferred option because bats and other wildlife still have free access. Sometimes the old shafts became unofficial rubbish dumps and were filled to the brim with all sorts of crap — even old cars. And then there was a phase when health and safety probably went a little mad, and the done thing was to plug them with concrete. Given our valley is about to become a resort, it's probably just as well someone did.

While I'm walking around the valley with the landscapers, I get another chance to look at the Clwyd Cap. Is the shaft really plugged? And if not, does it need plugging? Surely there's a detailed survey of such things somewhere? The other option is to lift it, brush away the shale, and see for myself. As we walk past, I bend to rattle the cage, and to my surprise there's quite a bit of give in it, but the landscapers don't seem to think it's a big deal.

"Probably a holding bolt gone rusty. Get one of the builders to put in new ones and the job's a good 'un. Oh, and it should have a sign on it warning people off."

I'm a bit nervous about the bolt situation, so back in the portacabin I create a temporary sign and tape it inside a plastic folder. When I return to fix it, I discover the cage is really very wobbly — only the trailing gorse bush seems to be holding it in place. I tie the notice to the frame and hope for the best.

Next morning my car has a flat tyre, and a banner has appeared between two trees in the garden of a Nankathes property overlooking the site: 'Stop the build — no Wheal Nightmare here!'

"Bit late for that," one of the electricians laughs. "Bloody pot-heads — can't even organise a protest with any sense of urgency." I only wish he was right.

All day long the phone rings and then stops. A vehicle's left parked across the site entrance for over an hour. It is as if the protestors have suddenly woken up again, and Sebastian is nowhere to be seen. Are the two connected? Once again I begin to wonder how close he really is to Serena. A spy in the camp? But he seems so genuinely glad of my friendship I can't quite believe it.

I find him propping up the bar in The Tinners after work. I drive there and ask if I can leave my Peugeot in their car park for a few days. Now the Easter holidays are over it isn't a problem, but it's far from a long term solution. Today's actions have pushed me well past hoping things will calm down any time soon.

I don't mention the new wave of protests, and although Ray raises an eyebrow when he hears me ask about my car he doesn't pursue the matter. Keith and I concentrate on the crossword, then Sebastian walks me home. Even then I daren't tell him what's been going on, and it makes me realise I'm in a very lonely place.

CHAPTER FORTY

At times like this, my best friend is action — that and a firm belief knowledge is power. Control what you can, ignore what you can't. And about a million other platitudes. Which is why I'm waiting outside St Pirans library when it opens, watching the young mothers gathering to chat after offloading their children at school. For a moment I envy them, but that isn't the life I've chosen and it's much too late to change my mind.

The small print on Luke's scan of the shafts told me it came from a British Geological Survey book on mining in south west England, and there's a copy in the local history reference section. Much of it I don't understand, but I begin to find my bearings when it mentions The Tinners, and a few pages later I discover the sum total of their knowledge about Wheal Nevek.

It doesn't amount to much. First it was opencast — I guess where our valley is — and later came the shafts, starting at the village end and extending for about a mile eastwards. No maps remain of the workings, but it's believed they followed the lode north towards the sea. That's all very interesting, but even though the book was written in the 1950s there's no mention of how — or whether — the shafts were closed off. I all but slam it shut.

I park behind the pub and with trepidation I walk onto the site down the new road. At least the entrance isn't blocked, but the workmen tell me they had to move an old fridge dumped there before they could get in.

Another irritation is that the notice on the Clwyd Cap is missing. I know I tied it on tightly, although when I find it clinging to a nearby gorse bush it looks for all the world as though it blew there. I take it back to the portacabin to wipe it dry then make tea for everyone and start dealing with my emails, so very soon the day begins to feel a little more normal.

The workmen leave at five, and I follow them up the valley. Soft spring is in the air, and I watch two wagtails hop from bush to bush as the sun releases faint hints of coconut from the gorse. I close my eyes and imagine the platform grassed over, yurts dotted around, the sound of laughter in the air. This will be a good place, it will.

At the old shaft I find I can wiggle the cage this way and that, but every time I try to lift it the metal frame bends alarmingly and is far too unwieldy to control on my own. I look around for inspiration, and under the hedge bordering the road I find a stout stick about three foot long. I poke it through and begin to scrape away at the shale. The loose pieces move easily, and I am so engrossed I don't see or hear Sebastian approach.

"That's a bit of a strange thing to be doing."

I look up at him from my crouching position. "My curiosity was piqued. And anyway, apparently there's a planning condition about old shafts, so I need to know whether it's plugged or not."

"That doesn't look the easiest way to do it. Can't you ask the workmen to cut the bolts so you can lift the cage?"

"There aren't any bolts. The landscape guys said they sometimes rust away. But I can't lift the cage on my own."

He grins at me. "Is that a hint?"

I stand up. "Not really, but seeing as you're here... One side of it's trapped in that bush, so we need to sort of hinge it."

The cage is octagonal, so we stand opposite each other and lift. Once we get it to chest height, it pivots quite easily and tips back onto the bed of gorse. I'm about to step forward when Sebastian raises his hand.

"No — be careful. If it hasn't been plugged, you could fall in — and fall quite a way at that. Let's clear the shale from one side to the other, very carefully."

So we kneel together and start brushing with our hands, but what we begin to feel about a foot in isn't earth and it isn't concrete. It's planks of wood.

"What the hell?" Sebastian rocks back on his knees.

"Not what you expected?"

His lips have almost disappeared under his beard and his eyes narrow. "They do use wooden battens when they're plugging, but underneath the concrete, not on top."

I point at a curved indent cut into the edge of the planks, the earth beneath it scooped smooth through use. "And not with a means of lifting it. Come on, let's take a look."

"Anna, you still need to be careful. Perhaps wait until the workmen are back tomorrow so you have some help."

"Aren't you going to help me?"

"Growing up around here, you're taught from a very young age not to mess with the shafts. They can drop hundreds of feet, be full of water … anything."

"But it won't hurt just to look."

"Okay. Just to look."

The planks are nailed into one solid board, so they lift easily until they rest against the raised cage. Not a scatter of earth falls; the edge of the hole has been worn firm and just below the lip hangs a sturdy chain ladder. There is no way of telling its length, as after a few feet it disappears into the darkness below.

I pull my phone from my pocket and shine the torch into the shaft. The links of metal glint, and there's mud on the treads that looks relatively fresh. I turn to Sebastian.

"I'm going in."

"Honestly, Anna, best leave it until tomorrow. The light will go soon and…"

"It won't take me five minutes to climb down and back up again, just to see what's going on."

"You don't know how deep it is."

I turn off my torch. "There's only one way to find out."

"Don't be so stupid. You hold the light and I'll go first. Get out of the way."

To be honest, I'm pleased I don't have to go down there alone. I kneel next to the top of the ladder, trying my best to shine the torch to illuminate the rungs and watching Sebastian's head disappear into the gloom below. He is nothing more than a shadow when he calls he's hit a flat surface, probably about thirty feet below.

"I won't move until you get here with the light."

I put my phone back in my pocket. "I'm on my way."

Despite being securely fastened at the top, the ladder sways as I descend, my palms slippery as I try to grip it. I swallow hard, but curiosity drives me on through the darkness and eventually I feel Sebastian's hand on the small of my back.

"It's all right, I've got you."

My feet on firm ground, I switch on the torch. We're in a wide space hewn out of the rock, its rough edges glinting as I flash the beam around. The floor beneath our feet is solid and fairly flat, although I can feel its roughness beneath the soles of my pumps.

To our far right are alien shapes, cubes of white plastic catching the light. We move towards them and I unclip the lid of the nearest one. It's filled with boxes of cigarettes, the lettering on the packets clearly eastern European.

I turn to Sebastian. He looks gaunt as I shine the torch into his face, his shadow impossibly tall behind him. "Smuggling? In this day and age?"

He leans against the wall and folds his arms. "It's something of a Cornish tradition."

"No wonder Serena and her friends don't want the valley developed."

"It's nothing to do with her." There's a hint of aggression in his voice.

"How can you be so sure?"

"I know her, that's all. Come on, let's get out of here."

Before putting the lid back on the box, I take a photograph. In the moment before the flash goes off, the space is completely dark. A darkness like never before. The torch comes back on and I stand and brush the dampness from my trousers.

"What are you going to do?" Sebastian asks.

"Tell the police. If you're so sure your sister isn't involved, you've nothing to worry about."

He grunts and I follow him back towards the shaft. All of a sudden his voice is low, urgent. "Anna — shine the light."

Then I see what he sees — the ladder has gone.

My legs begin to buckle, so I lean against the wall.

"They must have seen us come down."

"Well, they're in even bigger trouble now, whoever they are. I'm going to call the police." I fumble with my phone, but there is no signal. Not even enough to make an emergency call. "Shit. What now?"

It is a while before Sebastian replies. "We can wait or we can find a way out. Or at least perhaps a passage that runs closer to the surface so you can phone for help."

"That's a better idea."

"We need another form of light. We don't want to drain your battery." He rounds on me. "See — I told you we should have waited, should at least have been better prepared."

"I'm sorry." I begin to shiver, but he offers no comfort. Under the circumstances, I'm not surprised.

He takes my phone from me and prowls around the space like a caged tiger. "There must be something... They must have brought something down here..."

I sink to the floor and bury my face in my knees. I hear boxes being clicked open and shut, then Sebastian exhales. All is still for a moment, then he says, "Candles. Scented ones, mind. I have no idea how they got here."

Cecile bought some in Serena's shop. But I say nothing.

"Come here."

I stand and walk towards the light. Sebastian is stuffing the pockets of his coat with the candles and tells me to do the same. Once we can carry no more, he thrusts my phone into my hand and pulls out a silver vesta case, a flutter of cigarette papers floating to the floor. A single candle is lit, and he tells me to turn off my phone.

"Can't I have one too?"

"Maybe. Once I know how fast they burn."

I follow him down the tunnel away from the shaft. I'm completely disorientated; I have no idea which way we're going in relation to the surface. If only I could work it out, then perhaps we could reach one of the other shafts. But unless and until we have a choice of direction, it's pretty academic anyway.

Sebastian moves slowly, scanning the ground in front of him with the candle. Already he's having to stoop, and I have the impression our path is sloping gently downwards. But I can't be sure. I can't be sure of anything in this strange, dark world.

There is a scratching sound ahead of us and Sebastian stops. I almost collide with his back, and in the moment of confusion something warm and furry brushes the leg of my trousers and I scream.

"It's only a rat," he growls.

After a while, I lose perspective of space or time. My world is reduced to Sebastian's hunched back, a halo of flickering light around him, the ceiling getting lower and lower until I, too, am having to bend my head.

We see no tunnels to the left or right, although in one place there is a recess in the rock where the top of another shaft drops away. The hole yawns empty and black, and somewhere below I can hear running water. The candle is burning low. Sebastian lights another and we move on.

The only sound is the scrunch of our feet on patches of loose shale. At other times the floor is hard, uneven and roughly cut as the walls. The air is damp and quickly fills with the scent of lemon verbena. In different circumstances, the absurdity of it would make me laugh.

Eventually Sebastian stops. "We should take a breather." He slides down the wall, slowly extending his spine until it is straight again, tipping his head back against the rock.

I sit opposite him and massage my aching feet. Damp oozes into my trousers below my thin waterproof and I start to shiver. I want to cry, but this is all my fault so that isn't an option. And then, in the silence, I hear the distant pounding of the waves.

"Sebastian, listen."

He puts his head on one side. "The sea." His voice is flat.

"I read somewhere ... the workings ran towards the sea."

"Anything else you're not telling me?"

I shake my head. "There are no plans of Wheal Nevek, just of the shafts. And if we can hear the sea, we're probably well away from those by now. Perhaps there's a way out onto the cliffs. Or one of the caps near Wheal Catharine."

"Live in hope, Anna, live in hope." He hauls himself to his feet. "Come on, let's get going."

But now I can hear the sea, I do feel more hopeful. At least if we can get near the cliff face there may be enough of a phone signal. That's all we need. Just one tiny little signal to be able to call for help.

A short while further on, we reach a rock fall partially blocking the tunnel. Sebastian presses his boot against it, but it seems firm. Although it is almost thigh height, he scrambles over it. My world momentarily grows dark and my heart thuds, then Sebastian's face appears and he holds the light so I can see my way across. The rough tumble of stones rips my trousers, and I feel the warm stickiness of blood on my shins.

With every step the murmur of the waves becomes louder and the ceiling lower. Sebastian is bent almost double ahead of me and his swaying coat blocks off most of the light.

"Please ... I need my own candle. Surely we have enough?"

He turns and nods, angling his towards me. I fish in my pocket and in the flickering light straighten the wick. Our hands touch as the flame flares between them. His firm, mine trembling.

"I'm sorry," I tell him.

"So am I." He trudges on for a few steps then calls over his shoulder. "Serena sells these candles."

"She can't know you're down here."

"No."

It isn't long before the air changes. Not just the competing wafts of apple and lemon verbena but a hint of freshness from above. My candle gutters in what can only be a breeze. The wash of the waves is louder, coming from below.

Suddenly Sebastian stands upright and raises his candle above his head. I can see from the flickering light we're in some sort of cavern and I sink to the ground in relief, my legs shaking too much to hold me. I lean against the rock and watch as he explores, working methodically around, the light high and then low, as he looks for a means of escape.

I should be helping him. I lever myself up the wall. There has to be a way out — has to be. The light dips as Sebastian ducks down and picks up something. He looks at it for a moment and I walk towards him, stopping when he says, "No-one would ever find you here, would they?"

A chill runs through me. He takes a step closer and I can't read his look. All that's left of my candle is a tiny stub. With shaking hands I reach into my pocket to light another, but it falls to the floor with a soft rattle and goes out. The sea pounds, my skull pounds. I'm no longer sure which is which.

"Come on, I'll light it for you. Then we can take a proper look at this."

On the flat of his hand he holds a silver locket, tarnished by the years. The broken chain hangs over the edge of his palm. I pick it up and finger it, smooth and cool.

"I wonder…"

"It's hers."

"Hers?"

"The young woman I can't understand."

"How do you know?"

He shakes his head. "I just do." We stare at it for a few moments more, then he takes it from me and slips it into his pocket. "Come on, this isn't getting us out of here."

We find the continuation of the tunnel but it's been completely blocked, either by a fall or by human hand. The stones are packed so tightly we agree it's the latter. I try my phone but there is still no signal, so we search on.

There is an area of the cave where there is a definite draught and the sea sounds a little louder. We focus our attention here and behind an outcrop of rock find a narrow crevice. It's almost five feet up the wall and Sebastian holds his candle high so we can inspect it. It might be big enough or it might not. We look at each other, then Sebastian clears away a few fallen rocks so we can get closer to the cavern wall.

"Up on my shoulders, Anna." Sebastian hunkers down. "You're smaller than me."

"But how will you get up?"

"All we need is a phone signal. Stop wasting time."

I clamber onto his shoulders and slowly he stands, bracing himself against the wall. "It's bigger than it looks," I tell him. "Turn sideways, then I'll see if I can climb into it."

The answer is I can — quite easily, in fact. On my hands and knees I crawl away from the cavern, the air becoming fresher and colder until suddenly I am out in the starlit darkness. A different darkness; velvety, incomplete. I want to weep with relief.

I'm on a ledge on the cliffs. The moon reflects on the strip of sand below, the waves crashing as I gulp the salty air. With shaking hands I try my phone again, but there is no signal.

I crawl back towards the cavern. Sebastian is peering into the gap, holding his candle above his head.

"Still no sodding signal, but if you can get up you can get out," I tell him. "It's big enough."

"And where does it lead?"

"Somewhere on the cliff — there's quite a big ledge."

His voice is gruff. "Hold the candle." I edge back to give him space. His feet scrabble on the rock and he heaves himself up. His first few attempts are fruitless, but then he catapults forwards, his head almost landing in my lap. He struggles onto his hands and knees then crawls after me to safety.

Together we sit on the ledge, our backs to the cliff, drinking in the cold, sweet air.

"Do you know where we are?" I ask.

"All too well." There is a silence before he continues. "We're just around the headland from Porthnevek. The cliff's sheer above us. Sheer and unstable."

"So we'll need to find a way down."

"I can't go down, Anna."

"Why not? You've a good head for heights."

"I can't go down."

I am about to argue further, but I realise it could be purely academic. The first thing to do is work out if there is a way off the ledge. I flash the torch on my phone to our right, but the rock very soon becomes too narrow for safety. To our left it dips a little, and I crawl over Sebastian's legs to investigate.

A couple of feet below is a gully no more than a yard across. I lie on my stomach so I can take a better look. To one side of it are the remains of a path, narrow and precarious, but it winds down towards the beach until it meets a stack of rocks from a fall. If they're remotely stable, it should be a simple thing to climb down onto the sand. The moon has disappeared behind a cloud, but I can hear the waves and they sound closer. Time is against us — the tide has already turned.

I crawl back to Sebastian. "It's doable, but we'll need to help each other."

"I can't … the sea…"

"The sea's the problem — the tide's already turned. We may not have much time." And then I remember. "You're scared of the sea, aren't you?"

He nods.

"And why's that?"

"Why's anyone scared of anything, Anna? Why are you scared of going to sort out your mother's things?"

"That's different."

"No, it isn't. It's the memories — the memories being churned up. The damage and the hurt…"

I pick up his hand. "Memories can't kill us. A night on the cliff in this bitter wind or a rock fall could. Can you at least try? I'll look after you … no, we'll look after each other. It's not safe to attempt it alone, although I will if I have to."

He grasps my fingers tightly. "I can't let you do that. This place … it can't take you as well."

"Then you'll come?"

"I have no choice."

I loosen my grip and crawl back along the ledge. There is just enough moonlight to see what we're doing, but I flash the torch to show him the way. "We need to drop into the gully then use it to brace downwards towards the path."

"I'll go first," he says. "My height will be an advantage."

I watch him lower himself and a scatter of small stones dislodges, but no sooner than he's in the gully his feet reach the track. Once he's stable, he tells me to follow. As soon as I am over the ledge I feel his hands guiding me, his arms closing around me to bring me to safety.

He releases me and indicates I should go first with the torch. I point it at my feet and clinging to the rock wall I edge along, sweat pouring from me and dripping into my eyes. It's far narrower than I thought, and suddenly the beach seems a long way below. But inch by inch we make our way downwards until we're at the top of the rock fall.

I pause to consider our best option. Behind me, Sebastian is shivering. The cold's beginning to get to me too, so I drop to my knees and begin to crawl down backwards. A few of the rocks shift beneath me but mercifully they hold, and finally my feet find the softness of sand. As Sebastian begins his descent I take off my ruined shoes, hoping the damp chill will give my soles some respite from the throbbing.

I turn to look at the sea. The waves are licking perilously close to the headland. Sebastian is inching down the rocks, but I dare not tell him to hurry. He's heavier than I am and one false move could be disastrous. I can hear his breathing becoming more laboured as he approaches, then with a final rattle of stones he's on the sand.

I grab his hand. "Right — run!" For a moment I think he's going to resist, but my momentum drags him forwards and soon we are both racing across the beach, one moment soft, one moment firm beneath our feet. By the time we reach the headland we are flirting with the waves, spray soaking our trousers as we hurl ourselves onwards, the lights of Porthnevek tantalisingly just around the corner.

CHAPTER FORTY-ONE

Sebastian drops to his haunches on the soft sand above the tidal reach, shaking from head to toe. I crouch next to him and wrap my arm around his shoulders. "You did it — you did it." He buries his head in my chest, his hair damp with salt.

There are lights on in the bar behind us and a gentle throb of music as the door opens and closes, then the wash of the waves takes over again. I am beginning to ache in places I didn't know could ache, and the cuts on my legs and feet are stinging like hell. But now we are safe I don't want to move until Sebastian is ready.

Eventually he looks up. "It was here. Here on this beach."

"What was?" My voice is a whisper.

"My dad drowned."

I pull him closer. "Oh, Sebastian. I'm so sorry."

He struggles free then stands. "I don't deserve your sympathy. Ask anyone around here — it was my fault."

"But…"

His voice is terse. "We should go back to my place. Get warm and dry."

Nevek Cot is nearer, but it doesn't seem the moment to argue.

Somehow I manage to force my feet back into my shoes, and rather than cut through the village we take the path out onto the cliffs and back again. As we reach the chalets Sebastian wraps me into his coat so in the darkness I am part of his shadow, and together we thread our way through the parked cars and up the steps to his house.

It is only slightly warmer inside than out. I stand and shiver while he disappears up the open staircase and returns with a towel, a thick jumper and pair of khaki shorts.

"Best I can do," he mutters. "Bathroom's through the kitchen — there should be hot water for you to shower. I'll light the wood burner."

The shower is little more than a trickle, but it's enough to wash away the sweat and spray and to clean the dirt from my knees and feet. Afterwards I sit on the toilet seat with the towel wrapped around me, replaying the events of the evening, but they hardly seem real. How the hell did all that happen to me?

While Sebastian is in the bathroom, I boil the kettle to make some tea and hunt around the kitchen for something to eat. Even now he has some money, his cupboards are heart-wrenchingly bare. No wonder he's so thin. But there's bread, some cans of baked beans and a packet of bacon, so we won't have to starve. Not that I can actually face food at the moment. I sit as close as I can to the burner and wait for him.

When he emerges, the skin above his beard is paler than I have ever seen. I tell him the kettle's boiled, and he makes the tea then settles into his chair.

"Are you all right, Sebastian?"

He nods without conviction. "Your feet are a right old mess, though, and your knees. Need some salt water." He puts down his mug and returns to the kitchen area. I continue to gaze at the fire as the tap gushes and the kettle boils.

He sets a washing up bowl full of water in front of me. "Stick them in there. It'll sting at first, but it's best in the long run. Wash some up onto the cuts on your legs too. Like this." He cups water in his hand and closes it over my knee, and even though it almost scalds me, his skin feels cold against mine.

I look down at him. "I'm so sorry. Dragging you into this…"

"I'll live. My nephew's autistic. He relies on his mum. He needs her."

I return to watching the flames. "When did you realise Serena was involved?"

"When I saw the candles."

"And you were surprised?"

"Some things … fell into place. But I was in denial. Even after I found them, I suppose. But we had a lot of time to think down there."

"What do you want me to do?"

"You must do what you feel you have to."

But what is that? Could there be a bigger prize at stake here? Something worth gambling on for the sake of Wheal Dream? For my own sake, even?

The sting has gone from the hot water and it's starting to soothe my feet. I bend and wash some over my knees.

"You're going to struggle to walk tomorrow," Sebastian says.

"We're both going to be stiff as boards."

"Like a couple of old codgers."

We watch the flames some more.

"Sebastian, do you think there's any chance that if I didn't go to the police, Serena and her friends would drop the protests? I can't lie — it's going to be tough for me if they carry on when our guests arrive. They … they could take most of the stuff away, but I'd want some left down there when we seal the cap. Kind of as an insurance policy."

"You can trust Serena."

"Can I? Can you?"

"You can trust her because I'll never speak to her again if she breaks her word — and I mean it."

I close my eyes and whisper my thanks. Sebastian grunts.

We sit in silence for the longest time, and I'm almost asleep when he says, "Kip down on my bed for a while. I'll go to see Serena."

"It must be the middle of the night."

"I reckon under the circumstances she'll be awake. And she needs to know about your offer."

"But won't they just go up there, clear it all out?"

"You have to trust me. Anyway, it would be hard to eradicate every trace — and you've got that photo." He places his hand on my shoulder. "Go to sleep, Anna, and leave this to me."

CHAPTER FORTY-TWO

The moment I put my feet on the rug next morning, I realise Sebastian was right — it is going to be hard to do more than hobble. The soles of my shoes were almost in threads and my feet are cut from the roughness of the cavern floor, my heels and toes a mass of blisters. It's all I can do not to gasp in agony, but the house is silent and if Sebastian is back, I don't want to disturb him.

I peep down the stairs to see him dozing in his chair. The wood burner's gone out and his hand trails onto the threadbare carpet. Long, clever fingers; those incredible eyes, hidden behind almost translucent lids; and the kindest, truest heart... I stop and gaze at him as it slowly dawns on me that my feelings for him have taken something of a seismic shift, seemingly overnight.

He opens his eyes and glances upwards.

"Your turn for the bed," I say.

He stretches, rubs his arms. "There'll be time for that later."

I grip the rail and totter down a couple of steps, forcing my errant thoughts back to practicalities. "What did Serena say?"

"She wants to talk to you."

"Bloody great." The pain from my feet is shooting up my legs, but I continue my descent. "I think I need to soak these again."

"Yes. And they probably need a proper dressing. Make sure they don't get infected."

I lower myself into the other chair. Resting on its arm is the locket we found in the cavern. "We forgot about this last night," I say.

"Yes." Sebastian busies himself with the kettle.

I turn the necklace over in my hand, the chain slipping through my fingers. The locket itself is a plain silver oval and I feel for the catch. It springs open to reveal two curls of hair; one deep brown and the other white with age.

He peers over my shoulder. "That's what lockets are for. It's how they got their name. From locks of hair."

I nod and close it again. On the back is an inscription. I angle it to the light streaming in through the window to read it. A single word. *Thérèse*. It tugs at my memory and I feel myself frowning. Sebastian walks away as the kettle boils.

And then, it falls into place. A series of connections too wild to even imagine they'd be linked. As he places the bowl of water at my feet, I ask, "Could you have not been able to understand the grey lady because she was speaking French?"

His eyebrows shoot up. "Why the hell didn't I realise it was a foreign language? Of course, that could well be it. Why?"

"Her name was Thérèse. And I think… This is going to sound so strange… I think she was a lady's maid at Trelissick in Regency times. I … I played her part in the Christmas pageants we had. I wore a grey dress and cloak, although I expect a lot of servants did. I could be completely wrong… I mean … what would her locket be doing down a mine shaft? It's crazy."

"Not crazy; coincidence, serendipity … fate. It happens like that sometimes, Anna. Sometimes everything just fits." He sets the bowl of water at my feet and looks up at me.

Do we fit? I think. I want to say it, but I dare not. Instead I lean forwards and wrap my arms around his shoulders, my cheek resting against the softness of his beard. He runs his hands over my back; slowly, sensually, and I turn my head, ready to kiss him, but as our lips meet he pulls away.

"Don't think I don't want to, Anna, but it wouldn't be a good idea. You're far too precious to me."

"But that doesn't make sense."

He grips my hands. "It does. You know how I am. I can't hold down a relationship any more than I can a job. Oh, we might be all right for a few months, but come January … no-one's ever survived a January with me."

"But you said it yourself — I know how you are. I've seen it. And now I know the reason too. I'd be going in with my eyes wide open…"

"Anna, no. Now, get your feet into that water before it's too cold to do any good. I'm going to catch up on some sleep."

It's early afternoon by the time I make it to the portacabin, properly washed and dressed, my feet swathed in thick socks inside my wellies, the only footwear I can bear to put on. The sun is shining, the workmen whistling and my inbox full of emails.

I've been at my desk for about an hour when Serena appears at the open door, climbs the steps and closes it behind her.

"Where's Sebastian?" I ask her.

"He thinks I'm coming at four, but I wanted to talk to you alone."

I nod. "Sit down. I'll just finish this off so you'll have my full attention." Maybe she knows I'm buying time. Buying time to think, and to activate the voice recorder on my laptop. After a few minutes, I push it to one side so we are face to face. "Okay."

"I'm truly sorry for what happened last night. The person who saw you go down panicked. They didn't tell me for hours, and by then you'd disappeared. I was about to call some cave rescue guys I know when Sebastian showed up."

"He told you what I'm offering?"

"Yes, but I can barely believe it. Why would you do that?"

I sit back in my chair. "First, is it just cigarettes or are there drugs involved too?"

She snorts. "What do you take me for? I'm a mother of teenagers."

"So that's a no?"

"Of course it is." She folds her arms and some of the old feisty Serena reappears.

"Right. My reasons. Firstly, the protests are a pain in the neck and I want them to stop."

"They'd stop all right if there were police crawling all over the place."

"You almost sound as though you want that to happen."

"Of course I don't..."

"Well then." Combative or not, she can't look me in the eye. I carry on. "I also want our visitors to be welcomed in the village. I know it's too much to ask that for myself, but tolerated at least would be good. It's a pain having to drive to St Pirans when I want a pint of milk."

"Yes, I get that." Her voice is slow. "But you see now, don't you? See why we had to protect the valley? We rely on the extra money through the winter — life here's tough."

"I've seen that too. This isn't picture postcard Cornwall, however beautiful the scenery. But I'm sure the glampers will spend a small fortune if everyone's nice to them."

"That remains to be seen." She buries her chin in the collar of her coat, and finally she asks, "So are those your only reasons? Nothing to do with Sebastian?"

Her question catches me off guard, but I shake my head. "Not Sebastian, but something he said. About your son being autistic. Why hurt him too when I can see a way around this?"

When she finally looks up, there are tears in her eyes. "I'll talk to the others, see what I can do. To be honest, it's all been a bit of a strain. Matt's had a tough term at school, and what with everything else…"

I sit silently while she composes herself. I can't bring myself to step around the desk to comfort her — that would be a bridge too far — but maybe we have a beginning.

I hobble after Ray to the smokers' shelter outside The Tinners' side door.

"What's with you, Hop-along?" he grins. "Taken up fags to dull the pain?"

"I want to ask you something."

He lights his roll-up, shielding it from the wind. "That sounds ominous."

"No, it's about Sebastian. I had a feeling a while back you were going to say why he gets so low in January. He told me about his dad drowning, that it was his fault, but…"

"No way was it his fault. Far from it, in fact. And I should know — I was bloody there."

"You said … you were children when it happened."

"Yeah. Let me think; I was in the first year of junior school and Gun's a year younger. We're talking forty years ago, but there are some things you never forget." He takes a long drag. "It was January. Dry day, though, sunny, so we were playing football on the beach. Then along comes Gun's old man, drunk as a skunk as usual. They closed the pubs in the afternoons back then, so he'd probably been thrown out.

"He tried to join in with us but he was too pissed to kick the ball, then all of a sudden he asked who was up for a swim. Some of the older boys told him not to be so stupid, and he staggered off down the beach. We never thought he'd do it,

261

but next thing we knew he was wading in. Well, Gun just belted after him, trying to get him out. He was six, remember, trying to rescue this huge drunken shit of a man. Luckily a couple of experienced surfers were walking their dog and they managed to get Gun out, although he was only semi-conscious at the time. I've never been so scared in my life. I don't think his old man's body ever did wash up."

"God, how awful."

"Not Gun's fault, though. No way. But his mum fell to pieces and he and Serena were sent to live with their grandparents in Redruth for quite a while, so maybe ... who knows what kids think."

I follow him back inside to finish my orange juice, but my heart isn't in the drink, the chat or the crossword, so I limp back to the car park. I sit there for a long time, keys dangling from the ignition, pondering on how a moment of adult stupidity can blight a child's whole life. But if Sebastian has been blaming himself for his father's death for forty years, how the hell can I convince him he's wrong? A tear rolls down my cheek. I'm desperate to do it. Not just for him, but for me.

PART EIGHT: 1816

CHAPTER FORTY-THREE

The footman presented Mrs Daniell with a letter on a silver salver. "This arrived not twenty minutes since, Madam."

She looked at her husband before running her fingernail along the fold to open it. "It is from Lieutenant Colonel Gosset — it must be news of Gertrude's confinement."

He looked over her shoulder as they read it together, the words blurring in front of her eyes. She clutched at Mr Daniell's hand. "I must go to her, and quickly."

"Indeed you must, my dear, if she is so ill. But at least the baby thrives. What of Mary, my love? Should she stay here in the schoolroom or accompany me back to Truro and remain in Lizzie's care? Or indeed travel with you to London?"

"I cannot take her to what might be her sister's deathbed."

"I pray it will not come to that. But surely she can be useful in some way, and a trip would prove an excellent distraction. Captain Gilbert will not be transferred for some weeks and it would place her well away from temptation."

"I think it better she remain here with Miss Grafton, but we must at least tell her the news. Thérèse!" Mrs Daniell turned to her. "We must leave for London without delay. Gertrude has been delivered of another daughter, but the birth has left her with a dangerous fever."

"You are very pale, Madame; perhaps first you should rest a little." Thérèse ran to fetch Mrs Daniell's lavender.

"Ah, Thérèse, just dab a little on my temples then please fetch Mary."

"Is she to accompany us, Madame?"

Mrs Daniell frowned. "Of course not. This is not a pleasure trip."

Thérèse blushed deeply. "Oh, Madame, I know it is not my place to speak, but I think perhaps she should."

"Well, I disagree. She is best left here with Miss Grafton."

"But Madame…"

"Has something happened, Thérèse?" Mr Daniell asked.

She shook her head from side to side. "Perhaps. I don't know … I can't be sure … but while I was walking just now, I saw a man who looked very much like Captain Gilbert, except he was in a dark cloak and not a uniform."

"Damn the man! How dare he?"

"Monsieur … I could not be certain … maybe I was mistaken."

"Where was he?"

"On the path through the woods, just downstream of the lane."

Mr Daniell straightened. "Very well. I will take my gamekeeper and his dogs to hunt him down. And Mary will accompany you at least as far as Truro. If we cannot find the scoundrel, then maybe even to London." He turned to Mrs Daniell. "I am sorry, my dear, but in view of what Thérèse has said it is the only way. Now please rest while Thérèse packs. I beg of you, overnight in town so we can consider what is best for Mary and have a little time together before you leave. I will send two coachmen and two armed men with you, so if you wish you can travel day and night until you get there."

Mrs Daniell clutched his hand. "You cannot accompany us?"

"Sadly I have business here. But my heart will be with you every last mile."

It was almost dusk when the carriage arrived in front of the Daniells' Truro mansion, and Thérèse felt exhausted and sick. After the upset of the morning, even such a short journey had unsettled her stomach, and she was already dreading the long days — and possibly nights — on the road.

Mary was sent straight to her room, and Thérèse accompanied Mrs Daniell upstairs to complete the packing while her mistress took tea. Dresses suitable for a visit to London needed to be selected and brushed before being folded into a trunk with matching shoes and shawls.

By the time the task was complete, Thérèse felt more herself and ready to help Mrs Daniell dress for dinner.

"It will be *en famille*, naturally, but I think I should wear the lilac dress as it is Ralph's favourite. And, of course, the amethyst necklace he gave me for my birthday last year."

Thérèse looked around her. "Madame, the jewellery roll has not been brought up from the carriage. It must have been overlooked as it was hidden in one of the hat boxes. Shall I fetch it when I go downstairs for the hot water?"

"Please, Thérèse. It should not be left in the stables overnight in any event. Even if there is nothing of particular monetary value, a great many of the pieces were gifts from Ralph and I should not wish to lose them."

Thérèse took a lamp from the kitchen and made her way into the garden. The moon hung above the harbour, almost full, and together with the lamp cast eerie shadows under the trees. Before she had thought the garden secure, but Captain Gilbert's words about how easily the stable boy was bought were making her nervous. Mr Daniell's search party had come back empty-handed, although she was certain the captain would have known he was being hunted down. And who was to blame for this turn of events.

She almost ran to the stable entrance, which was closed by night, and leant against the wooden door. If only she had some way of warning Coates. If he returned by next Sunday he might wait for her, and she would not be here. The perfidious stable boy would surely tell the captain and the excise men would pounce. Did she have enough money to pay the lad off? Certainly, she had coins in her reticule, but she knew not the cost of silence. Or how to ask for it in this foreign tongue. She fingered the locket around her neck, wondering what Paul would do.

Enough. She could not keep Mrs Daniell waiting. She opened the door into the yard, the sweet smell of hay greeting her. The boy emerged from the shadows.

"Mam'selle Thérèse?"

"I need the hatbox. In the coach."

"I will find it for you."

She shook her head. "No. I know where it is."

"Very well." He walked ahead and opened the double doors to the carriage house. The hatboxes were lined up on the seat inside and she selected the medium-sized one and tucked it under her arm.

Her heart was in her throat, filling it almost too much to speak. "Monsieur Coates. Did you see him?"

The boy nodded. "This morning."

"Where is he, please? Do you know?"

He pointed towards a spot on the harbour, close to where a ketch was moored, and grinned, saying something she did not understand.

She shook her head and took a coin from her reticule, holding it up. "Where is he? Now."

He took her outside onto the wharf and pointed to Lander's Inn at the far end of Quay Street. She understood. She gave

267

him the coin and then took out another, putting her finger to her lips. He nodded, and pocketing both of them he went back about his work, whistling.

What could she do? What should she do? Thérèse merely picked at her supper in the kitchen, drawing sympathetic looks from Mrs Leigh, who took it to be apprehension over the long coach journey. She had already given her a vial of peppermint oil to soothe her stomach and now advised her to rest until Mrs Daniell called for her to be made ready for bed.

Instead, Thérèse indicated she needed fresh air and took her cloak to go into the garden. There was a wrought iron seat just outside the arc of light that shone from the butler's pantry and she sat there for a while, trying to pluck up the courage for what she knew she must do.

There was no doubt in her mind she had to warn Coates. Even had they not been leaving for London with the dawn, tomorrow may be too late. But for a woman to enter an inn alone was a difficult thing, and this was not the welcoming hearth and kindly landlord at Porthnevek. This was a town establishment, likely full of sailors — possibly even soldiers. What if she went inside and could not see Coates? If he had taken a room, would he not dine in it? Or perhaps he would be about his business elsewhere.

But find him she must. She rocked forwards, clutching her arms around her body. It was nothing to do with any feelings she may or may not have for Coates, it was her duty. He had been good to her, and she owed him this at least.

She had to act before she was needed by Mrs Daniell. She stood and brushed down her dress and cloak. The lamp trembled in her hand as she threaded a path through the trees towards the stable gate. For once the boy was nowhere to be seen, but she felt his eyes on her all the same. He would surely interpret her actions badly, but would he keep his silence? Or would that cost more pennies from her purse?

Lemon Quay was quiet as she made her way past the ketch anchored opposite the stables then turned up past the green. At the side of Lander's Inn was a door marked 'parlour' and she opened it and stepped inside.

The room was small and cosy with a red rug in the centre of the wooden floor. An elderly couple were dining near the fireplace, the man's cheeks flushed beneath his powdered wig. A clergyman sat alone in the corner with his pipe and a glass of wine in front of him, but he did not look up from his book as Thérèse entered.

There was a small bell on a side table and she rang it, her heart thudding as she waited. Before long a maid came, a round-faced woman in her middle years, her dark hair scraped back under a mob cap.

"I have a message for Coates," said Thérèse.

The maid told her to wait and then disappeared down a darkened passage, closing the door behind her.

Each minute seemed interminable. The cleric's pipe smoke mingled with the aroma of roast beef, the clatter of cutlery drowned by noisy conversation from the room next door. Thérèse stood with her eyes cast down, wishing herself anywhere but here.

The door to the passageway opened and after a moment the woman beckoned to Thérèse. As she looked she could see Coates standing behind her, and she started to tremble with relief. Just two steps and she could tell him, then return to the safety of the Daniells' mansion with a clear conscience.

Once the door to the parlour closed behind them, Coates spoke. "My dear Mam'selle Thérèse, what brings you here?"

"I must warn you…"

"But you're shaking." He turned to the serving woman. "Please bring some wine to my room. The lady is unwell and needs reviving."

With his hand beneath her elbow, he led her up the stairs to a room at the front of the inn. The four poster bed was richly curtained and there were two chairs in front of the fire. He settled her into one before sitting down opposite.

"Please excuse this intimacy," he said, "but it is better we meet in private."

"Indeed, Monsieur Coates. I would not have come had the matter not been urgent."

"And how did you find me?"

"The stable lad." A smile fluttered across Coates's face. "But he is not to be trusted," Thérèse continued.

"I pay him well."

"There is someone who threatens to pay him better."

There was a knock on the door and Thérèse jumped, but it was only the maid carrying a tray with two glasses and a bottle of wine. Coates thanked her then poured Thérèse a drink.

"Your good health, Mam'selle."

"Your safety, Monsieur."

"My safety means that much to you?"

Unable to meet his gaze, Thérèse looked into the fire. Eventually, she said, "Your safety is a matter of urgency, Monsieur Coates."

"For what reason?"

And so Thérèse told him; about Mrs Daniell's refusal to receive Captain Gilbert, of Mary's assignation in the garden and their sudden removal to Trelissick because of it, coming last to the captain's threats of this morning.

"Then he knows of our friendship," Coates murmured. "Who else, I wonder, for he cannot be alone. Miss Mary, perhaps?"

"She has said nothing to me…"

"The foolish girl may be too wrapped in her own sorrow to see its worth. But worth it has, make no mistake, Mam'selle Thérèse. Despite my best intentions, I fear I have compromised you."

"It matters not. Tomorrow at dawn I leave for London with Madame. Her daughter there is gravely ill, so we may be gone for some weeks. No Truro gossip can reach us there."

"And I will not be able to reach you either." He poured her another glass of wine. "Thérèse, in all this time you have not asked for news of Paul."

She gave a small smile. "Sometimes it is better to travel in hope than to arrive."

"But if I had news, would you wish to know it?"

Thérèse's heart stilled in her chest. "Good news or bad?"

"Both." He was gazing at her intently. "You are ready, Mam'selle?" She nodded, swallowing hard. "Paul is alive —" Thérèse clutched her glass tightly to her, spilling wine on her dress — "but he is a sick man. He needs you to care for him, Thérèse. He needs you more than Mrs Daniell does. I am sorry. I would have found a way to break this to you more gently, but in view of Gilbert's threats we have no time. We must leave tonight."

Thérèse's voice shook. "Leave, Monsieur?"

"It is a good moon. I will have them ready my horse and we can be away within the hour to find a safe place closer to the harbour at St Pirans. Then as soon as we can, we will sail for Roscoff."

"But Monsieur Coates, I cannot... Madame Daniell..." Thérèse choked back a sob.

He took her glass from her and held both her hands. "The wine is making you emotional, clouding your judgment. You have already warned me of danger, so I must flee. I may not be able to return for many months, and in that time who is to care for Paul? You often speak of duty, my dear Thérèse, and it seems to me your duty is clear."

She stood up and the room shifted slightly. "I must return to the house and explain."

"You cannot. If Gilbert already has the excise men waiting, they will follow you when you return to the inn and I will be done for." Tears spilled down her cheeks and Coates turned away. "Fear not. I will ask for paper and ink so you can write a note to be delivered an hour or so after we leave. We should be a safe distance from Truro by then, and if perhaps you hint we sail from Falmouth, should they try to follow they will be on the wrong trail."

Eventually Thérèse nodded. "There is much sense in what you say, Monsieur."

"Trust me, Mam'selle. That is all I ask." His eyes burned coal-black into hers, but she had to turn away.

CHAPTER FOURTY-FOUR

Coates's horse Blaze walked quietly along the quay then turned up Lemon Street. Thérèse, balancing uncomfortably in front of him, was hidden in the folds of an old-fashioned cloak he wore over his coat, the wine and the scent of his sweat having a strange and unnerving effect on her.

"It is as well you are small, Mam'selle," he had told her as he'd climbed up behind her in the inn yard. "But you need only stay hidden until we leave the town. All the same, we will travel first by the Falmouth road to lay a false trail."

"Monsieur, you frighten me." She stifled a sob and he bent his head so his chin rested on the soft fabric of her mob cap.

"We must take every precaution, that is all. I will keep you safe, I promise."

But her tears were for Mrs Daniell and for all she was leaving behind. It would not be long before she was missed, and there would be panic until the note arrived. Then anger and recriminations that she could leave her mistress at such a time. After all the kindness shown to her, Thérèse felt sure her heart would break. But Coates was right — her duty was to Paul, and her letter would explain.

Before long the horse turned from the cobbled street onto a track. The sounds of the town faded and she peeped from the folds of the cloak, glad to breathe fresh air. Coates shook his head. "A little longer, Mam'selle, for we will shortly pass through Higher Town, but then we will be on the open road and free."

She covered her face again and leant further into his warmth. Never had she been so intimate with a man, and the comfort in it surprised her. This close to him, with his arms either side of her holding the reins, she did indeed feel safe. And he was taking her back to Paul. She just wished her heart felt gladder at the news, but she supposed it was the shock. Maybe it wouldn't do to think too much at the moment, because above all her duty was clear.

Coates was good to his word, and past Higher Town he pulled the cloak away from her head so she could see. He upped the horse's pace to a trot, the moon flitting between the clouds, lighting the desolate moorland around them.

Suddenly Coates pulled the horse to a halt, listening intently. In the distance behind them were hoofbeats, fast and insistent. Coates swore then urged Blaze into a furious gallop, reins in one hand and the other across Thérèse's chest as he bent forwards over her.

"If we can get ahead," he gasped, "there is another way ... along the stream ... we can lose them ... but we must get ahead. Damn this moon!"

Instinctively Thérèse dropped to the horse's haunches and clung to its mane, giving Coates full control of the bridle again. "Good girl," he whispered, "clever, brave girl." She could not tell if he was speaking to her or to his mount, and she closed her eyes to the sheer terror of the earth flashing beneath them.

The horse veered to the left and started to descend into a gully. Now there were trees on either side, but the shouts of the excise men were still behind them. For a moment or two the thundering hooves stopped, allowing them to gain a little ground, but then they heard a scatter of stones as their pursuers headed into the valley too.

They were splashing through water now, the spray stinging Thérèse's cheeks. Coates's voice was close in her ear. "When we escape, they may bring hounds. But this way they will lose the scent." Thérèse shuddered. To be hunted down like a deer or a hare … was this Coates's life? A part of it he'd hidden from her? What had she agreed to?

Another sharp turn and they were threading upwards between trees, their pace slowed to a walk. The noise of the men was behind them now, still in the valley, and Thérèse felt her heartbeat slow.

"We are not safe yet, Mam'selle, simply a little safer. But I know a place we can hide close by."

Once they were out of the wood Thérèse sat up. The terrain had flattened into high moorland and to their left she could see a mine chimney and engine house. There was something familiar about them, but it wasn't until she saw another mine ahead that she knew where they were.

"It's Porthnevek," she exclaimed.

"And Wheal Nevek will be our hiding place."

"Wheal Nevek? But it is closed off…"

"Which makes it perfect. I can hide Blaze in the outbuildings and we will go below and make our way towards the sea."

"Below? You mean, into the mine?"

"I know it well. I told you I worked there with my father when I was a lad."

A deep unease stirred within her, but she slapped it down. This was no time to doubt him, for now he was all she had.

Underground the blackness was intense. Only the distant crash of waves beating against the cliffs gave Thérèse any sense of where she was. She put out her hand, the rock damp beneath it, the roughness of its cut scraping her fingers as she traced an arc above her head.

Something was scurrying behind her. A breath of fur touched her ankles and she stifled a scream. She must be braver than this. She closed her eyes and pictured the gleaming expanse of ocean that lay ahead — with Paul on the other side of it.

A light flared in front of her — Coates's face in profile as he bent over a stub of candle, her guide in this strange subterranean world. The flame settled and she stepped forwards into the circle of light.

He scooped more scraps of candle from the floor and placed them in her hand, closing his fist around hers. "Follow me," he said, before turning away.

The flame climbed the walls ahead of him, quartz sparkling in the bouncing light. It circled him with a halo, like some strange angel in this place without stars and sky. A shiver ran through her from head to toe, and she forced her mind back to the sea. She paused for a moment to listen for it. Yes, it was there. Very faintly, but she was sure she could hear it.

She had no way of measuring distance except by the echo of the waves. The tunnel narrowed where a tumble of rocks spewed from the wall. Coates tested it with his boot. "It is solid enough," he said and clambered over. Darkness closed around Thérèse.

"Pass me a candle."

She reached out and he touched the ends of her fingers as he took it. A rustle of the fabric of his coat. A flare. And once again they had light.

He held the stub high and Thérèse scrambled over the rocks, their sharpness digging into her palms as she steadied herself. What if there was another fall? Panic clasped at her chest, but she knew she must not allow it to take hold. Therein lay the path to madness.

Time stretched as they edged forwards. Coates's silence seemed to become increasingly heavy, as if his words were being crushed by the weight of stone above. Perhaps he was concentrating, navigating them through this unfamiliar land. Or perhaps he was remembering the flood that had killed his brother.

The roof lowered after a while and they had to stoop. Coates bent over the candle, the flickers behind him dim. Thérèse wanted to ask him to light a stub for her, but she dared not. Something about his manner made her cautious. And every last scrap might be needed to take them to the end of their journey.

Thérèse's shoulders were hunched, her back aching, but she knew it must be much worse for Coates with his height. She considered crawling, but the floor was too rough so she repeated to herself over and over to keep moving. And to trust him.

All of a sudden, Coates was upright in front of her. He held the candle above his head and it failed to reach the furthest corners of the cavern. For the first time, his mouth curved into a smile. Thérèse leant against the wall and straightened her spine.

"What is this place?" Water was trickling somewhere to her left, its music almost lost in the wash of the waves below. Below. Not distant. Not above. Below. Her heart sang a silent prayer of thanks.

Coates walked the perimeter, tracing the walls with the light, a curious zigzag up and down, up and down. She sank onto her haunches as she watched him. The flame guttered.

"Bring me another candle."

She followed the last flickers across the floor, then darkness closed around them. She stopped. "Monsieur Coates, where are you?"

Footsteps. His breath warm in her ear. "No-one would ever find you here, would they?" he whispered.

She shivered. "What do you mean?"

"Only that we are safe. And we should rest for a while. I have a little brandy in my flask to warm you."

"No, thank you, Monsieur. I will rest but am not sure I shall sleep, however tired I am."

He held out his hand and grasped hers through the darkness. "Let us save a candle." He led her slowly until they reached the wall of the cavern. She heard a rustle of fabric as he unbundled the cloak he'd been carrying. "The floor is dirty and rough, but I can at least offer you some warmth." He wrapped it around her and lowered them both onto the surface of the rock, propping himself against the wall. "You will have to take my legs for a pillow, I'm afraid."

"Monsieur, it is not proper."

"None of this is proper, Thérèse, but needs must."

"But you ... you will be cold if I have the extra cloak."

"If you are safe and warm, that is enough for me."

CHAPTER FORTY-FIVE

Despite her words Thérèse did sleep, albeit fitfully, and when she woke, she was aware of a pale grey light filtering into the cave.

She sat up abruptly. "Monsieur, Monsieur ... look!"

"I know. I have been watching the dawn. And watching you sleep."

To cover her embarrassment, Thérèse leapt to her feet. "There is a gap in the rock — like a window."

"Exactly like a window, to give us light and air. I do not remember it, but maybe there has been some sort of collapse in the cliff. It's high up, though; we should still be secure."

"I am very thankful."

Coates stood too, brushing down his breeches. "I must go back to water Blaze and to find us some food. You must be hungry."

"A little. More thirsty, but last night I heard water somewhere in the cavern."

"Have a care, Thérèse; take some if you must, but it likely carries traces of poisons. I will bring us something to drink as well."

"I cannot come with you?"

"It is better not to — you would draw too much attention. Remember I am known here, and alone I can slip unseen into the houses of friends."

"You have no family?"

He turned away and spat on the floor. "My mother's back broken by labouring on the bal, my brother killed in one of these very shafts and my father dead trying to escape the threat of the asylum, with a price on his head put there by interfering..." He passed his hand over his eyes. "I may have found myself capable of love, Thérèse, but I have no reason to love mine owners."

Her breath caught in her throat. What could he mean? All she could do was shake her head and tell him she was sorry.

"It is not your fault. Being here makes me think of them, and it makes me angry. Try to rest some more while I am gone. After we have breakfasted, I will ride over the cliffs to St Pirans and secure our passage."

He bent to pick up some stubs of candle, and Thérèse watched him disappear into the blackness at the far end of the cave. His footsteps stopped and she heard the rasp of his tinder, a flare illuminating his profile for a moment until the candle was lit and he turned away.

At first she explored the parts of the cavern where the light permeated. She found the trickle of water running down the wall, but it had a blueish tinge and she was not so desperate as to risk sickness. The rocks nearest the gap were covered in dried bird droppings; perhaps there had been a nest here last summer, but its occupants were long gone.

She gazed up at the source of the light. The narrow crevice was half hidden behind an outcrop of rock, and its lowest point was almost level with her eyes. Although it was little more than a crack, if she stood in the right position and angled her head she could see the sky, distant and a clear pale blue. She was not sure how such a tiny sliver of the outside world could make this place bearable but it did, and after a while she went to fetch the cloak so she could sit closer to it.

It was as she was folding it into a makeshift cushion the letter fell out of a hidden pocket. She knew it immediately — the creases in the inn's cheap paper, her own handwriting. But how? She had seen Coates pass it to the groom with her own eyes, heard him give instructions, although of course she'd been unable to understand them.

She sat down with a thump. Could he have made a mistake? Handed the man another letter in error? But what letter? No. Far more likely this was deliberate, but why? Why? And worse, now Mrs Daniell would never read her carefully composed words of apology and thanks, would always think her ungrateful. Her sobs began to echo around the cave.

She had to pull herself together, to think. Coates was her protector, her friend. Why had he exchanged the letters? Again she came back to it being a mistake on his part, but that seemed uncharacteristically careless. Neither option rang true, but the fact of the matter was she held the evidence in her hand.

Thérèse heard a distant scuffling in the darker part of the cave and the hairs on the back of her neck stood on end. But slowly the sound became footsteps and a flicker of candlelight appeared, behind it a smiling Coates, carrying a flagon of ale and with a bulky bundle strapped over his chest.

"Breakfast, Mam'selle," he said with a small bow, before setting the ale at her feet and blowing out the candle. "I see you have moved nearer the light. That is very wise, if a little draughty."

She held up the letter with a shaking hand. "Monsieur, have you played me false, or is this some mistake?"

He crouched next to her, unwrapping the bundle. "I am sorry, but it had to be done."

"But why? You cheated me! I even saw you give the groom a note."

He sat on the floor and pulled a hunk of bread from the loaf. "Thérèse, hear me out. You are right to be angry, but I have acted in your best interests, I assure you."

"How can this be?"

"You will need money. To be honest, we will both need money. Perhaps, if all goes well, I will not return to Cornwall but make my home in Roscoff. And if all goes awry, I may not be able to return." He shrugged. "It is of little matter; with my father gone, there is no-one to detain me here."

"But I do not understand... I saw you give a letter to the groom."

"There have been kidnappings recently, or at least, rumours of kidnappings. So I have simply asked the very rich Mrs Daniell for a ransom for the return of her devoted Thérèse. A ransom she will surely pay. But regretfully I will not be keeping my side of the bargain."

Thérèse's mouth opened, but shock choked back her words. Coates shrugged. "She can afford it. The price of one of her dresses would keep us for months, but of course I have asked for a little more than that."

"But she will be frightened for my life! She is a dear, dear, lady — how could you do this to her?"

"She is a rich, rich lady. And she will forget you as soon as she finds another maid."

"No!" Thérèse jumped to her feet.

"It is the way of the world, Thérèse. But perhaps the fact you are so unworldly matters not now you are under my protection."

"I do not want your protection!"

"Then do you at least want my ale? My bread, my cheese?"

She stamped her foot. "I want nothing."

"Thérèse, please…"

"You will take me back to her. Or to the inn at Porthnevek, where I am known and they can send word."

Although she had her back to him, she heard him stand and walk over to where she stood. She wrapped her shawl more tightly around her, shaking.

"And what of Paul?" he whispered, close in her ear. "Would you leave him to die alone in a gutter?"

"How do I know you're not lying about that as well?"

"You don't. I could very well be lying about … everything." His words were bitter, sharp. He moved away and she heard him unstop the flagon and take a draught of ale. "I'm going to St Pirans. Eat, drink and think about what I've said. Hopefully by the time I return, you will understand."

CHAPTER FORTY-SIX

Mrs Daniell made her way downstairs on her husband's arm. It was early in the morning, but already she felt dishevelled after half the night spent weeping and the other half in a laudanum-induced stupor. Mrs Leigh had helped with her toilette as best she could, but she wasn't Thérèse. No-one could ever be Thérèse.

If it hadn't been for Gertrude's illness she would have kept to her room, but in this, as in all things, her family came first and somehow she needed to gather enough strength for the journey. Mr Daniell led her to the morning room, then with promises to return as soon as possible, went to find his secretary to apprise him of the situation.

Last night seemed like some surreal nightmare. The moment she had returned to her bedroom, she had known something was wrong; the fire had been allowed to burn low and there had been no nightdress warming in front of it. Neither had her hairbrush and ointments been set out on the dressing table. She'd rung the bell, and after a short while Mrs Leigh had appeared and gone to check Thérèse's room, which she'd found to be empty.

At once it had been established her maid had appeared out of sorts and had gone to take the air in the garden. Mr Leigh and Matthew had been dispatched immediately to see if perhaps she had fainted or fallen, but although Mrs Daniell had watched the bobbing lights below for some time there had been no trace of her. It was as they had returned to the hall Matthew had spied a note slipped under the door. Her husband had come to her, looking grave; Thérèse was being held for ransom.

Even as she'd wept her thoughts had been for her maid; how frightened she must be in the hands of a dangerous stranger. She imagined her bound on the floor of some dark cellar, her cries muffled by a gag around her mouth. Oh, how she wished she had told her of the rumours — especially how the last kidnapping had ended well. At least that may have brought her some comfort.

It brought Mrs Daniell a shred of comfort too. Initially her husband had been for calling the constables to chase the rogue down, but Mrs Daniell had begged for caution. The ransom was large, but not impossibly so. Would it not be better simply to pay and have Thérèse returned? No-one ever need know they had been victims of such a crime.

In the end, Mr Daniell had agreed. Much as it pained him to line a criminal's pockets, he recognised Thérèse's value and the money would be left as instructed in a gap in the wall of the engine house at Wheal Nevek at dusk, and Thérèse would be returned the following morning. It was the location as much as anything that convinced them the perpetrator was indeed John Coates.

"Then it is not only money, it is revenge," Mrs Daniell had cried. "It scares me all the more that Thérèse might come to harm. We know he blames us for his brother's death, and even though they claimed estrangement, likely for his father's too. Oh, Ralph, that these things have come to haunt us!"

This morning, the pain was no less sharp. The morning room door opened and Mrs Leigh bustled in with a tray of tea and pound cake, urging her to eat before the journey.

Mrs Daniell shook her head. "I cannot."

"Madam, you must, or you will make yourself ill and you will be no use at all to Mrs Gertrude."

Mary appeared behind her in her best travelling dress and matching bonnet. "She is right, Mama. Whatever has befallen Thérèse, we should not delay our departure because of it. You have me as companion, after all."

Mrs Daniell grasped her hand. "And I am thankful for it."

Mary sniffed. "Perhaps now she has gone, I can find a way back into your affections."

"But, Mary, you were never…"

She was silenced by Mr Daniell marching into the room accompanied by Mr Leigh and the stable boy. The lad was clutching his cap and looking around him, wide-eyed.

Mr Daniell sat down beside his wife. "There has been an interesting development, my dear."

"Yes?"

"It seems yesterday evening Thérèse asked this lad if he knew where John Coates was."

Mrs Daniell gasped and fell back into her chair. "But why?"

"I would have thought that was obvious, Mama," Mary said. "She has been out to trick you all along. After all, she lied to you about Capt—"

"Thérèse would not lie. There must be some reason… Perhaps Coates sent her a message to lure her into his clutches…"

Mr Daniell shook his head. "I fear not. Tell Mrs Daniell what you told Mr Leigh, boy."

"About Mam'selle Thérèse, sir?"

"About Mam'selle Thérèse."

"She knew John Coates, Madam. When you were in church on Sundays, very often he would wait for her on the quay and they would walk out together."

"No!" The room swam a little in front of Mrs Daniell's eyes and Mary's voice came from a distance, calling for her mother's salts.

Her husband took her hand. "So you see, my dear, this is no more than a ruse to rob us."

Tears sprang to Mrs Daniell's eyes. "I do not believe it. I will not believe it. Can you not see, it is not Thérèse who has tricked us, it is Coates who has tricked Thérèse."

"Mama, do not be so ridiculous."

"Mary, hold your tongue," said Mr Daniell. "Boy, you can go back to your work. There is much to do to prepare my wife's carriage, for she leaves within the hour."

When the family were alone in the room, Mrs Daniell turned to her husband. "You believe me, don't you?"

He looked uncertain. "I admit the possibility. I was not going to pay the ransom, but your words have made me reconsider. Coates could well have been playing a long game, with Thérèse being so new to the country and so trusting."

"She is not trusting," Mary pouted. "She is devious — she's a witch…"

"Mary — enough. If you continue in this vein, you will not accompany your mother to London and I will send you to your aunt in Hereford for a dose of discipline instead."

Mary gazed into her lap. "Sorry, Papa."

Mrs Daniell held out her hand to her. "It is not my daughter who speaks with such ill will, it is her poor battered heart. The young have not our experience to know who to trust, Ralph my dear. It can be a hard lesson to learn."

Mr Daniell looked at her, his brown eyes misting. "You were but eighteen years old when you put your trust in me."

"And I thank the good Lord in heaven for it every day. But now all our prayers should be for Thérèse."

CHAPTER FORTY-SEVEN

After Coates left, Thérèse sat perfectly still for the longest time. Her thirst had left her; her thirst, her hope, her zest for life, it seemed. She had been tricked, that was certain, but of the extent of the trickery she was unsure.

How long had Coates been playing her? Their growing friendship had felt real enough, and maybe it was. His increasing regard had surprised her at first and perhaps she should have been more cautious, but she had warmed to it, warmed to him, and if she was honest with herself, this too was part of the hurt.

She wanted to believe he was acting in her best interests — he'd said their best interests — by asking the Daniells for money, and there was no doubt at all they could afford to pay. But the worry he was causing Madame cut through her like a knife. A worry that would not end, for Thérèse would not return to her once the ransom was paid, and she would fear her dead and mourn.

No wonder Coates would not come back to Cornwall. This was a crime for which he would hang. He had taken great pains to keep their escape secret, but at least two people at the inn knew. How much had their silence cost him? Oh, could everyone be bought in this wretched country?

She wanted to go home. Home as it was, not home as it might be now. Home with her father, and with Paul a whole man. She put her hand to her throat to finger her locket, but it wasn't there. She searched inside her bodice, but it must have fallen from her neck. Or more likely Coates had taken it while she slept. Anger blazed inside her once more.

She stood and began to pace the cave. What could she do? She was captive here as sure as if she was locked in a cell. Even with a light she would never find her way back through the labyrinth of tunnels, and Coates had taken all the candles. What if he simply took the ransom too, and didn't return for her?

There was a way out, but although she was small enough to slip through the crack she could never climb the cave wall to reach it. But there was one rock close by; perhaps there were more and she could drag them, make a pile...

Deciding on a course of action made her feel better, but she would need all her strength so first she would eat and drink. She sat back down on the cloak and lifted the ale jug to her lips. It was bitter and strong, unlike the small beer at the servants' table, but it was liquid so she gulped it down. She tore some bread from the loaf and broke some cheese from the block. Coates had not left her his knife. Perhaps he did not trust her either.

Was she right, or was she wrong? So many small memories weighed this way and that. She ran her hand over his cloak. He hadn't had to be so tender last night, so solicitous of her. If he'd only wanted the ransom, then he hadn't had to keep her alive at all. And if he'd wanted her... She shuddered. He could have taken her. But he hadn't.

She put her head in her hands, the image of Mrs Daniell's sweet face filling the dark space. She couldn't be sure of Coates, but she could be sure of her mistress. And perhaps she could even verify the story about Paul. Why had she not thought of it before? Mr Daniell traded all over Europe — he must have contacts too.

She began to prowl around the cave, looking for rocks. Those she could lift were quite small and of varying shapes, but slowly the pile grew below the gap in the wall. The shaft of light was beginning to fade; either it was eventide or the day was becoming stormy. The pounding of the waves below was certainly louder, and as she worked the wind whipped a curtain of fine spray through the hole.

At last she had piled all the stones she could find. They wobbled as she tested them with her foot. The soles of her boots were smooth; she would be better in bare feet, but she would need them outside so she would have to risk it. One careful step at a time.

She reached up and clutched at the ledge. It was slippery beneath her hands, but there was no going back now. She couldn't risk Coates returning and seeing the stones. She gripped its sharp edge as best she could and felt her way onto the first rock. It was solid and it held, giving her confidence. The next wobbled, but it had a flat edge and she was able to move one foot onto it at least.

She leant into the wall of the cavern, breathing heavily. Outside she could hear rain, mixing with the thunder of the waves. How high up was she? Would the cliff be sheer below her? Or sheer above? She felt sick to her soul but she pushed on, one slow foot after another, until she needed to rest again.

Now she could see properly through the crack. The rain was hammering down, but at least there was a ledge outside. And the ledge must lead somewhere. If she could just take one more step...

She lifted her boot, but it found only air. Her whole body unbalanced, her fingers clawed at the floor of the crevice but a lump of shale came away in her hand and she was falling,

falling backwards into the darkness until her head met the floor of the cavern with a loud crack.

There was no more light, only pain, and cold, the wind and waves screaming around her. And then, from a long way off, Coates, the anguish in his voice following her towards a tunnel of light.

"Thérèse, oh, Thérèse my love, what have you done?"

She was looking down on them, circling higher and higher, as he cradled her limp body in his arms. The warmth and light were claiming her, her father beckoning her on, but the moment he did so Coates raised his face, a roar of torment escaping his lungs as tears streamed down his cheeks.

She felt her soul hesitate, then she was lost.

PART NINE:2016

CHAPTER FORTY-EIGHT

I sit in my car for a long time, staring at the house. It's a very ordinary house; 1970s, red brick, neat lawn in front. Above the garage to the left of the front door was my bedroom. There's a swag of lilac fabric in the window now.

This very ordinary house in the suburban outskirts of Gloucester is the only place I've ever called home. But even then I left, went away. Did Helen drive me out? Or even if she didn't, have I always believed she did, muscling in on Mum like that when Dad did his bunk? An uncomfortable thought creeps into my brain — have I been punishing her?

I think how fiercely protective Serena is of Sebastian. She'd kill for him, I'm sure of it. I know he finds it claustrophobic, but I'd wager there've been times she's been his saviour, dragging him back from the brink. Helen's never protected me, but perhaps I've never needed her to.

Families, families. So very complicated. It's the history we carry, the memories. On the ledge on the cliff I told Sebastian memories couldn't hurt him. He found the courage to face at least some of his demons head on, and I have to do the same.

The clock on the dashboard tells me I have half an hour to drive the three miles to the village where Helen lives. In that time, I somehow need to put the past behind me and forgive her for the biggest crime of all — not taking my mother away — she never did that, Mum wouldn't have let it happen. But she did rob us both of our home.

Even after I left, I could always come back. At the end of every glamping project, I came back. This house was my sanctuary, my anchor. When my marriage broke up, when my best friend died ten years ago, this was the place I ran to. Not just to my mother but to these four familiar walls, knowing they'd comfort me.

Two and a half years ago, that security was ripped away. Helen and her husband wanted to move to a village, but they couldn't quite afford it. So she persuaded Mum to sell, give up her independence, and live in the granny flat of the house they were coveting. I may have been given a share of the proceeds, but I wasn't given a say in the matter. I'm not sure poor Mum was either. Looking back, it was the beginning of the end for her. That's the hardest thing to forgive.

I gulp the bitterness and anger back down. Today is no day to let loose those emotions, so perhaps I'll just bury them again. I'll drive down the road, be as nice as I can to Helen, then I'll coat myself in steel and we'll sort through what's left of Mum's possessions. And after that, we can say goodbye and get on with our lives.

Later, I take the cardboard box from the back seat of my car and lock it in the boot. I have a strong urge to protect what I have left of my mother's life.

I let Helen keep the photograph albums; after all, she has children to pass them on to. I have a single framed picture of Mum, Helen and I outside the front door of our house. It was the day I left for university and a neighbour took it. It had pride of place on Mum's dressing table, along with Helen's wedding photo. Helen's keeping most of the furniture too — she has plans to turn the flat into an Airbnb. But there are some precious things ... like the chair that was always in Mum's bedroom, the Edwardian bureau she used as her desk... I don't want strangers using them, so I'm putting them into storage until I can find a home for them myself.

Otherwise, it's an eclectic mix. A slow cooker I may or may not use, but in which Mum always prepared a one-pot meal when I came home so we had more time to talk. A tiny cup and saucer in the shape of a strawberry that belonged to my great grandmother. Mum's favourite mug; we bought it in a garden centre as it was decorated with her birth flower, lily of the valley. It was only later we noticed the word lily was spelt with two ls and oh, how we laughed.

I need to tell Cecile I won't be taking the job in Italy, and I figure it's best to do it in person. She's been an amazing boss and I will be sorry to leave, but I can't see another way.

The strange thing is, I wasn't even sure about that until I was driving away from Helen's house. I was tired and crabby and completely fed up with the world. All I wanted to do was go home. And when I thought of home, I thought of the rugged cliffs and sparkling sea at Porthnevek. The first time I met Sebastian he said they claimed people, and in my case he was right.

At first, Cecile and I talk about Wheal Dream. We're on target for the bank holiday, and the permanent manager arrives next week. It's quite a relief not to be worrying whether he can go into the village or not.

"You never did say what ended the protests," Cecile says. "Did they just give up?"

"Well, I eventually managed to get to the bottom of their objections, so I was able to sit down with the ringleader and sort things out. You saw how the village dies in the winter — I guess in the summer they'll all be too busy making a living to worry much about it anyway."

"And once they see how much our guests spend…"

"Exactly. I want it to work for them as well, I really do."

"You said that with a great deal of passion, Anna."

"It's a pretty special place, and despite everything I've become quite attached to it."

"So attached you don't want to go to Italy?"

I take a deep breath. "No, I don't."

"I suppose I knew it the moment you started prevaricating. There's no way I can persuade you?"

"No. I know my decision to stay in Cornwall means I'll have to hand in my notice, and I'm sad about that, but it's time I put down some roots."

There is a pause, then she says, "It's really too soon for me to mention this, but last week the board approved another property in Cornwall, and I think I've found somewhere. It's very early days — we haven't even put in a formal offer. And it's different; there's a house to be renovated as well. The timing may not be right, all sorts of things…"

"But?"

"But if it comes off, I'll give you first refusal."

"That's amazing!" I grin at her across the desk.

"Don't go counting your chickens yet, Anna."

"Don't worry, I won't."

CHAPTER FORTY-NINE

I've saved the best part of my trip up country until last. Julie at Trelissick was curious when I asked her about the letters mentioning Thérèse, Elizabeth Daniell's French maid, but when I told her I just wanted to extend my knowledge of the era she was more than happy to show me the photocopy, which had come from the archives of one of the Oxford colleges.

It was simple in the extreme.

My dearest Thomas,

Thank you for your letter. I am sorry to hear your mama has been unwell and send all good wishes for her recovery.

Thérèse is quickly becoming accustomed to life at Truro and at Trelissick. She is a pleasant girl and willing to please, although her English still needs much improvement. But that is of little matter, as it is a delight to converse in French and it is good for the children to be able to do so.

Do send more news of your mama's health.

Your cousin, Elizabeth

The smallest of clues. But added to the fact we know Elizabeth Daniell visited the miners of Wheal Nevek with her maid, circumstances definitely link Thérèse to the area. Today I'll discover if there is anything more.

Just stepping inside an Oxford college more than four hundred years old is daunting for a graduate of a modern campus university. There's nothing familiar about the narrow arched entrance, cut into an enormous wooden door, but the porters are friendly enough and point me in the direction of a decidedly twenty-first-century building housing the library, archives and reading rooms.

I had expected the archivist to be someone old and dusty, but Anthony Sargeant is a lively thirty-something in a flowered shirt and pink chinos. Before I've even had time to draw breath, he's dragging me off to the dining hall to see one of Thomas Chalmers' paintings.

It stands out because it's by no means a portrait, and the subject is a woman. Anthony explains all the other pictures are of former college masters, so I ask why this one is here.

"The same reason as the rest of the Chalmers archive. A late nineteenth-century master was an expert on his work, and it was at his specific request this was hung in the hall instead of his portrait. It's by far Chalmers' most famous painting, although it was controversial at the time."

"Because it's a woman?"

"No, because she's French."

The hairs on the back of my neck stand up as we move forwards to study the picture more closely. It's a sizeable canvas with a small figure in grey clinging to a tree at its heart, behind her the aftermath of battle on a massive scale. The gold plate screwed to the frame tells me it's called *The Leavings of War* and it's dated 1815.

I turn to Anthony. "It's Waterloo, isn't it?"

"Yes. Early in his career Chalmers was primarily a war artist. This painting was exhibited in the Royal Academy in 1816 as part of a collection to celebrate Wellington's victory, but once it got out the model was French it was only allowed to remain once Chalmers explained the figure represented the mothers, wives and sisters of every nation who had lost their loved ones in the battle."

"So would he have actually been at Waterloo?"

"Without a doubt. There are letters to prove it, although I understood you were specifically interested in his correspondence with his cousin Elizabeth Daniell."

I nod. "Yes, that's really why I'm here."

Three letters are laid out in the reading room, and Anthony gives me a pair of white cotton gloves to wear. The paper is cream in colour and soft to the touch, almost like a fine linen, and folded in half like a modern notelet, with the writing on the inside. Turning the letter over, I can see it has the address and seal on the reverse.

The first is the one Julie showed me a copy of at Trelissick, but somehow reading the real thing makes me feel closer to Elizabeth and Thérèse. I remember the touch of the maid's dress on my skin, the rustle as I walked. Come on, Anna, stop being so fanciful. You're here to find out some facts.

To my disappointment the second letter doesn't mention Thérèse at all, but I remind myself that although there was some connection between her and Chalmers, she was, after all, only a servant. This letter is clearly designed to be read to Thomas's ailing mother and describes a great ball held in the house to celebrate Elizabeth's son Will's leave from his navy ship and the betrothal of her daughter Lizzie.

The final letter is longer and comes from an address in London. I scan the first part about someone called Gertrude's health improving, but then I come to Thérèse's name. I have to read the next sentence twice; it seems Thérèse was kidnapped by a notorious smuggler, the ransom paid, but she was not returned to them as promised. I sit back to try to take it in; maybe she even met a grizzly end in the mine workings where we found her locket. If that's the case, no wonder her ghost is wandering the cliffs.

I check myself. That's Sebastian's story, not mine. I return to the letter and read on.

For Ralph, that was the end of the matter. I knew he doubted Thérèse as soon as we discovered she had been walking out with Coates, and he believes they have secured a passage across the channel. There is a part of me that longs to believe it, for it would mean she is happy and safe, but I cannot bring myself to consider her dishonest in any way. That was not our Thérèse, dear Thomas. You and I both know her loyal, trusting nature, and it would have been easy for a felon like Coates to dupe her and lure her away. She was such a stranger to the ways of this land. I fear I should have protected her more, and the guilt will remain with me always.

Personally, I'm with Ralph on this one; Thérèse was French, after all, and presumably she wanted to go home. Who wouldn't prefer that to a life of servitude? And with a sexy smuggler thrown into the bargain ... well, I'm assuming he was sexy, but my Porthnevek smugglers were anything but. Perhaps eighteenth-century smugglers used the mine workings too — the letter is dated April 1816, so it would have happened after Wheal Nevek was closed — and it would explain the locket.

I am lost in my thoughts when Anthony comes in, carrying a cardboard folder. "When I was preparing the letters, I noticed they mentioned someone called Thérèse and there are a few sketches of her in the archive. It's probable she was the model for *The Leavings of War*, although it's hard to be certain."

I move the letters carefully to one side and he sets the folder on the table, untying its pink ribbon. The first sketch is of a young woman sipping from an elegant two handled cup with a sprigged floral pattern. Above Chalmers' signature are the words *Thérèse drinking chocolate*. I never in a million years dreamt I would see her face. Her hair is tucked into a mob cap, and she has a small, straight nose and large eyes. I gaze at the sketch in wonder.

"Incredible, isn't it?" says Anthony. "When you see a picture of someone from so long ago you've already read about."

"Breath-taking."

In the next two sketches, Thérèse is bent over a large piece of dark fabric and in one of them it seems to flow like water over her lap. That Chalmers had a great deal of talent is beyond question, and I shake my head in awe. But there is better to come. Anthony turns the page again. This drawing is called *Thérèse at the window*, and above the square neckline of her dress a locket can clearly be seen.

It takes me a moment to recover my power of speech, then I look up at Anthony. "I think we may have found her locket."

"What, at Trelissick?"

I shake my head as I scrabble in the inside pocket of my handbag and pull out a small plastic box, which used to contain a pair of my earrings. I hand it to him and from his pocket he pulls a magnifying glass to take a closer look at the painting.

"You could well be right. Where did you say you found it?"

I didn't, and I don't want to. What can I tell him? "The steward at Trelissick told me Thérèse would have accompanied Elizabeth Daniell to visit poor and sick miners at Porthnevek. It was there."

Luckily, he doesn't question me further. "Incredible," he murmurs, "absolutely incredible."

Yes, that just about sums it up.

301

CHAPTER FIFTY

Sebastian and I are sitting on the promontory opposite Wheal Clare when I tell him I'm staying in Cornwall. He pauses, his pasty halfway to his mouth.

"I know."

"How can you know? I've only just made up my own mind."

"Because I saw your face the very first time you walked out onto the cliffs. I'll never forget your expression as long as I live."

"So that's not the reason you're holding out on me?" It's the first time I've alluded to the morning after our cave adventure and part of me inwardly cringes at doing so, but I need to somehow bring the conversation around to our relationship. Or lack of it.

He shoots me a glance. "I'm not holding out on you. The answer's no, and you know very well why."

"So you're going to let the prospect of a difficult month or so every year mean we can't have ten good ones?"

"No. I'm not letting us kid ourselves for eight months then have it all blow up in our faces and it hurt even more. I'm not prepared to take the risk."

I fold my arms. "Well, I am." I'm tempted to ask him how I can continue just to be friends when I fall for him a little more every time I see him, but that would be downright cruel. And anyway, I have another trump card. Or at least, I hope I have. But for the moment, I take another bite of my pasty and watch the foamy skirts of the waves lick back over the sand below as the tide recedes.

I still don't know quite how I fell for Sebastian. Was it a slow burn that suddenly came into focus when I knew absolutely I could trust him? Or was it our experience down the mine and on the cliffs that brought the best of him into sharp relief? Or am I simply ready to meet someone I want to keep, in a place I want to be? Whatever the reason, the man sitting quietly beside me has made me want to stop running. But to make it happen, he needs to face up to something too.

I wait until we've finished our pasties, sweeping the crumbs from my walking trousers onto the rock.

"Shall we go?" Sebastian asks.

"There's something I want to show you first. After what you told me about your dad, I wanted to know more so I asked Ray. But his story didn't quite tally with yours, so I had a look online."

He turns to face me. "Online? This happened way before online."

"Newspaper archives are online. And Alwyn Godrevy isn't a common name."

"I don't like you digging. You have no business to."

"You've made it my business by setting it up as a barrier between us."

"Jesus, woman, will you stop at nothing to get what you want?" There's a flash of anger in his eyes that reminds me of Serena. I put my hand on his arm.

"I wouldn't do it if I didn't care about you so very much. Listen, just hear me out. Then I promise never to speak of it again unless you want to."

There is an endless silence, but then he covers my hand with his own. "Deal."

It is more than a little awkward to pull the printout from my pocket, but I don't want to break our contact. I shake it out and hand it to him, hoping the grainy image of his father won't upset him too much.

"It's a load of crap."

"You haven't read it."

"I've read the headline."

I look over his shoulder, but I know it by heart: *Schoolboy hero fails to prevent tragic accident.* "It tallies with Ray's story. And you know Ray was there. You were playing football with him just before it happened."

He fingers the edges of the paper. "I'd forgotten that."

"Then perhaps there are other things you've forgotten too. Or at the very least, not quite remembered right. You were only about six, after all."

"But Mum always said ... it was my fault. It was why she made us go away to live with Gran and Pops. Couldn't bear to have me around." He gazes out over the sea. "I don't suppose she ever really could afterwards; she was certainly never the same. Winters were hell as I got older — we'd both go downhill. Both pretty incapable of anything. Probably why I did so crap at school.

"Serena kept us afloat, but sometimes it was just too much and we'd be packed off to our grandparents again. They were pretty strict but I guess they had to be, and it was probably only them who stopped us from being put into care." His expression is grim as he looks at me, his eyes hard, but then the lines around them soften a little as he raises his hand to wipe a tear from my cheek. "Hey, there's no need for that. I got through it. I lived."

"But you're still letting it blight your life. If only you could stop blaming yourself…"

"How can I, when it was my fault? If I hadn't been fooling around at the edge of the sea, trying to get his attention, he'd have never gone in."

"That's not how Ray tells it. That's not how the guy the journalist interviewed tells it, and he was the one who hauled you out."

He stands, stuffing the paper into his pocket in an untidy ball. "I'm going for a walk." Dry-eyed now, I watch him as he disappears down the path towards St Pirans. The only thing I can do now is wait.

I am surprised when Sebastian asks if I'll take him to Trelissick. It is almost a week after our unsatisfactory conversation on the cliffs, but nevertheless I have a flicker of hope because Ray told me that for the first time ever, Sebastian wanted to talk about the day his father died.

We visit the house late on a Tuesday afternoon when I know it will be quiet. At this time of year, most of the visitors are in the garden admiring the azaleas. Liz is on duty in the hall and appraises Sebastian with quick eyes as she welcomes us. Not for the first time, I am aware what an odd couple we would seem through other people's eyes, but I don't give a damn. If I've learnt one thing since I came to Cornwall, it's what a person is like inside that matters.

We wander around the rooms, Sebastian almost silent while I gabble on, info-dumping everything I know about the Regency era here. His hands are deep in his pockets as he follows me, and after a while I come to realise he is listening, but not to me.

I stop in the door to the orangery, blocking his way. "She's here, isn't she?"

"No. I thought she might be, but she's not. Perhaps she's been able to move on."

"And have you?"

He jumps back, no doubt as startled by the force of my challenge as I am. Half under my breath, I mutter an apology.

I stand aside to let him pass and he makes straight for the door onto the terrace, while I trail miserably behind. Together we gaze over the parkland towards the Fal, the estuary shimmering towards the distant hump of Pendennis Castle guarding its entrance.

"She'd have seen this too," he murmurs. "Did she look down that river and long for home? Or long for love? We'll never know for sure, but she took a chance."

"So next you'll say, 'and look where it got her.'"

"Night doesn't always follow day."

"How exactly do you mean?"

"I mean, some chances pay off." He sinks onto the low wall, facing me. "Anna, are you really sure? It's not just how damaged I am, it's all the other stuff about me you don't get. The gulf between us, it's potentially huge — we're just so different. And yet ... I don't know ... something about it feels ... right? Jesus ... I wish I was better at this sort of thing."

I sit down next to him, wrapping my arm around his shoulder. "We are right. God only knows why, but we are." I smile at him. "After our adventure down the mine I knew I could trust you with my life, and that made all the difference to me."

"You needed proof?"

"That's me, I'm afraid."

There's a sparkle in his eyes as he looks down at me and says, "So my chances of getting you to believe in my ghosts?"

"Minimal," I laugh.

But all the same, in the very last moment before he kisses me I look up to the first-floor windows and see someone looking down. A grey shadow, nothing more, that vanishes almost as soon as I'm aware of it. Then Sebastian's lips are on mine, his beard tickling my skin, and I abandon myself to the moment.

HISTORICAL NOTES

First, I would like to be clear about what (and who) is real, and who is not. And also to say that even where people exist in the historical record, I have no way of knowing their character — or even what they looked like — so everything in that respect is a product of my imagination.

I have kept the structure of the Daniell family (births, marriages and deaths) as accurate as I can, except for the addition of the fictitious Chalmers cousins. Ralph Allen Daniell was a successful businessman, following in his father's footsteps, and a significant property owner in Cornwall (and elsewhere) at the time. The family's main residence was the country house at Trelissick, now owned by the National Trust, but they also kept The Mansion House in Truro, which in the present day has been converted into offices, although it retains many original features.

The historical research into the family and their homes and business interests has been fascinating and frustrating in equal measure. The truth has been slippery, to say the least, with different sources giving different dates, even for quite important events. And the fact 'Wheal Nevek', at one time the most profitable mine in Cornwall, has been quite literally wiped off the map, did not help either.

Little by little, and with a great deal of help from the Courtney Library at the Royal Cornwall Museum, I managed to piece together the most likely sequence of events to make the Daniells' circumstances in 1815 and early 1816 as real as possible. They were certainly living in a newly extended Trelissick, and Wheal Nevek was certainly closed, Ralph Allen

Daniell having failed to convince Lord Falmouth and the other land owners it was worth the investment to keep it going. And it is in the parish records that Elizabeth Daniell gave poor relief in the area at the time.

Background on Regency Cornwall was easier to come by. The most pleasurable source was reading some of Winston Graham's later Poldark novels, in particular *The Twisted Sword*, which is set in exactly the right time period and includes a few chapters about Waterloo. As I looked back to the historical record I realised just how good Graham's research was, so I felt I could rely on his work for the look and feel of the time.

Absolute gold dust, though, was a schematic drawing of Truro in 1811 by June Palmer, included in her book *Truro During the Napoleonic Wars*. This and its sister volume, *Truro in the Age of Reform*, were invaluable sources of information, so all the shops and businesses Thérèse visits in the town are real.

Captain Frederick Gilbert was named by a Facebook competition winner, Lynn Folliott, and I chose her entry because one family who lived at Trelissick after the Daniells' time was called Gilbert, and I liked the co-incidence.

In terms of the mining history around 'Porthnevek', the most useful source of information was AK Hamilton Jenkin's *Mines and Miners of Cornwall* (volume 11). It gives a detailed account of the various mines in the area, including 'Wheal Nevek', and the schematic of the mineshafts Luke gives Anna exists as well. I'm afraid to say that while walking in the area I've become a real bore about it all. But history does matter to me, and I love to picture it how it would have been two hundred years ago.

A NOTE TO THE READER

When I first visited 'Porthnevek' at the very end of 2011, little did I know Cornwall would become my home. My husband Jim and I were there to look for a holiday property and we immediately fell in love with the village, its shabby surfer chic, and its very real and in no way picture-postcard sense of community.

Over the next few years, we spent more and more time there and in 2017 finally crossed the Rubicon — or in this case the Tamar — and moved to Cornwall full time. My heart feels at home on this wild patch of north Cornish coast in a way it never has since I left my native Wales to go to university many moons ago. You could say, as Sebastian does to Anna when they first meet, that it has claimed me.

Inevitably I wanted to set a book there, and the idea for *The Forgotten Maid* was gifted to me on a plate one afternoon in a pub not unlike The Tinners. We were still getting to know the locals, and I was chatting to one of them when he started to tell me about a farmer from many centuries ago who he'd met while walking his dog. The man had been most aggrieved because he had just sold an animal at market but had dropped dead before being able to spend the proceeds.

The tale stayed with me because of the way it was told — as if it was the most normal thing in the world. And to its teller, it was. Having an open mind about such things and an interest in consciousness beyond matter, I had no reason to disbelieve him. He gave me permission to use his gift as a template for Sebastian, but had no idea of the details of the story. Imagine my surprise when I was well into my first draft and he told me he'd had a conversation with a maid who was scrubbing the steps of the Mansion House, the Daniell family's former home in Truro.

I would, however, point out that in just about every other way I have made Sebastian as unlike the real man who talks to ghosts as possible. Although for people who know the area well, Porthnevek, St Pirans and The Tinners (as well as some of its other locals) may well be recognisable.

I hope you feel at home here too, and thank you for investing your precious time and money in the first Cornish Echoes story. The second in this series of standalone dual-timeline novels, *The Lost Heir*, will be released next year. In the meantime, if you feel so inclined, ratings and reviews on **Amazon** and **Goodreads** are important to authors. Reviews don't have to be lengthy or erudite — a few words will do — but rest assured they are all appreciated.

If you have any questions about *The Forgotten Maid*, or would like to consider it for your book club, please contact me via **Twitter: @JaneCable**, **Facebook: Jane Cable, Author**, or **my website**. There is more background information about *The Forgotten Maid* and my other books there. I am also happy to visit book clubs and libraries, virtually or in person.

Jane Cable

janecable.com

Sapere Books is an exciting new publisher of brilliant fiction and popular history.

To find out more about our latest releases and our monthly bargain books visit our website: **saperebooks.com**

Printed in Great Britain
by Amazon